Livvy and the Enchanted Woodland

Connie Lacy

Wild Falls Publishing

~ ~ ~

Atlanta, GA

ISBN-13: 978-1-7374552-4-0

Published by Wild Falls Publishing
Atlanta, GA

WildFallsPublishing@outlook.com

For my sister Susan and my brother Hugh

~~~

Also by Connie Lacy

1

Looking across the cotton field, Livvy caught sight of Daddy and her brother Preston, somber as mourners at a graveside service. Daddy broke off a stem, holding it for his son to examine, then flung it to the ground, spitting in disgust.

There was no need to hear their words. She already knew the particulars. The loan Daddy took out for seed, fertilizer and that worthless arsenic pesticide was coming due. But boll weevils had laid waste to the cotton crop. In spite of all their efforts to keep the vile insects at bay, the cotton bolls had been eaten from the inside and the leaves chewed down to nothing. As if that wasn't bad enough, the drought, like an uninvited guest from hell, refused to leave, turning the red Georgia clay into a veil of dry orange dust that coated everything, from the leaves on the trees to the glass in the windows.

They'd hoped 1930 would be a better year than 1929. But they'd been wrong once again. Was it fate or just bad luck? Either way, it was a bitter pill to swallow. Losing the farm loomed larger with each passing day.

Livvy took off for the forest pushing the wheelbarrow. There'd be plenty of time later for the endless gnashing of teeth over how to avoid foreclosure while putting food on the table. Grandma used to say it didn't do a lick of good letting everyday worries wear you out, that life was a heap of ups and downs; you had to take pleasure in the ups and hang on tight for the downs. Easier said than done. Sometimes you just had to leave your real life behind.

That's why Livvy hurried home from the store as soon as her sister arrived for the afternoon shift. She'd changed out of her work dress and slipped into hand-me-down overalls and a faded shirt, tying her thick mane into a ponytail to keep it off her neck. Her hair was the color of a sassafras tree in the fall, the bright orange conspicuous now amid the verdant green of summer.

Reaching the woods, she filled her lungs with the scent of tall pines, leafy oaks and hickory trees. A chorus of cicadas welcomed her like an old friend. The air was different here. Fresher. Sweeter. Her skin cooled beneath the leafy canopy.

Her new forest sculpture was nearly finished. Positioned in an airy strip of woods within the larger forest, shafts of sunlight streamed through the branches above, casting her creation in a shimmering glow. Using sticks and twigs woven together with wild grape, honeysuckle and jessamine vines, she'd created a large round doorway like something in the book of fairy tales Grandma used to read her when she was little. It was a foot thick, six feet tall, and open in the middle so you could see the dense forest beyond. The sides were lashed to two pine trees for support.

She got down on her knees and plaited more lengths of vine mixed with twigs before weaving them into the structure.

As she worked, her mind drifted back to the day she designed her first work of art in this same neck of the woods. She was eight years old. It was fall and the ground was a lush golden carpet of fallen hickory leaves.

Now, as Livvy worked on the big doorway, she could almost feel her white-haired grandmother tramping alongside her on that long-ago day, a firm grip on her walking stick. Grandma said if you were quiet, you might hear the trees talking to you. She believed in signs and omens and magic.

"Looks like a fairy might've been here before us," her *grandmother said. She gestured at several smooth stones lying prettily among the leaves, giving her granddaughter an encouraging nod.*

Livvy rounded up more stones, then arranged them in a starburst pattern. When she stood to admire her handiwork, Grandma suggested a finishing touch.

"Since Mother Nature provided the ingredients, I think you should add a little seasoning of your own! Like a signature on a painting."

She pulled her small embroidery scissors from her pocket, snipping a lock of hair from one of Livvy's long pigtails and placing it in her granddaughter's hand. The little girl tucked the red hair beneath one of the stones. As though Mother Nature had taken notice, a gust of wind whistled through the trees, sending a quiver down Livvy's back. She locked eyes with her grandmother.

"Magic happens all the time," Grandma whispered. *"You just have to look for it."*

It was a moment Livvy would never forget. It was also the last time they hiked through the woods together. Her grandmother died that fall just the way she always prophesied she would go – suddenly and without warning, determined not to fade away little by little.

Over the past few months, the connection to her grandmother had grown stronger again. When the idea took root in her mind to build a doorway, she wondered if Grandma might be sending a message that there was so much more out there besides what existed within the confines of Livvy's monotonous life.

Looking at it now, there was a hint of enchantment about her creation, the space around it radiating an aura of possibility.

She smiled as she completed the final section. For the first time since Grandma died, Livvy felt the urge to add something of herself to one of her creations. She removed the ribbon from her ponytail, letting her hair spill onto her shoulders. Reaching into her pocket she withdrew Grandma's little scissors, now darkened with age, and clipped several strands of hair. She braided them with jessamine tendrils, weaving the braid into the sculpture.

As she got to her feet, she was wonderstruck by the sight of a rainbow flickering around the inside edge, making it look like a fairy door. At the same time, a vibration traveled down her spine triggering an urge to step through the doorway. She stopped in her tracks when she heard hoofbeats approaching from the other side, hardly breathing as a horse cantered toward her, a rider on his back.

The man pulled up on the reins, apparently as startled by her appearance as she was by his. He looked like a city slicker in a tweed jacket over a shirt and tie, with dark pants and black boots that came to the knee. He wore a tan cap on his head that reminded her of a picture she'd seen of the famous golfer

Bobby Jones. The smokey grey horse danced nervously as the rider stared at her through the doorway.

"The ginger girl," he said.

He had a warm voice, but what a strange accent. Definitely not from around here.

"Ginger girl?" she said.

"Your hair."

Ginger. That's what the British called people like her, or so she'd read. Not in a nice way either. To be fair, Grandma, whose white hair had once been the same bright orange color, used to say Livvy was a redhead through and through. She had a light sprinkling of freckles across her cheeks and nose, blue eyes, and an independent streak that some mistook for a bit of a temper.

"Well, sir," she replied, "I'm sure you know we don't get to choose the color of our hair. I think it's pure meanness to make fun of folks for something they don't have any say-so about."

"I'm not making fun, I assure you. I saw a girl in a dream when I was a boy. She was standing in the woods, her pretty red hair lit by the sun. You remind me of her."

There was a faraway look in his eyes.

"Where are you from?" she said.

"Kinston."

"I visit Kinston a lot and you don't sound like you're from Kinston."

"I daresay I *am* from Kinston. But you don't speak like anyone I've ever met. Where are *you* from?"

"From here. Where else?"

She wasn't sure what to make of him. He didn't seem feebleminded, but he obviously didn't grow up in Kinston.

From the way he talked and the odd way he dressed, he had to be an Englishman. As much as she wanted to solve the puzzle, she wasn't sure she could trust him.

"I better go." She retrieved the wheelbarrow and headed back the way she came.

"Wait! I have to ask, did you erect this… this…"

"Yep," she called out over her shoulder, continuing on her way.

"It has a mythological air about it," he called back. "Rather like an enchanted doorway."

She smiled, wondering why she hadn't made a run for it the moment she saw him. That's what she always told her little sister to do. Maybe it was because he'd been so captivated by her doorway.

Feeling a little giddy, she spent the rest of the day cutting more vines with her pocketknife, an idea for another artwork forming in her mind. She kept her eyes peeled for the interloper as she hauled the load to her special place, dumping the vines in a pile not far from the doorway. That way, she could get right to work when she returned tomorrow.

As she started for the farm, she recalled how he'd described the little girl he saw as having "pretty red hair." Which left her with a warm glow.

The warm glow faded, however, the closer she got to home. It was the home she'd grown up in, but it was no longer the welcoming place of her childhood. There were too many people now, all jostling for space, all of them on edge. Except her two young nieces who didn't fully understand how bleak the situation was.

Dusk had settled by the time she arrived. Lamp light streamed through the windows like all was well within. From a distance the clapboard house looked the same as always. Like most homes in Burgess County, it was unpainted, the faded boards blending with the outbuildings beyond. There was a modest barn, a hog pen, chicken coop, smokehouse and two outhouses, one of them added when her brother's family moved in. The house had three chimneys and a wide, covered porch along the side. But even after all these years, there was no running water or electricity. There used to be flowers in the yard when she was little. Now it was mostly dirt with a smattering of weeds, some hardy fig bushes and two big pecan trees – one in front, the other out back. The sense of possibility she'd experienced in the woods vanished, replaced by dread.

Walking along the edge of the field, she could see that Daddy and Preston had plowed under the dead cotton plants. The earthy smell of freshly turned soil filled the evening air. She washed up at the pump in the yard, drying her hands on her overalls as she stamped dirt from her shoes.

The spacious kitchen had a high ceiling and large windows which helped disperse the heat. But the wood-burning stove on the far wall hadn't cooled down yet from cooking a big supper and the room was too warm for comfort.

When she strolled in, the children had already been excused. The adults were still seated around the long, rectangular table. It was clear she'd interrupted a serious conversation about finances.

Her brother Preston's eyes settled on her as she took her seat across from him.

"It would be a big help, Livvy, if you and Inez could bring in more money at the store."

Pushing forty, his brown hair showed flecks of grey and his lined face made him look older than his years. He and his wife Clara and their four kids had lost their own farm, returning to live here so that Mama and Daddy's house was now bursting at the seams. Clara sat beside him darning socks, keeping her eyes on her needle. They were both rail thin.

"I hope that's not all you've got up your sleeve for making the loan payment." Her older sister Inez aimed a challenging stare in Preston's direction.

"Me and Daddy are working on some ideas. It would just be helpful if you could contribute a little more."

"We can't raise our prices," Livvy said, digging into the cold plate of food they'd saved her.

"We can if we want to!" Inez said, her hackles up.

In her will, Grandma Hopkins left the general store to her granddaughters without naming them. There were two granddaughters at the time – Inez and Livvy. Ruthie was born a few years after Grandma died, but everyone said she was part owner as well.

"If we raise prices, we won't sell as much," Livvy argued.

"We can mark some items up by a penny."

Inez was a self-professed old maid at forty-one. She'd helped Grandma run the store, then managed it by herself until Livvy was old enough to pitch in.

"I went along with you in the spring, Inez. You saw what happened. People are doing without. I haven't sold a single piece of cloth all summer and not one pair of pants. I only sold two Moon Pies last week. We can't pay our bills if we don't earn any money. I think we ought to lower prices."

"Are you crazy?"

Daddy pushed his chair back as if to say enough was enough. He gestured for Preston to join him outside for their after-supper cigarette. That meant they were going to have a private man-to-man. As they eased out the door, Clara took her darning and made a quick exit. Then Inez stalked from the room in a huff.

"Don't mind her," Mama said to Livvy. "She's a little tetchy this evening."

Ruthie sashayed into the kitchen at that moment. At fourteen, all she saw was blue skies ahead. "Inez has been tetchy since before I was born."

Livvy stifled a laugh.

"You arrived just in time to wash dishes, young lady," Mama said. "Go find your nieces to give you a hand."

Ruthie's reply was a whine bordering on a groan as she grabbed several buckets to haul water from the pump. She got a stern wag of the finger from Mama.

Ruthie was right. Livvy remembered a time when Inez always had a smile and a laugh. But once the handsome boy she was in love with in high school abandoned her for another girl, the smiles and laughter faded away and her habitual scowl hardened the lines in her face.

Unlike her big sister, Livvy had once been married. She and Hank Sloan wed after she completed two years at Young Harris Junior College. But when he was killed in an accident at the sawmill, Livvy became a widow at the age of twenty. That was six years ago. Her mother encouraged her to keep her eyes peeled for another man. "You're still young, Olivia," Mama would whisper. "You don't want to end up like Inez."

That night both windows were open in the little lean-to bedroom she and Ruthie shared. With not even a hint of a breeze, the windows weren't much help. How Ruthie could sleep was beyond her.

Lying on her bed listening to the crickets sing, she banished family discord from her mind, thinking back to a more intriguing topic – the unexpected encounter in the woods. She tried to picture the stranger in her mind's eye. Besides his unusual clothing and odd accent, he was tall in the saddle, clean shaven, with dark hair and an easy smile.

The sense of enchantment had been so strong, she could've sworn she'd felt her grandmother's presence. Was it possible she'd merely been swept up in the moment, imagining the rainbow in the doorway? Imagining the meeting with the mysterious stranger? She sighed thinking about it. Surely the encounter was more than just a wishful flight of fancy. She found herself hoping the Englishman and his magnificent horse might surprise her in the woods again one day soon.

2

There were so many Hopkins around these parts, the community was known as Hopkinsville. It's not that the Hopkins were rich, but unlike the sharecroppers, the Hopkins owned their own land. Now with the crop failure, Livvy's branch of the Hopkins clan was on the verge of losing their farm.

It helped that her family had some extra income from the store. Located at the main crossroad just half a mile from their house, the store had been in business on the same spot since Livvy's grandfather built it to give his wife something to do after their children were grown.

While the faded sign above the door read Hopkins General Merchandise, the structure resembled a small house with two windows facing the road except for the fact that the front was plastered with ads for everything from Coca-Cola to Ivory Soap. There was a plank porch along the front and a wooden pen with chicken wire on the left side in case customers paid for purchases with chickens or the occasional pig. The store's only neighbor was the one-room schoolhouse across the street.

Unlocking the door, Livvy flipped the sign over to read "open" before unfastening the shutters to let the sunshine in.

No need to light the lamps. If they were lucky and a thunderstorm moved through this afternoon, Inez might have to light them later on.

The ice in the half barrels used for soft drinks had melted, the bottles now floating in tepid water. Ice delivery was scheduled for this afternoon. She wondered how many more years it would take before electricity arrived out here in the country.

She was just putting cash in the register when her first customer arrived.

Mae Glover was about Livvy's age. A widow with three small children, she only came when Livvy was behind the counter, arriving early with a small cloth-covered basket. Mae was a pretty Black woman, always neat in appearance. But a good many white folks were none too friendly to her or any of their Black neighbors.

"Morning, Mae," Livvy said, giving her a welcoming smile as she closed the cash drawer. "What can I do for you?"

"Morning, Miss Livvy. I need a box of salt, please."

Livvy retrieved the blue box on a shelf behind her as the door opened again.

The new arrival stood on the threshold, glaring. He was a wiry old man with cloudy glasses and thinning grey hair who loved to brag that his pa was a hero of the Confederacy.

"Be with you in a minute, Mr. Singletary," Livvy said, then handed Mae the salt. "I'll add it to your account, Mrs. Glover."

She knew Mae had brought eggs to trade, which she could only do when Livvy was there. Inez brought her own eggs every day, refusing to accept anyone else's in payment. That's not why Livvy didn't accept the eggs though. She knew it wouldn't do for Mr. Singletary to witness the exchange.

Understanding flashed in Mae's eyes, prompting a quick "thank you" before she walked through the open door without looking in Mr. Singletary's direction.

"Now, what can I get for you?" Livvy said, smiling at the sour man.

"Don't believe you can get anything for me. I won't be doing business where Coloreds shop."

He was building up to a mean-spirited stemwinder and Livvy was relieved when she caught sight of someone approaching the entrance.

Coy Whitaker smelled like money in his expensive shirt, sleeves rolled up to the elbows and new tan slacks. His sandy blond hair was slicked back just so, reminding her of a movie star in one of Ruthie's magazines. His family hadn't always been well off and Livvy suspected he liked to remind people of how far they'd risen.

"Livvy, Mr. Singletary, how's everyone getting along this morning?"

Coy had been dropping by the store more often lately, buying something with each visit, always stopping in while Livvy was on duty. Tall and good-looking with a big booming voice, she barely recognized the little boy he'd been when they attended school as children. His family had avoided the privations so many had suffered these past few years. They sold their farm before the drought began, using the proceeds to buy part ownership of the sawmill. Livvy suspected they had other income as well.

"I was just telling Livvy I don't take kindly to her serving Nigras," Mr. Singletary replied.

"Times are hard, Mr. Singletary," Livvy said. "The store is barely making any money as it is. We can't afford to turn any customers away." She stopped herself from blurting, "including mean old bastards like you."

She was surprised when Coy took her side.

"We don't want to drive the store out of business, now do we, Mr. Singletary? That would be a real shame." Then he turned to Livvy. "I need a fifty-pound bag of flour for Mama. Too heavy for you to carry."

He walked directly to the back of the store, his leather shoes pounding on the bare wooden floor. He hoisted one of two large flour sacks onto his shoulder and carried it to the register before Mr. Singletary could respond.

"I'll also take a case of Co-Cola," Coy added, lifting one of the wooden crates from the stack by the door and setting it on the counter with a thud. "And a pack of Camels."

The older man turned on his heel and stalked out. Coy waited until he was out of earshot before speaking.

"Old man Singletary's not a bad fella but he don't like mingling of the races."

Livvy was pretty sure Coy agreed with Mr. Singletary on that issue, finding it interesting that he took her side today.

"Thank you, Coy," she said, giving him his cigarettes and ringing up his purchases.

"Can't let the store go bust," he said, handing her the cash.

He tucked the cigarettes in his shirt pocket and set the large bag of flour on top of the drink crate as he headed for the open door.

"By the way," he said, looking over his shoulder. "You know what you need to do, don't you? Get a gas pump. Lots of folks have cars now. That'd bring customers in, for sure."

"Wish we could afford it."

"I'd buy my gas from you."

There was an unmistakable glint in his eyes.

Through the window, she watched him load his purchases into the back seat of his Model A. It was a brilliant blue and looked nice and shiny when it was freshly washed. But like all the other automobiles around here, driving on dirt roads day in and day out left it covered in a thick layer of dust. He tapped a cigarette from the pack of Camels, lighting it with a match before sliding in behind the wheel and driving away.

Closing the door, she remembered Mama's admonition about finding a good man. She'd never considered that Coy might fall into that category. He was a couple of years younger than her, and she remembered him from their school days as a snot-nosed little meany who called her carrot head and freckle face. Still, it was his family who gave her late husband a job at the lumber mill. And they were kind after Hank died, sending an expensive spray of flowers for the funeral. They also paid Livvy a death benefit which everyone said was mighty generous. Of course, she was obliged to give Hank's family a share and there were funeral expenses to pay. What was left over, she put in the bank hoping to use it for an art degree.

*

The house was in an uproar when Livvy got home. As she approached she could hear Mama playing "Blessed Assurance" on the piano. But it was not a happy sound. A woman was sobbing, interrupted by a man's voice. It was Clara crying while Preston tried to calm her down, telling her everything would be all right. Mama pounded away on the piano attempting to drown them out. Preston raised his voice to be heard and Livvy got the gist of the conversation.

He had hired on at the sawmill and was trying to convince his wife that they needed the money.

"What if you get yourself killed like Hank did?" Clara wailed.

"I won't let that happen, sugar."

Livvy didn't blame her sister-in-law one bit. If she'd known her own husband's life was in danger, she would've pitched a fit too when he told her about his new job.

The crying continued as Mama raised her voice in song. Livvy slipped into her bedroom to change clothes, finding Ruthie sprawled on the bed looking at *Silver Screen Magazine*.

"When can I start working at the store?" Ruthie said, oblivious to all the noise and drama. She was the beauty of the family with high cheekbones, big green eyes and golden brown hair.

"I can stock the shelves, clean up, wait on customers. I'm sick and tired of churning butter, doing laundry, sweeping and mopping. Not to mention cleaning the dang chamber pots."

Livvy pulled her dress off, tossing it on a chair and grabbing her overalls and a shirt. "You know how particular Inez is."

Ruthie looked up from her magazine. "Y'all seem to forget, I own one third of that store. I've been trying to decide which third is mine. Maybe the part that has the cold drinks and candy."

"You ought to be a clown in the traveling circus."

"You and Inez both worked at the store when you were fourteen."

"I don't know what you're fussing about. We make sure you get your share of the profits."

"Minus what we give Mama and Daddy. And their share's gotten a whole lot bigger lately."

"We have to help make a living around here. You do want a roof over your head, don't you?"

Ruthie sighed, setting her magazine on the bedside table.

"All right," Livvy said. "You can help me at the store in the morning. But the chores still need to be done. We'll talk with Mama about re-arranging who does what."

She gave her grinning little sister a wave and headed out the door. Tiptoeing into the kitchen, she snitched a couple of leftover hoecakes before trotting off toward the woods as the first strains of "There Will be Peace in the Valley" wafted through the open windows accompanied by Clara's bawling.

*

She'd worked up a sweat by the time she arrived at her enchanted doorway. That's how she'd begun to think of it. She looked upon it with satisfaction, walking this way and that, studying it from different angles. The air behind it seemed to ripple in the distance. Then she stepped through the opening, smiling at the idea of passing through a fairy door as though it might take her to another world.

Her next project wouldn't take as long. Using her knife, she cut long sections of vine she'd gathered the day before, stacking them alongside two scrub oaks a few yards from the doorway. There were some low branches that would serve her needs.

Excited to see the sky clouding up, she got to work arranging the vines on the ground side by side until they measured about five feet across. Then, starting at one end, she wove lengths of vine from one side of the rectangle to the other, then back and forth, back and forth like she was making a loosely woven basket. She continued until she'd created a long rectangle of crisscrossing vines. Then it was time to hang it. It took her a while to get the loose vines tied securely around the trunk of each tree above the bottom branches. When it was completed, she'd created a hammock. Not that it would hold anyone's weight, mind you, except for birds and squirrels.

Standing up, she stretched to loosen her back muscles. Then she walked a short distance away to gauge the effect. Not much to look at yet. She needed wind. Daddy mentioned they might get a thunderstorm this afternoon. Sure enough, she looked up to see the sky darkening.

From her bib pocket, she withdrew a handful of wild plums she'd picked on her walk to the woods – about the size of cherries. Sitting cross-legged on the ground, she devoured them, spitting the pits out, amused thinking about little plum trees growing on this spot one day.

She bided her time, keeping watch on the sky. The clouds grew thicker and darker, then a breeze picked up. Her new creation swayed gently. More wind. That's what she was waiting for.

Looking in all directions, it dawned on her she was also on the alert for a horse and rider. Which was embarrassing. A childish fantasy. Life was hard, she was lonely. So she was letting her imagination carry her away to a world of make-believe where an Englishman dropped by an enchanted forest to visit a red-haired Georgia girl. Not that she would admit it to anyone, but there was no denying she longed to escape a life filled with endless disappointment.

She had almost forgotten the finishing touch – embedding strands of her hair. She used the small scissors, then braided her hair into the vines. After which, she once again felt a strange quiver down her back.

That's when a sudden gust of wind whipped her hair into her eyes. She brushed it back, a grin sprouting on her face. Then a noise drew her eye toward the doorway. Through the opening she spied a horse and rider galloping toward her. He pulled up on the other side of the door just as the hammock began to flail from side to side as though strung from the timbers of a ship caught in a mighty tempest. The wind raced through the treetops, the branches careening wildly, a loud whooshing noise filling her ears. She watched the hammock whip back and forth, her hair flying in all directions.

"Well, this is a bit of a how-do-you-do," the stranger called out, his voice carried off by the wind.

Which made Livvy laugh. A strange remark made even stranger by his accent. He seemed as entranced as she was by the sight of the thrashing hammock.

A bolt of lightning split the sky. A quiet voice in her head reminded her that lightning could be dangerous but she was too enthralled to pay any heed.

"There was a cloudless sky until I arrived in the woodland," the man said, holding onto his hat.

She laughed again.

The horse jerked sideways, ready to bolt. But the man held tightly to the reins.

"You have a most creative mind," he said. "Who would think to create a vine hammock just as a storm passes through? A kinetic work of art."

He was right. This creation came alive in the wind.

Another flash of lightning stabbed the sky, followed by a rumble of thunder. The horse twirled around.

"It's all right, Bailey," the man said, patting the animal's neck.

"He's smarter than we are. He knows to get out of the storm."

"Perhaps I might take you home?"

"I won't melt."

He laughed. "A great relief, indeed."

"But thanks for the offer." Her mind told her to go but her legs hesitated.

"By the by, my name is Gordon Collins."

He gave her a lopsided grin, which reminded her of a little boy who likes a girl but isn't about to admit it.

"Livvy Sloan," she replied.

She waved as he took his leave. The rider and his beautiful horse disappeared into the trees, a dark sky visible in the distance. Bailey was undoubtedly relieved to be heading for home. Wherever that was.

A big fat raindrop landed on her head. Then another, followed by another bright flash of lightning and a crack of thunder. Raindrops splattered on the ground. She felt so alive.

She walked at a leisurely pace, the deluge soaking her to the skin. She wanted to relive the last ten minutes – the thrilling sight of her vine hammock whipping in the wind and the arrival of the mysterious stranger. Why did he dress like he was going to town when he went horseback riding? And his mount was the finest horse she'd ever seen. Maybe she should've let Gordon Collins give her a ride home. She tittered at the thought of sitting behind him, her arms wrapped around his waist. She hadn't felt this girlish since, well, since she was in high school. She needed to get a hold of herself.

"By the by," she whispered, chuckling. "Who says by the by?"

The rain was still coming down when she reached the farm. She watched Daddy hurry from the barn to the house. He removed his hat and scraped mud from his shoes on a cast iron boot scraper at the edge of the porch, calling out to her.

"Lordamercy, Livvy. Your hair's so red I can spot you a mile away even when it's raining. What were you doing out in that gulley washer?"

Before she could reply he made it plain that her forest excursions were not as stealthy as she thought.

"Building another nature construction?" he said, giving her a playful wink she hadn't seen in a long time. "Cecil and Vernon ran across a big thingamabob as they were checking their rabbit boxes. Had to be your doing." He shook his head before turning to go inside. "Bad enough you're roaming around the woods by yourself, but downright bone-headed to stay out during a thunderstorm. The older you get, the more you remind me of my mama. She had that same fiery red hair when she was young and listened about as well as you do."

Pride welled up as she removed her mud-caked shoes at the edge of the porch, setting them aside before ducking into her room. Daddy was a sly dog, chewing her out while making her feel special all at the same time.

You could tell he'd been a good-looking young man with a square jaw and warm brown eyes. He still had a thick shock of hair. Now it was white instead of brown. And, although he'd been a bear of a man in his younger years, he'd turned into a beanpole just like his son and grandsons. The culprit – too much work and not enough food to go around.

Once she'd changed into dry clothes, she lit the lamp and lay on her bed to read, knowing the kitchen was overflowing with helpers. She couldn't keep her eyes focused on the page though as she relived the events in the woods. She eventually drifted off to sleep dreaming about riding behind the stranger on his smokey horse, racing through the trees, rain falling in slow motion around them.

When she awoke, the tantalizing smell of fried chicken filled the air. She shook herself awake, pushing the dream from her mind. Reaching the kitchen, everyone was digging in. No one had even bothered to call her to supper.

There were eleven people seated elbow to elbow. Daddy sat at the head of the table, Livvy on his left. Then came Ruthie, and on her left Preston's two brown-haired daughters, eleven-year-old Nettie and nine-year old Faye. Mama was in her place at the end of the table by the stove, her food-spattered apron still tied in place, beads of sweat dotting her brow. Across the table, her grumpy sister Inez sat on Daddy's right, then Preston and his wife Clara. Their teenaged sons Cecil and Vernon sat on Clara's other side. This was how Thanksgiving used to look. Now it was an everyday sight, except there wasn't as much goodwill and not nearly as much food.

Tonight was an exception. Besides fried chicken, there was also mashed potatoes, gravy, biscuits and corn.

Livvy claimed the last piece of chicken – a back with precious little meat on it. But latecomers couldn't be choosers. She served her plate, keenly aware of the tension in the air. Inez sat ramrod straight, not saying a word, her plate only half filled. And it was plain that Preston and Clara had not made up since their spat.

"Thank you for the chickens, Aunt Inez," Cecil said.

The poor boy was trying to lift everyone's spirits, not realizing he'd just lit a fuse. Inez set her fork down.

"I'm real glad y'all think Flossie and Maisie taste so good. When Daddy said we should celebrate Preston getting the sawmill job with a fried chicken supper, why, I just jumped for joy watching Mama wring their necks."

Her chickens were like pets to Inez. She had names for all of them.

After a moment, Daddy broke the uneasy silence.

"You said last week they hardly laid eggs anymore, Inez."

She raised her eyes to the ceiling in exasperation.

"And we do appreciate it," he went on, then sank his teeth into a chicken leg.

Inez wasn't one to bury her resentment, forgetting that she wasn't the only one forced to make concessions. They were all compromising in one way or another.

Livvy, herself, had seen her savings depleted. She'd planned to pay for two more years of college at the University of Georgia. But she'd withdrawn money every year to share with the family to make ends meet. And, despite having precious little left in her account, from the look of things she'd be withdrawing more money very soon. Her hopes of studying art had been stubbed out like one of Daddy's after-supper cigarettes, crushed into the dirt by the toe of his shoe.

3

It started out as a quiet morning at the store. Only a couple of customers stopped by, one to buy a spool of thread, another to purchase hinges for a door. Livvy kept busy tidying up and changing out displays. She hung a blue flowered dress in the front window and set a nice straw hat on top of it. She was rearranging the men's hats when Ruthie burst through the door.

"You hear the news?" she said, looking like a dancing sunflower in the yellow dress Mama made her last year.

"What news?"

"Old Mr. Singletary was arrested last night for running moonshine."

"Mr. Singletary?"

"Yup. Heard Coy Whitaker talking with Reverend Blackwood just now sitting in their cars in the middle of the road."

"Mr. Singletary is a deacon of the church."

Ruthie snickered as she gazed around the store as though she were the owner come to check on her employees.

"What'll I do first?" she said.

"You can continue rearranging these hats. Just try to put something different in front so customers don't see the same thing every time they come."

The door opened again and Coy sauntered in, the shiny buttons on his shirt catching the sunlight. He nodded first at Livvy, then Ruthie.

"Morning, ladies!"

"Ruthie just told me about Mr. Singletary," Livvy said.

"The revenuers caught him with a trunkful of hooch just outside Atlanta. Now they're searching high and low for his still."

"Did you know he was a bootlegger?"

"I heard rumors."

"I guess Mr. High and Mighty is getting his just deserts." Livvy couldn't help but recall how Mr. Singletary said he wouldn't shop at a store that served Coloreds. "Now what can I help you with this morning?"

He glanced at Ruthie then raised his eyebrows at Livvy. "Can we step outside for a minute?"

They moved onto the porch and he pulled the door closed, striking a match to light a cigarette.

"I was thinking about that gas pump," he began. "You said you couldn't afford it. But what if I make you a loan so you can have it installed? A pump, a storage tank and the first fuel delivery, just to get you started."

Her mouth dropped open.

"A no-interest loan," he added.

"Why would you do that?"

"Just want the store to be successful, that's all. And I know for a fact you'd pay me back." He gave her one of his patented Coy Whitaker smiles, then took a puff of his cigarette.

She was left momentarily speechless.

"Think on it for a spell," he said.

She remembered to thank him as he left.

"Appreciate the offer, Coy."

Ruthie was laughing when Livvy returned.

"Believe Mr. Whitaker is sweet on you, Livvy!"

"What are you talking about?"

"Even through that dirty window, it was plain as day that he was looking at you with lovey-dovey eyes."

"Funny, I didn't notice any lovey-dovey eyes and I was standing right in front of him." She shook her head and slipped behind the counter.

"That's because you were staring at the dirt."

Livvy got to work, telling Ruthie to do the same. She spent the rest of the morning mulling over Coy's offer. So many things to consider. If they could sell gasoline, who knows – they might actually make some money. He was right. More and more people had cars and trucks these days, many of them second hand, but all of them with gas tanks that needed filling. Daddy had been driving over to Kinston to fill up ever since he bought his used Model T pickup. That's where Preston went too. If they had a pump at the store, she could sell it to them at cost. And if people drove to the general store for gas, they might come inside and buy other items.

Not knowing Coy very well, she wasn't entirely sure about his motives. He said he just didn't want the store to fail. Seemed logical. It was good for the community to have its own general store. Saved folks from having to make so many trips to town. Which is what they'd have to do every time they needed a plug of chewing tobacco or a bottle of castor oil if Hopkins General Merchandise went out of business.

She was also trying to figure out whether her little sister might be right about Coy. He'd certainly been coming around more often. And his offer of a loan came across as awfully kind. Still, if he did like her, seemed like he might ask her out. Maybe he was working up to it. She should think about how she wanted to reply.

*

When Livvy got home that afternoon Preston was riding Uncle Tyrone's corn planter as their two mules pulled it back and forth across the field.

Mama stood on the porch, hands on her hips, her brow even more furrowed than usual. Her face reflected years of hard work as a farm wife, her long grey hair in a whirl of a bun on the nape of her neck. Until a few years back, she'd been more full-figured, but the lean years had taken their toll and her dress hung loose on her thin frame.

"Uncle Tyrone let Daddy borrow his planter?" Livvy asked.

"Borrow? Not hardly. Rented it to him. Tyrone wouldn't give his own brother a helping hand even if it was judgment day."

"How did Daddy pay him? And how'd he buy the corn seed?"

"I asked the very same questions when they got home. How in tarnation did you get money to buy seed and pay Tyrone? Leon says, 'don't you worry about it, hon.' Lord, give me strength."

She looked up at the hazy sky before turning on her heel and bustling inside. Livvy followed her into the kitchen to find something to eat.

"Picked some tomatoes this morning," Mama said, slipping a clean apron over her head. "You can have one."

Livvy gave her mother a squeeze and kissed her on the cheek before grabbing the smallest tomato and a hunk of bread. On her way out the door, she was nearly knocked over as Preston's older daughter, Nettie, charged in with a basket of laundry fresh from the clothesline. Her little sister Faye was chasing after her.

"Nettie dropped a pair of pants in the dirt, Granny," Faye tattled.

"Did not," Nettie cried.

"Heavens," Mama replied. "A little dirt won't hurt anyone."

Nettie stuck her tongue out at Faye, both of them giggling as they waited for further instructions. When school started again, Livvy would need to help Mama more with the chores. But for now at least, she was enjoying her freedom.

She stopped by the barn where the wheelbarrow was parked inside the door, pushing it in front of her as she made her escape.

Once she left the farm behind, her mind was filled with speculation about whether Gordon Collins would show up on his fancy horse again. If he did, she was dying to ask him a few questions. Like where was he really from? And if he did live in Kinston, what in the world was he doing there? Because he was most definitely not from around here. And why, all of a sudden, had he started visiting her woods?

Well, it wasn't *her* woods although she thought of it that way. Nobody else came through there except her nephews. Cecil and Vernon ranged far and wide checking their rabbit boxes. The rabbits and squirrels they trapped helped keep the family fed. That and Mama's garden.

The forest land used to belong to Daddy and his older brother Tyrone, all the way to a stream called Sweet Creek that flowed to the river. But Uncle Tyrone claimed their father left it to *him*. Somehow he came up with money to hire a lawyer and ended up with title to the property. Relations between Leon and Tyrone had been cool ever since. It didn't surprise her in the least that Uncle Tyrone had charged his brother to use the checkrow planter.

At least Uncle Tyrone hadn't razed the trees for farmland. Instead, he'd built a rudimentary irrigation system from the stream to keep his soybeans from withering in the field while his brother's crops turned brown and died.

Finished with her food, she veered east toward the little brook. She spent a good hour gathering smooth stones, then pushed the heavy wheelbarrow the short distance to her growing art gallery.

After dumping the rocks on the ground, she plopped down, pulling a slightly squashed Moon Pie from her bib pocket. She enjoyed the treat while letting her eyes wander. The hammock now hung at an angle. One of the anchor vines had unraveled. Thankfully, the storm hadn't done any damage to her special doorway.

She took a few minutes to repair the hammock, then turned to her new project. Clearing the space in front of the doorway took longer than expected. She used her hands to scrape the pine straw, leaves and sticks away. By the time she finished, her hands were filthy and she was done in.

Movement in the distance drew her eyes. A doe darting between the trees – a rare sight these days because of overhunting – but not what she was looking for. Collapsing on the ground, she stared through the doorway, listening for hoofbeats. All she heard was cicadas calling for a mate.

Heading for home, she tried not to be disappointed. She shouldn't have been surprised. Judging from his clothes, his speech and his horse, Gordon Collins was not a poor man. She glanced down at her worn overalls and considered how she must appear to such a man. Like a country bumpkin. Which is exactly what she was by any measure.

At supper, the usual dark cloud seemed to have lifted, at least temporarily, even though there was no meat tonight. Preston's kids had left the table and Ruthie was just getting up to leave. As Livvy filled her plate, Ruthie giggled softly.

"I told everyone about Mr. Whitaker's visit to the store," she said.

Livvy rolled her eyes.

"Livvy pretended she didn't know what I was talking about," Ruthie continued, then looked across the table at Inez. "You said he asked about Livvy's work hours so he'd know when to visit."

"That was a month ago," Inez said. "Haven't seen hide nor hair of him since."

"You want the real lowdown?" Livvy said, looking around the table. "Coy came by to…"

"Coy!" Ruthie crowed, as if using his first name meant they were spooning.

Livvy held her hand up for Ruthie to shush.

"Coy stopped by yesterday to buy a sack of flour and a case of soft drinks. As he was leaving he said he thought we'd get more customers if we had a gas pump. Of course Inez and I have talked about that more than once. But the cost has always been out of the question."

Inez nodded.

"Today, he came back." She looked at Inez then. "He offered to give us a personal loan to pay for a gas pump, a storage tank, and the first delivery of gasoline. I was going to discuss it with you this evening."

"A personal loan?" Inez said, leaning forward.

"A no-interest personal loan. He said *he* would buy gas from us. He thinks a lot of folks would instead of driving all the way to Kinston. It's possible if people come by for a fill up, they might walk inside to buy something else. Groceries, a pack of cigarettes, a frying pan."

Inez nodded her head slowly, thinking hard.

"And speaking of loans," Livvy said, looking at Daddy, "who gave you a loan to buy that corn seed? And isn't it a little late for planting?"

Daddy sighed deeply, staring at his wife at the far end of the table. Mama lowered her chin, eyes fixed on her husband, waiting.

"The bank," Daddy said.

"We already have one bank loan we can't pay," Mama said, her voice a little shaky.

"We've got to make money somehow, Bess."

"But what did you use as security for the loan?"

"We don't aim to default. And it's only the middle of July. There's plenty of time to get a corn crop in. The soil was wet from last night's rain. Which is a good sign."

Livvy resumed eating, preferring not to watch the unspoken messages fly between her mother and father. She also didn't want to contemplate what would happen if last night's rain was a fluke and the drought continued. Instead, she focused her mind on Coy's offer.

The others had abandoned the table by the time she carried her plate to the wash tub. Ruthie, Nettie and Faye carried buckets of water into the kitchen, reporting for dishwashing duty.

When she stepped onto the porch, she stood still, enjoying the view of lightning bugs blinking beneath the branches of the pecan tree. When her eyes adjusted to the dark, she noticed the red tips of Daddy and Preston's cigarettes as they smoked and talked in low voices. Why were they being so secretive? Maybe she should find out.

Staying in the shadows, she eased all the way around the house, ducking below the windows until she reached the opposite corner. From there she scampered unseen to the truck which was parked halfway between the house and the pecan tree. She sat on the running board, straining to hear their words.

"Once the loan is paid off, we can wash our hands of it," Preston said. "We just have to be careful. Old man Singletary got sloppy."

Shuddering at his words, Livvy got to her feet and marched toward the pecan tree.

"I don't believe my ears," she whispered.

"You need to mind your own business," Preston barked.

His face was too shadowed to see, but she could hear the righteous indignation in his voice as though *she* was the one guilty of wrongdoing.

"I can't believe you're willing to risk going to prison," she said.

"Not going to prison," Daddy replied.

"Does Mama know about this harebrained idea?"

He dropped his cigarette and ground it into the dirt with his shoe. "One way or another, we have to make some money. You got a better idea?"

"Losing the farm would be better than…"

"No! No it wouldn't!"

She turned to Preston. "But you're starting at the lumber mill next Monday. That'll bring in some money."

"Not nearly enough."

"Does Clara know you're becoming bootleggers?"

"That's between me and her. Don't you stir up any trouble, you hear?"

4

Once the mules and the hog were fed the next morning, Daddy and Preston drove off in the truck with the boys riding in back. Clara was bluer than blue and Mama stomped around the kitchen like she was killing spiders. Inez squinted as the truck disappeared down the road, then glanced at her mother. She looked like she was about to say something but held her tongue for once, wandering out to feed her chickens. Eager to clear out, Livvy wolfed down some scrambled eggs then grabbed a biscuit to eat on her walk to the store.

Ruthie was full of questions when she reported for duty. Livvy pretended she had no idea where the men were off to. The last thing they needed was for Ruthie to learn the truth. She liked to jabber with anybody and everybody. But as much as Daddy and Preston wanted to keep their new business venture quiet, it would only be a matter of time till word leaked out.

As soon as Inez arrived midday, the first question out of her mouth was where the men had gotten off to that morning.

Livvy feigned ignorance again and changed the subject to the gas pump. Inez immediately offered to call the owner of a general store in Kinston she'd visited to pick his brain about how to go about having a storage tank and pump installed.

"The money is what I'm interested in," she said. "How much it would cost and how much we could make."

Livvy was glad to let her sister look into it and relieved when it was time to go home. She'd planned to sneak in and out of the house before starting for the woods again today. But once again her mother caught her foraging for food in the kitchen.

"Watch your step," Mama said, moving a bucket of murky water out of the way and leaning the mop against the wall.

She had just finished mopping under the table. All the chairs were turned upside down on the table's surface.

"I've got something for you," she said, wiping sweat from her face with her apron as she retrieved something wrapped in brown paper from the sideboard. It was a folded piece of green fabric. "I've been saving this cloth for a while. I want you to have it so you can sew yourself a pretty dress."

"I've got three work dresses for summer and three for winter. And I've got church dresses too."

"All of them are faded, some threadbare." Her mother smiled, holding the cloth out to her. "You don't have anything nice enough for a date." Mama glanced over her shoulder to make sure they were alone and lowered her voice. "Like I've said before, you don't want to end up like Inez. You need to have something special to wear if Coy Whitaker comes calling."

Livvy rolled her eyes.

"Listen here, daughter, Coy's got a future ahead of him. One thing's for sure, the bank's not breathing down his neck.

From all I hear, he's taken a fancy to you. And that's nothing to sneeze at. It broke my heart when Hank died, but you don't want to be a widow for the rest of your life. Even if Coy doesn't make your heart flutter like Hank did, you could have a good life and a family of your own."

Funny how everyone assumed Hank had made Livvy's heart flutter. Their marriage wasn't as romantic as Mama assumed. When they began dating, Hank didn't seem overly smitten. His sister spilled the beans, explaining to Livvy that Hank was trying to mend his broken heart when he asked her out. The girl he was head over heels for had dumped him for a college boy and he thought Livvy might be a good second choice. Which hurt her feelings at first. But they gradually settled into an affectionate relationship. One thing she appreciated about Hank was that he respected her artistic aspirations, saying he approved of her getting a four-year degree. That was a rarity in a farming community where women were expected to turn their attention to keeping house and making babies once they tied the knot. He promised to get a job in Athens so she could attend the University of Georgia. Unfortunately, right after they married he took the sawmill job instead, saying he could earn more money before they moved to Athens in time for classes in the fall.

Livvy hugged her mother. "You're the best mama this side of the North Pole!"

Mama laughed and resumed mopping the floor.

"You need to take a break," Livvy said. "Why don't you let me finish up for you?"

"It'll be done in two shakes. Then I'll have a nice glass of ice tea on the porch." She waved her hand in dismissal.

Livvy grabbed a leftover biscuit and took the fabric to her bedroom, ready to get a move on. Changing into her overalls, she thought about the sorrows in Mama's life. Their first-born died in infancy, smothered in the sheets of the family bed. Mama always blamed herself. Their son Garnett was killed on the battlefield in the Great War. She blamed herself for his death too, as if she could've saved him from being drafted and shipped to France. Mama also worried she hadn't done enough to teach Inez how to get along with people, men in particular. She fretted about being too old to be a good mother to Ruthie who came along as a mid-life surprise when she was fifty, causing her no end of embarrassment at church that she and Daddy were still more than a little affectionate. Now, Livvy guessed Mama blamed herself for Preston's struggles. Hell, she might even hold herself responsible for Livvy's troubles. Poor Mama.

She concluded then that she would make herself that new dress. And if Coy asked her out, she would say yes. But the sewing would have to wait. Her pretty river stones were calling.

Upon reaching her special area of the woods, she took several slow, deep breaths and rolled her head in a circle to relax her neck. She could see the spiral design in her mind, crowding out the burdens of everyday life. Fatigue and worry evaporated like dew on the wildflowers by the roadside as the sun climbed higher every morning.

Choosing a spot to the left of the hammock, she began by placing a small dark grey stone in the center. Then she added more dark stones, creating spiral arms, using slightly larger stones as she proceeded, then smaller stones for the outermost edges. She left spaces so that when the spiral was about five feet across, she started at the center again, creating another spiral that fit in between the rocks of the dark spiral. This time, she used light colored stones. Starting in the middle again with smaller stones, she graduated to larger ones as she went, then scaled the size of the stones smaller before reaching the outer rim.

Eager to see what it looked like from a bird's eye view, she climbed the sitting tree – so named because it grew at such a slant, you could scoot up the leaning trunk into the branches and sit for a spell. She gazed down upon her new creation. The dark and light interlocking spirals resembled something out of a fable, a design with a celestial quality to it, a design that might have a hidden meaning.

Climbing down again, she separated three strands of her hair and snipped them with Grandma's scissors, tucking them beneath the center rock. As she straightened up again, a quiver zipped through her body, followed immediately by the unmistakable sound of hoofbeats approaching.

Gordon Collins waved in greeting

"Halloo!" he called out, reminding her of a horse whinnying.

For an instant, it made her think of the centaur she'd read about in a book on Greek myths when she was growing up. Which made her chuckle. She was always chuckling when the stranger with the English accent turned up.

He came to a halt and dismounted – the first time he'd done that. He pulled his cap from his head as he walked toward her. His tousled hair was a rich brown in the dappled sunlight. The dashing smile was there, as usual. But now she could also see his lively eyes, eyes that appeared to be on the lookout for adventure.

"You're just in time," she said, sweeping her arm in a grand gesture toward the arrangement of stones.

He studied her creation, then nodded vigorously. "What an extraordinary design! It reminds me of a galaxy in the cosmos."

"A galaxy?"

"I've seen a photo of a galaxy shaped like your work of art, whirling around in a spiral."

"An actual photograph?"

"Yes, of the Andromeda Galaxy, taken by a Welshman. Scientists used to think the Milky Way was the only galaxy and that Andromeda was a nebula within it. Now they say there are other island universes as well."

She studied her spiral of smooth stones with new appreciation. "I wish I could see that picture."

"It's in a magazine. Perhaps I could bring it with me next time. Are you a stargazer?"

"I don't know much about the heavens but I like looking up at the stars."

"I enjoy looking up at the night sky as well. I'm an amateur astronomer."

She smiled, not sure what to say. Anyone whose hobby was astronomy came from a whole different world than the one she lived in.

"I started in this direction yesterday afternoon but got turned around," he said. "Oddly, Bailey and I couldn't seem to find our way to the woodland."

"I was back and forth to the brook hauling rocks." She pointed toward the small stream.

"I didn't know there was a brook nearby. Of course, I didn't know about these woods until the other day. You'd think I'd know my way around as long as I've lived here."

"How long have you lived in Kinston?"

"All my life."

"You don't sound like any American I've ever met."

He laughed at that. "Definitely not a Yank. But you *do* sound like an American."

"American, born and bred."

He opened his mouth as if to speak, then closed it again. For a second, she imagined he was mesmerized. How silly of her. Here she was in her overalls, her hair disheveled, hands covered with dirt. She liked that word though. Mesmerized. It was a romantic word. The idea of a man being mesmerized by her struck a chord. Although it wasn't likely to happen even under the best of circumstances, especially not when she was traipsing through the woods looking like a field hand.

"It's getting late and I must go," he said. "Will you be here tomorrow?"

"There's something I need to take care of tomorrow. I'll be back the day after."

"Then I shall bring my magazine with the Andromeda picture." He donned his cap and remounted his horse. "Until then!"

She watched him go, filled with anticipation. Maybe Mama was right. It was time to spruce up. She needed to get busy on that new dress.

*

The truck rumbled into the yard that evening. Livvy listened through the window as the men stopped by the water pump to wash up. She heard Preston say he was leaving right after supper, cautioning Cecil and Vernon to keep their mouths shut.

"Don't even talk about it with each other," he said. "Someone's bound to hear. Understand?"

"Yes sir."

Waiting until they clomped across the porch and into the house, she slipped out of her room and headed toward the pickup, casual as you please. When she reached the truck, she strolled around to the other side. There was something in the bed covered by a blanket tied down with rope. She lifted a corner, discovering the truck was loaded with crates of canning jars. She didn't need anybody to tell her what that clear liquid was inside them.

She entered the kitchen as bowls full of poke sallet, boiled potatoes and butter beans were passed from hand to hand, followed by a plate of crackling bread. The flurry of activity was accompanied by chatter from the kids, including an "I don't like poke sallet," from nine-year-old Faye, followed by her mother's quick retort, "You'll eat what's served and be thankful for it."

Poke sallet wasn't Livvy's favorite either, but she knew they were lucky Mama's garden was so productive. She had insisted Daddy and Preston put barrels around the house to catch what little rainwater they got and kept a bucket below the pump in the yard to catch dirty water. Which was put to good use watering the garden. She always said, "waste not, want not."

"This crackling bread is awful good," Cecil said.

"Mm-mm," Vernon agreed, his mouth too full to speak.

Cecil definitely took after his granny, always wanting to smooth things over. Vernon was kind-hearted too. The boys were only a little shorter than their father and could've passed for twins except Cecil was an inch taller than Vernon. They had their mother's grey eyes, minus the nervous melancholy, and their father's thick brown hair and long legs.

Inez wasn't as prickly as usual, catching Livvy's attention as she passed the beans.

"I found out how it works," she said. "I'll tell you after supper."

By her tone, Livvy guessed Inez wanted to start selling gasoline as soon as possible. She'd been chomping at the bit to make more money. Now she saw her chance.

Livvy was thankful the usual dinnertime edginess was largely absent but noticed Clara giving her husband meaningful glances as they ate. When Preston had cleaned his plate, he pushed away from the table, announcing he had an errand to run.

"I need to talk with you first," Clara said, keeping her voice low.

"Can it wait till I get back?"

"Won't take five minutes." She stood too, leading the way from the kitchen toward their bedroom at the back of the house.

Livvy waited a minute, then rose as well. She thanked Mama for supper before easing out the door while everyone else finished eating. Passing right by her bedroom, she moseyed out to the pickup, planting herself on the driver's side running board so no one in the house could see her. She didn't have to wait long.

Preston heaved an irritated sigh when he rounded the truck.

"I'm late already and I'm not interested in anything you have to say."

She stayed put, blocking the door. "I saw what's in the back." She pointed to the truck bed.

"Move, Livvy!"

"It's not just your own life you're risking, Preston. If you go to prison, what'll happen to your family?"

"Get out of my way." He gave her a stern look.

"And what about Daddy? What about Cecil and Vernon? You want them to end up behind bars?"

He shook his head and started around the front of the truck heading for the other side. She jumped up, opened the driver's door and slipped in behind the wheel.

"I'll pry you out of my way, if need be," he said, yanking the passenger door open.

"If you're known as a bootlegger, what do you think that'll mean for the rest of us?"

"My patience is worn thin, Livvy."

He slammed the door, stalked back around the truck, and stood threateningly beside her.

"One last chance. Move now or I'm dragging you out."

"Clara deserves to know."

"She knows."

"And Mama deserves to know you're turning your sixty-five-year-old father into a criminal."

"Dammit, Livvy!"

"Not to mention Cecil, who'll be a criminal at the age of sixteen, and Vernon, who's only fifteen. You're setting a fine example for your sons."

He hung his head, taking a deep breath.

"As I just told Clara, this is only for a little while. But my family's not going to end up moving from shack to shack with no place to call home."

She started to speak but he held up his hand. "I know what I'm doing, Livvy. I've done it before."

"Before?"

"Ten years ago, after Prohibition began, me and a friend had a still. Never got caught. Gave it up when the farm started producing enough to make a living. Of course, that was before the damn drought knocked me down flat. Anyway, time's a wasting. Don't force me to pry you out of the truck."

She slid off the seat and stepped aside. Without another word, he hopped in, cranked the engine and whirled the truck around before speeding away.

Standing with her arms crossed over her chest, she surveyed the cornfield. There'd been that good rain the night before planting, but not a drop since. It was too early for seedlings to be showing. She hoped to goodness it would be a successful crop. It occurred to her they might've chosen to plant corn instead of soybeans, like some of their neighbors had done, so they'd have corn for the still.

Ironic. That's what it was. Daddy didn't even drink. Never had. He had one cigarette a day which he rolled himself after supper. He was a family man, plain and simple. Never had any high aspirations. Working the farm, having family around him, spending time with Mama – those were the things that made him happy. But he had his pride. And repeated crop failures had taken their toll. When Livvy told him losing the farm was better than going to prison, he told her in no uncertain terms she was wrong.

When she started toward the house, she was surprised to see Mama waiting for her on the porch. She motioned for Livvy to walk with her to the garden, out of earshot of any busybodies.

"You going to start on that new dress?" Mama said.

"Thought I'd cut it out tonight and sew it up tomorrow when I get home."

"Good."

Reaching the potato patch, her mother turned to face her.

"I want you to know Leon told me what they're doing. Your daddy and I don't keep secrets from each other. Clara knows too. I admit, neither of us is happy about it, but Leon and Preston believe they can save the farm this way."

"But Mama..."

"Let me finish. Leon wishes he'd switched over to corn or soybeans last year like Preston said. But he thought the arsenic would kill the boll weevils. It killed some, but not nearly enough. He also prayed we'd get more rain this year. We didn't. Now we're in a pickle. He and Preston are trying to get us out. Giving them a tongue lashing won't help, Olivia."

"If we're in a pickle now, we'll be at the very bottom of a *barrel* of pickles if all the men in this family are hauled off to prison."

"Don't badger them!" She was dead serious.

Twilight had deepened and their features were in shadow. Which was a good thing because skepticism was plain on Livvy's face.

5

Cutting out fabric was usually a quiet task. But Inez strolled into the kitchen as Livvy was pinning pattern pieces onto the material Mama had given her. Thankfully, her big sister didn't look like a steel trap about to snap shut. She looked younger, her features softer, and her hair looked like she'd taken a little more time with it. It was red too, but more of a strawberry blonde, worn short with waves that framed her face, a couple of grey hairs visible on top.

"I reached Mr. Beasley who owns that store in Kinston. He explained everything. Gave me the number of a man at Texaco who estimated how much it would cost."

"A pretty penny, no doubt."

"Got to spend money to make money. Since Coy only drops by the store when you're there, ask him when we can meet to talk about the loan."

Livvy agreed to set up a meeting, conveying a sense of calm she didn't feel.

Inez cleared her throat before changing the subject.

"I'm glad you're sewing yourself a dress. I reckon Mama's right; you'll end up like me if you don't make an effort. Take my word for it, you'll turn around and be forty years old wondering where all those years went."

Lord! Now Inez, herself, was warning her about finding a man.

Sure enough, Coy stopped by the next morning, smelling freshly showered and shaved, his clothes neatly ironed. Livvy was positive his mother wouldn't stoop to using a hot iron, guessing their maid handled the sweaty housework.

"Need a tin of chewing tobacco for Daddy."

Livvy reached for a small red tin from a nearby shelf. "Inez and I talked about your offer. We'd like to sit down with you to discuss the particulars."

"Well now, that's good to hear, Livvy." He pulled cash from his billfold. "I'll check with our lawyer and we'll set up a meeting."

She took the money, handed him his change and gave him as warm a smile as she could muster under the circumstances. His mention of a lawyer caused her a touch of uneasiness. She and Inez should have a lawyer too. But that was too expensive.

She spent the afternoon sewing in her parents' bedroom, which also served as the living room. There was a sagging couch that had seen better days and two matching chairs on one side, the iron bed and chest of drawers on the other. While Mama and Daddy slept in here, Inez, Nettie and Faye slept in what used to be Mama and Daddy's bedroom – part of the rearrangement of the house when Preston's family moved in.

There was plenty of light streaming through the window, thus, no need to light a lamp. While she was intent on making the dress, she missed the forest. As her feet pumped the treadle she considered ideas for her next art project. What if she created the silhouette of a person? Maybe an entire figure. It could be attached to a tree. A nymph. Like a dryad from

Greek mythology she'd read about. Visions of tree nymphs paraded through her mind to the rhythmic thumping of the sewing machine. She couldn't wait to see Gordon's face. Realization dawned that his reaction had become part of the thrill of completing her artworks. She would get busy tomorrow gathering her materials.

When she finished sewing, she tried the dress on, pinning the back together where the buttons would go. Gazing at her reflection in the cloudy mirror, she had to agree – the fabric was meant for her, just like Mama said. It was the color of green apples. With her hair fixed and wearing her best shoes, she just might look presentable enough to sit down in a smart restaurant.

She spent the evening doing all of the hand stitching to finish it up.

*

Coy pulled up in front of the store the next morning as Livvy unlocked the door. Sitting in the driver's seat, engine idling, he called out to her.

"Is Monday afternoon good for you and your sister to meet?"

"Monday's fine."

"I'll pick y'all up here at one o'clock. We'll talk with the lawyer at my house."

He flashed a broad smile, waved and drove off, dust billowing up behind him.

She had to remind herself that she was the one who'd been dreaming of getting a gas pump. She agreed with Coy that it would likely bring in more customers. But drawing up the papers made her nervous. Did they really know what they were getting into? But dang it, plenty of general stores had gas pumps. Like that man Inez talked with in Kinston. This was a logical expansion of their business.

*

She hadn't intended to wear her new dress that afternoon. It didn't make a bit of sense. Her plan was to have it ready in case Coy asked her for a date. Yet when she slipped into her bedroom after work, the new dress looked so pretty hanging there on the wardrobe that she had a sudden hankering for Gordon to see her in it. Not Coy. She wanted Gordon to know she wasn't just a hayseed in overalls with wild red hair.

Naturally, she couldn't do her forest work in a dress, even an old one. So, after changing into her overalls, she folded the dress and placed it inside a paper sack, her good shoes underneath. She dropped her hairbrush in as well. She stopped by the barn, set the bag in the wheelbarrow and tramped off toward the woods.

She proceeded directly to her little woodland, as Gordon called it. Finding some thick bushes in the densely wooded area by the creek, she wiped her hands on her pantlegs before transforming herself into a city girl. Or some approximation thereof. She left the overalls in the wheelbarrow and smoothed her dress. She didn't want to soil it by sitting down, so she remained standing as she brushed her hair into place. Too bad she hadn't brought her lipstick. She hadn't used it in a long time, but today might've been a good day to apply a touch of red.

While she waited, she figured out how she would weave her materials together along the tree trunk. She calculated the quantity of sticks and vines she'd need. Strolling in the shade, she let her eyes roam the forest, listening for the sound of hoofbeats. But all she heard was the rustle of leaves and the mating call of a Bobwhite in the treetops – "bob bob white!"

"Bob bob white, yourself!" she called out, frustration making her irritable.

She'd been so looking forward to surprising him with her feminine appearance. But he must have more important things to do than ride out to see the country girl in overalls. He was an educated man, a man who would have friends more like himself. And despite his enthusiasm for her creations it made sense that he would have a girlfriend. Maybe even a fiancée. Who knows – he might even have a wife!

She changed back into her overalls before heading off with the wheelbarrow. A couple of hours later, having accumulated a sufficient pile of sticks, branches and more vines, she sat in a shady spot to rest. Peeling the hardboiled egg she'd brought, she ate as she selected a place for the new creation. A small oak to the right of the fairy door would be ideal for her tree nymph.

With time to make a start, she got to work, so captivated, she continued until the light had faded. Then she wiped her hands on her overalls, set the bag with her new dress and shoes in the wheelbarrow and started for home, thankful she knew the way even in the dark.

As she approached the cornfield, she heard Preston's voice near the truck.

"If you get stopped, tell him you borrowed the car and didn't know what was in the back."

"Yes sir." It was Cecil's voice.

A door slammed and the engine sputtered to life. Headlights swung around as Preston's beat up Model T bounced out of the yard, Cecil driving. Then another engine cranked and Daddy's truck rolled by, Preston behind the wheel.

*

Sunday morning everyone was expected to attend church. Livvy begged off, certain the spirit was more likely to move her if she were in the woods rather than sitting on a hard wooden pew listening to Daddy snore while Mama poked him in the ribs. When the rest of them took off, she breathed a sigh of relief. As a peace offering, she volunteered to clean up the kitchen, tackling that first thing.

Next, she pulled the whetstone out from under her bed, took it to the porch where she sat to sharpen her pocketknife. In her handwritten will Grandma had bequeathed her fancy hair combs and mirror to Inez. She'd left Livvy her embroidery scissors, her whetstone and her wooden handled pocketknife. Nothing fancy, but, as it turned out, just exactly what would bring Livvy the most satisfaction.

Her chores completed, she threw on her overalls, retrieved the wheelbarrow and started off in her favorite direction. Her spirits improved as soon as she reached the trees. She meandered through the woods, stopping here and there to load more twigs into the wheelbarrow, cutting more vines as she came across them. When the barrow was full, she made for the woodland, anxious to get to work.

The figure would be her own height – about five, eight. Last night she'd gotten a good start, but it still resembled a large fuzzy caterpillar clinging to the side of the tree. Today, she began on the head and face, molding a forehead, nose, mouth and chin. Leaving indentations for eyes, she created cheekbones using more of the sticks she'd broken into small pieces and woven together with vines.

The longer she worked, the more absorbed she became, and the more determined she was to give it an otherworldly quality. She forgot to listen for hoofbeats, forgot to wish Gordon would appear, forgot about dreading a life alone, forgot about the stressful plans for the store, forgot her fears about the moonshine business and the looming loan payments. Her body seemed to become one with her art.

Blood pumping, she stood back to gauge the effect. It reminded her of a female figurehead on the bow of a sailing ship from the past. They were thought to bring good luck to the ship and its crew. Her nymph leaned away from the tree, hovering over the woodland, her chin held high. Her eyes appeared to be gazing into the distance as though she were keeping watch.

Now to add the finishing touch! She clipped several strands of hair, coiled them together with a tendril of honeysuckle and braided it into the figure. As she tucked it into place, a vibration traveled through her body, followed by the sound of a horse racing through the forest.

She waved, anxious for her new friend's reaction.

Gordon dismounted and bounded toward her.

"As I live and breathe! Another woodland artwork! A dryad, is it not?"

"It is."

He backed up, moving a few feet to one side, then the other, never taking his eyes from the tree nymph.

"I confess, I'm greatly amazed by your artistry!"

She couldn't wipe the smile from her face. She was elated by his response. She was also relieved he'd returned.

"I brought my Kodak," he said. "If you have no objection, I'd like to take some photographs. I can share them with you once they're processed."

"I'd love that."

He dashed back to his horse, withdrawing a black camera from a saddlebag. He released a mechanism as he returned so the front of the camera expanded.

"If you'll stand next to your beautiful tree nymph."

"I'm not dressed for a picture." She looked down at her faded overalls, wishing he had come yesterday when she was wearing her pretty dress. "And my hair's a mess." She pushed an unruly lock behind her ear. "It may come as a surprise to you, but I normally wear dresses. Except, of course, when I'm out here in the woods."

Gesturing enthusiastically for him to proceed, she moved out of range while he photographed the tree nymph from different vantage points, doing the same for the doorway, the hammock and the rock spiral. She couldn't suppress the pride that welled up. She also couldn't wait to see the pictures.

When he finished, he stowed the camera, returning with a magazine. "You wanted to see the picture of the Andromeda Galaxy."

"Yes, I did!"

He found the page and started to pass the magazine to her.

"My hands are filthy," she said. "Can you hold it so I can see?"

"Of course. Considerate of you to think of that."

He held the magazine in front of him, the pages facing her so she could see the dramatic black and white image of the spiral galaxy.

She gasped, eyes wide. "How in the world did he take a photograph of something so far away?"

"He used a powerful telescope and a very long exposure. Not an easy thing to do. It's called astrophotography."

She sighed in admiration. "Wouldn't it be something to look through a telescope like that?"

"I've had the opportunity to do so and can say unequivocally that it's an awe-inspiring sight to behold."

"Lucky you." She stepped back as he closed the magazine. "Thank you for showing me."

"Watching the amazement in your face was thanks enough."

She walked over to her rock spiral and examined it with fresh eyes.

"I want to apologize for not coming yesterday," he said. "Bailey seemed confused again and we took the wrong path."

She looked beyond him to where the horse pawed the ground impatiently. Interesting that he was blaming that beautiful animal.

"I'm going to build a second figure – a male partner for the nymph," she said. "Would you care to help?"

"Indeed, I would!" Excitement was clear on his face. "Tomorrow?"

"Tomorrow."

He said his farewells, commenting that it was getting late. Then he looked up through the trees. "The light is always brighter here in your woodland."

The hazy sky looked normal to her for a mid-afternoon in late July.

That evening, it was time for Preston to leave for the lumber mill. He would share a room with three other men during the week and drive home on Friday evenings to spend weekends on the farm. He carried a knapsack to his car surrounded by his family. Livvy stood with Mama, Daddy, Inez and Ruthie on the porch watching as he hugged his daughters, telling them to help their mama and their granny. He reminded the boys about keeping up with all their chores. Then he turned to Clara. Preston wasn't one for public displays of affection, but he wrapped his wife in his arms and held her close, whispering something in her ear. Then he was off, his loved ones waving until his taillights disappeared around the bend.

*

Monday afternoon Inez arrived at the store ahead of schedule wearing a quiet tan dress belted at the waist with a hem that reached a few inches below the knee. While she never wore makeup, her face seemed to have more color than usual.

Livvy had worn her least faded work dress, the blue print, and had left her hair on her shoulders, not wanting to appear as though she was putting on airs.

Ruthie was giddy standing behind the counter like she was the proprietor as her two sisters walked out the door.

"Don't leave the store unattended," Inez cautioned her. "Not even for a minute."

"Don't worry. I know what I'm doing."

Coy beamed as he walked around the dusty car to open the doors for them. "Ladies!"

Inez hopped in back, Livvy in front, both of them tying scarves over their heads to protect their hair. Coy made small talk as they drove the two miles to his family's home. It was an imposing two-story white frame house with neat black shutters and thick bushes bordering a wraparound porch. Not ostentatious exactly but sitting on a hill overlooking a pasture with cows grazing in the distance, it made Livvy aware of the chasm between the Whitakers and the Hopkins.

Coy's mother greeted them at the front door, smiling like they were long-lost relatives come to visit.

"Welcome to our humble home." Then she turned to Coy. "Mr. Thompson is waiting in the dining room."

It was hard to come up with a polite response considering Mrs. Whitaker was clearly fishing for compliments. Their home might be humble compared to John D. Rockefeller's mansion, but it was probably the fanciest house in Burgess County.

Coy led them along a wide central hallway past a door that opened onto a parlor furnished with an overstuffed sofa, matching chairs and a Persian rug on the floor. Livvy was surprised to catch a glimpse of Mae Glover in a white apron with a feather duster in her hand. A few more steps along the hall brought them to the dining room. Standing at the far end of a polished oak table was a balding man in a grey pin-striped suit, the paunch protruding from his jacket a sure sign of a well-fed man. He nodded at Coy, who responded by shaking his hand before making the introductions.

"Mr. Thompson, this is Olivia Sloan and her sister Inez Hopkins, co-owners of Hopkins General Merchandise. Ladies, this is our family attorney, Lester Thompson."

Thompson studied the sisters like he was trying to see a resemblance. Formal nods were exchanged as they sat down in upholstered chairs, Coy on Mr. Thompson's right, Inez and Livvy on his left. Inez gave Livvy a tiny lift of her eyebrow as if to say, "they can easily afford to give us a loan."

Coy gestured for Mr. Thompson to begin.

"I've drawn up a loan agreement after discussing the matter with Mr. Whitaker. The term of the loan is twenty-four months at zero percent interest. Which is unheard of, ladies, except among family members. You should consider yourselves most fortunate to be the recipients of such magnanimity."

He handed Inez two long sheets of paper, then gave a copy of the document to Coy and kept one for himself. Livvy leaned closer to Inez so she could study the typed paragraphs marching one after another all the way down the first page and continuing onto the second page.

"First, I must ascertain that you two are indeed owners of Hopkins General Merchandise."

Inez spoke right up. "Our grandmother left the store to me, Livvy and our sister, Ruthie. But since she's only fourteen, Livvy and I make all the decisions and run the store."

"We'll need to see verification of ownership before the contract is signed."

Inez nodded.

"Now," he continued, "what this contract says, in essence, is that you're borrowing the still-to-be-determined sum of money to purchase a gas pump, the requisite tank to store the gasoline, and any additional equipment needed to operate said gas pump, along with your first fuel delivery. The contract also says you agree to repay Mr. Whitaker in monthly installments over the two-year loan period. Your first payment will be due two months after all parties sign the contract. It's your responsibility to determine the total cost, including delivery and installation so that we may specify the loan amount. It is also your responsibility to add a rider to your insurance policy covering the newly installed equipment. You will want to read the document over carefully. Once you've satisfied yourselves as to its contents, why then we can hold a second meeting wherein all parties will sign the contract."

"We'll know the price tomorrow," Inez said, surprising Livvy. "A man from the refinery is coming out to show us pictures of the pump and the tank. We'll agree on where they'll be installed, and he'll give me the exact cost."

"Excellent. I'm available Thursday afternoon to sign the documents, at which point Mr. Whitaker can write you a check."

He lifted a brown leather briefcase onto the table, slipped his copy of the contract inside and buckled the straps before getting to his feet.

"Thursday at one-thirty right here. If you have any questions before then, you may call my office in Athens." He handed his business card to Inez.

On the drive back to the store, not a word was spoken about the loan. Instead, Coy talked non-stop about his trip to Athens the previous weekend to spend time with college friends. About how they'd played a round of golf and gone to the Varsity for hot dogs afterwards. Although Inez was sitting in the back seat again, Livvy knew her sister well enough to imagine how she was rolling her eyes listening to Coy prattle on.

As he brought the car to a stop in front of the store, Livvy thanked him for his generosity.

"We consider ourselves most fortunate to be the recipients of such magnanimity."

He laughed. "Mr. Thompson's got a way with words, don't he?"

She only spent a few minutes in the store before walking home. The anxiety in her belly was causing her to question whether she was cut out to be a businesswoman. Yet people took out loans every day. Businesspeople especially. But it wasn't just the loan and the gas pump that bothered her. There was her naivete thinking she needed a new dress to be ready for Coy to ask her out. He wasn't going to ask her out. He'd just emphasized to her and Inez that he and his family were way above them, first, by arranging the loan meeting at his luxurious home, then by reminding them he was a college graduate who played golf with other University of Georgia alumni.

There was also the fact that he was two years younger than Livvy. He was twenty-four years old, good looking, with enough money that he could loan the poor Hopkins sisters cash to turn their country store into a filling station. Coy Whitaker could take his pick of any girl in the county. There was no reason for him to condescend to ask a poor widow for a date.

On top of all that, she couldn't help but think of Gordon. She preferred his company. But he was even less likely than Coy to see her in a romantic light. Gordon was fascinated by her artwork. She must seem like an interesting oddity to him. He didn't know any other country girls in overalls who spent their time in the woods creating art with sticks and vines. No doubt, it made for lively dinnertime conversation.

She heaved a sigh.

Lost in thought, she didn't hear a car approaching from behind until it pulled up alongside her.

"Hey!" It was Coy, his elbow resting on the open window, a cigarette in his hand. "Let me drive you the rest of the way home." He gestured with his head for her to get in.

She moved quickly to the other side of the car, sliding onto the seat beside him.

Instead of continuing to her house, he stopped in the shade of a half dead birch tree, taking a drag on his cigarette as he killed the engine.

"This has nothing to do with our business deal," he said, pulling his right knee up onto the seat so he could face her. "Did you know I was crazy about you back when we were in school?"

She shook her head, trying to remember any interactions they might've had, but came up blank.

"Yeah, I was a little kid to you," he said. "You didn't know I existed."

"I hope I never hurt your feelings."

"It's just the way things are. Upperclassmen don't notice underclassmen."

"Now *you're* the upperclassman," she said.

He chuckled, seeming pleased with her comment. "Anyway, I just wanted to ask if you'd like to go out Saturday evening. We could drive over to see a picture in Athens."

She wondered what Coy would think of her woodland creations. Would he be impressed like Gordon was? Or would he think she was off her rocker? Maybe she should give him a tour and find out. Right now, though, she needed to answer his question. She didn't know what his intentions were. It pained her to think he might be between girlfriends and was merely looking for some easy entertainment in the meantime.

Regardless, she had told herself if this moment came, she would say "yes." And that's what she did.

6

Cornbread slathered with fig preserves made a good late lunch. Later than usual today because of the meeting with the lawyer.

After pulling on her overalls, Livvy retrieved the wheelbarrow, calling out a hello to Nettie and Faye who were busy tossing hay down from the loft. The men were nowhere to be seen.

Still no seedlings showing as she skirted the cornfield. It would probably be a week or so before they poked up through the soil. Another rain is what they needed. And soon.

She tried to imagine going out with Coy. It had been a long time since she'd been on a date. She'd only ever dated Hank. And they were humble outings like playing horseshoes at his family's house on a Sunday afternoon. It wasn't at all like going out with a man she barely knew. Thinking about it didn't help. With a shake of the head, she nudged all thoughts of Coy from her mind.

Working with Gordon on the second figure would be fun. He seemed genuinely enthusiastic about helping her. Once she passed the tree line, she hurried to gather more twigs, vines and pinecones. With what was left over from her previous foraging, there should be enough.

Since she was running a little late, she thought he might be there before her. But he hadn't arrived yet. Which gave her time to organize her materials. Coaching him on how to thread the twigs, pinecones and vines together would be the first step. Her ears were on alert for his approach, but after waiting nearly an hour, she got started.

Eventually she concluded that something must've come up. But she was soon engrossed in her work and the afternoon slipped away as she shaped the new figure on a tree opposite the first one. This one had broader shoulders and a square jaw with a longer nose than the female figure. She wanted him to look masculine. While the lower half of both bodies were undefined – looking like they were growing out of the trees they were attached to – the upper half of the bodies, along with their heads and faces, had to be distinct. She fine-tuned the new creation until she was satisfied.

It was getting dark when she backed away to get a better view. The new figure definitely looked male. A little shiver of excitement ran through her body when she realized her two creatures appeared to be gazing at each other. Her heart warmed to think she had created a pair of woodland lovers. She wished Gordon could've been here to work with her.

As usual, she snipped a few strands of hair, twirled it with a bit of vine which she then tucked into the shoulder of her new artwork.

She turned her head, listening. Was that the sound of a horse approaching? No. Just her imagination.

*

"The best place for the pump is right here."

Mr. Scoggins was the Texaco representative. His easy-going manner matched his casual attire – grey trousers, a short-sleeved white shirt and a tie that was a little too short.

He told them the metal tank that held the gasoline should be placed where the animal pen now stood on the left side of the store. A pipe from the tank to the gas pump would be laid beneath the boardwalk, the pump just in front of it.

"Of course since you don't have electricity, we'll be installing an older model. You'll have to use a hand pump to fill the cylinder at the top of the gas pump. Then you put the nozzle into the customer's fuel tank and gravity makes it flow from the jug down into the customer's tank."

"Is someone going to show us exactly how to do it?" Inez said, sounding like she'd had a couple of extra cups of coffee before coming to work.

"I'll train you myself once the pump and tank are installed. You just have to know where the cap is. On the older vehicles, it's under the front seat. On some newer cars, it's on the hood. Depends on the make. If you don't know, just ask the customer. Nothing to it."

He spent the better part of an hour explaining how the installation would be done and showing them pictures of the equipment. He handed Inez his business card, telling her to call him when they were ready to pay.

By the time he left, Livvy was prickly from the heat and her head hurt. She didn't often have a cold drink, but pulled an RC Cola from the ice barrel, holding the cold bottle against her cheek for a moment before opening it.

Inez, on the other hand, paced the store with a girlish step.

"We should have a grand opening sale," she said. "We'll have a special opening day price for gas. We can spread the word at church. Lord, we need to fix up the store!" She whirled around, taking in the shelves and barrels. "We can put candy in a jar by the cash register and pull the cold drink barrels closer to the front so folks will be sure to see them. And I'll set a basket of eggs right up front!"

Livvy took a big swallow of her drink, leaning against the front counter, imagining all the extra work.

"We also need some new signs," Inez said. "How many years has that Camels cigarette sign been hanging out front? And that rusty Coca-Cola sign? It goes without saying, the windows need washing." She beamed with energy. "It'll be a fresh start!"

"Those are some razzle-dazzle ideas."

Inez beamed as she continued talking.

"Mr. Beasley over in Kinston held a drawing once for a prize just to get people to come into the store. He chose three items customers could choose from if they won. He said lots of folks came inside to put their names in the jar and a good many bought a little something."

Livvy felt like she was watching the Inez she used to know when she was a little girl. The Inez who smiled and talked and laughed. The enthusiasm was infectious as Inez clapped her hands like a little girl on Christmas Eve.

*

The dirt burned Livvy's feet right through her shoes as she walked home. She imagined sitting in Mama's rocking chair reading a book. But Mama and Clara were doing laundry today – two large tubs and the wringer set up in the kitchen. The girls were making a racket hauling baskets of wet clothes out to the clothesline. Tomorrow would be ironing day with

Mama and Clara both using hot irons to press pants, shirts and dresses, turning the kitchen into an oven.

Livvy made herself scarce since the women had the girls to help them. Besides, if Gordon came to the woods today, she had to be there.

She changed clothes, swung by the garden to snitch a cucumber and washed it at the pump before trekking off toward the forest, eating as she went.

She was alone in the woods. No sign of Gordon. She sat down so she could enjoy the view. The male and female tree nymphs gazed at each other, the fairy door behind them. The hammock hung limp off to the left, waiting for a breeze. On the ground in front of it was the galaxy rock spiral.

If her grandmother were sitting beside her, Livvy thought she would smile at the sight.

She'd been longing for magic in her life when she fashioned her artworks. Something that would transport her from a humdrum existence. Gordon's arrival had seemed a part of it all. It was almost like she'd summoned him through the enchanted doorway.

Yet he was a real man. Albeit a man unlike any she'd ever known. And while he seemed to admire her creations, she was certain he wouldn't be drawn to a country widow who finished junior college and ran a general store. It was likely he wouldn't return, that their friendship had run its course. His excuse about being unable to find his way back to the woods was his way of gently pulling away. She didn't blame him.

She needed to move on to her next project. What would she create this time?

Getting to her feet, she squinted as she raised her face toward the sun. A blurry vision floated before her eyes.

"A boat," she whispered.

Right there in front of the doorway with the two figures on either side as if they might climb in and glide through the doorway together.

*

The next morning Livvy braced herself when, a few minutes after unlocking the store, Inez arrived with Ruthie in tow. Normally, Inez enjoyed spending time with her chickens in the morning as she collected their eggs. But preparing for the gas pump now topped her priority list. There would be no more peace and quiet at the store for a while.

Setting their sack lunches behind the counter, her sisters took their tools outside so they could move the animal pen, making way for the storage tank. The pen would be hidden out back instead.

Livvy had put cash in the register and started cleaning the inside of the windows with vinegar when she saw Coy's car pull up. She set the cleaning rag aside and wiped her hands on her apron as he burst through the door.

"I see y'all are getting ready for installation."

"Yeah, Inez hasn't been this happy since she went to the high school prom!"

He laughed. "Can you sell me a bottle of brilliantine? I've got a big date coming up this Saturday and I need to look my best for the lady." He winked, pulling his billfold from his pocket.

She chortled as she hurried to the hair product shelf. "Anything else?" she asked, scooting behind the register.

"That'll do it."

As she took his money, she noticed a wagon drawn by a lone mule come to a stop through the window. Her old school friend, Arlene, climbed down, her husband Wade handing the baby to her while their two little boys sat in the wagon bed. The last time Arlene visited the store she'd arrived in Wade's Model T.

"Thanks, Livvy," Coy said. "Got business to tend to."

He held the door for Arlene, then trotted out to his car, nodding at Arlene's husband.

"Good to see you, Arlene," Livvy said. "It's been a while. Loretta sure has grown."

Livvy hoped the cheerful greeting would hide her concern. In truth, Arlene, who had been a dark-haired beauty in her teens, was now thin and pale, and the baby appeared listless in her arms. She wasn't about to ask what happened to the car.

"Hey, Livvy." The words sounded as though speaking was a chore. Her eyes darted around the store like she was checking to see if anyone else was there. "Funny seeing Coy Whitaker here. He used to say he was gonna marry you one day."

"When did he say that?"

"Back when we were in grade school. He was in love with you from the first day he walked into the schoolhouse."

Livvy glanced out the window as Coy drove away.

"Of course he was younger than us and small for his age." Arlene tried to smile but failed. "I need some milk, Livvy. And some flour." She heaved a tired sigh and lowered her eyes. "But I'll have to put it on our account."

There'd been no payment on their account in months and Livvy could tell by looking at her, there would be no payment anytime soon.

"That's fine. I know times are hard. We've got three jugs of milk in the ice tub. Brought them in myself this morning after milking the cow." She moved to the cold drink barrel, pulling the containers out, wiping them with a rag before setting them on the counter. "And I'll get you a twenty-pound bag of flour."

The baby whined, laying her head on her mother's shoulder.

Arlene's voice caught in her throat and her eyes brimmed.

"Thank you," she whispered.

Livvy retrieved the flour, tucking it under her arm so she could carry the milk jugs, and followed Arlene out the door.

Wade took the bag of flour from her, avoiding meeting her gaze.

"You can return the jugs when you have a chance," she said, handing them up to her friend once she was seated next to her husband.

The baby began to cry as Wade snapped the reins.

She had spent the entire morning cleaning and there was still a lot to do. The three of them worked all afternoon shifting stock, washing counters and shelves as they went. Inez waited on a handful of customers, taking the opportunity to announce they'd soon be selling gasoline, telling them they could fill up their tanks close to home.

After supper that night, there was more work to do. Because there hadn't been a drop of rain since the corn was planted, Daddy organized everybody except Mama and Clara into a water brigade. Cecil and Vernon used the two wheelbarrows to haul buckets of water from the rain barrels along the edge of the house to the field. They set a bucket at the end of a row, then went back for more water, using whatever containers they could find. Meantime, Livvy, Inez, Ruthie, Nettie and Faye followed Daddy's instructions, using bowls and pots to scoop water from the buckets and pour along the rows.

They continued until it was too dark to see. Ruthie groaned when Daddy announced the hand watering would continue for as many nights as it took to water all the rows. Mama wasn't happy either. She'd walked out to the field as they were finishing up.

"Leon, if you drain the rain barrels, what am I going to water the garden with?"

Daddy didn't answer.

"It's the garden that's filling our bellies," she said. "That and the rabbits and squirrels the boys bring home. But because they're busy *elsewhere*, they haven't had time to make their rounds lately."

Still no answer.

"And if you don't mind my saying so," Mama continued, "it's a fool's errand trying to water an entire cornfield by hand. You know as well as I do it's not nearly enough."

"Dang it, Bess!" Daddy snapped. "Better to try something than to sit around doing nothing."

*

Saying he could do without the truck Thursday, Daddy let Livvy borrow it. She drove to the store, Inez and Ruthie beside her.

Inez was practically walking on air in her best dress – the dark gold one that hugged her figure in a flattering way. And she'd styled her hair using Grandma's pretty hair combs. In contrast, Livvy seemed all thumbs, bumping several cans off a shelf, knocking two brooms to the floor with a loud clatter and dropping a jar of mayonnaise, shards of glass embedded in the goopy mess, some of it splattering the hem of her purple dress.

They left Ruthie in charge at one-fifteen so they could drive to the Whitaker home. Their scarves were tied under their chins so they wouldn't look like scarecrows when they arrived. Mae Glover answered the door, silently showing them to the dining room where Coy and Mr. Thompson were waiting.

Inez had brought Grandma's will and the family Bible where the births of all three granddaughters were recorded. She also had last year's tax bill for the store in case it was needed to establish ownership along with the invoice the Texaco man had given her spelling out the equipment to be installed and the total cost.

After writing the amount on the document, Mr. Thompson provided a short explanation of each paragraph of the loan agreement. Then Inez, Livvy and Coy each signed the contract which had been prepared in triplicate. The original went to Coy, one copy went to Mr. Thompson and one to Livvy and Inez.

"The next step," Mr. Thompson said, "is for Mr. Whitaker to write you a check."

Coy opened a leather checkbook, nodding his head enthusiastically. Using a dark fountain pen, he filled in the amount, signing with a flourish and waving the check in the air to dry the ink. Then he reached across the table to hand it to Inez before shaking the sisters' hands.

Next stop – the bank. They re-tied their scarves and drove to Kinston.

For the first couple of miles all Inez could talk about was how they were modernizing the store to attract customers so they could make more money. Eventually she grew quiet, watching Livvy behind the wheel.

"Who taught you to drive?" Inez said.

"Hank did while we were dating."

"When I was young, all we had was a carriage and a wagon. But I want to be a modern woman too. I want you to teach me how to drive an automobile."

"Be happy to." Livvy was glad to see her sister bubbling over with spunk again.

They parked in front of a two-story red brick building in the middle of downtown that housed the bank. Leaving their scarves in the truck, Livvy followed Inez inside.

A middle-aged man waited on Inez at the first window to deposit the check while Livvy was assisted by a young man at the third window. She was withdrawing money to pay for the flour and milk she'd given Arlene. It would go in the till when they got back to the store. As the teller counted out her little bit of cash, she asked him if he knew of any Englishmen who lived in town.

"Englishmen?"

"You know. From England? With an English accent?"

"Can't say as I do." He slid the bills across the counter to her.

"Does the name Gordon Collins ring a bell?"

He shook his head. "Sorry. Is there another transaction I can help you with?"

"Have you lived here very long?"

"I was born and raised here, ma'am."

She was rooted to the spot, trying to square what Gordon had told her with what the cashier had just said. Realizing he was ready for her to move along, she obliged, joining her sister by the door.

"Let's celebrate," Inez said. "Mr. Beasley's store is just around the corner. We can drop in and get a soda. That way I can thank him in person for his advice."

The exterior of Beasley's General Store was painted white with a new roof above a tall yellow gas pump where Mr. Beasley could fill customers' tanks even when it was raining. Located in downtown Kinston, the store had electric lights. It also had a couple of ceiling fans that turned slowly to keep the air moving. In addition, there was an electric drink machine that kept the drinks cold all day, every day. No ice deliveries required.

Inez wasted no time finding the proprietor. He was seated in a wooden chair in the center of the store where a checkerboard took pride of place on a small table.

"Mr. Beasley?" she said.

"Yes'm." A ready smile appeared on his face as he got to his feet. He wasn't a tall man, but he was trim with a friendly face and neat dark hair, a bit of grey at the temples.

"We spoke on the phone. I'm Inez Hopkins. This is my sister, Livvy Sloan."

His eyes lit up. He was about to say something when the bell above the door jangled. "I'll be back in a minute," he said, hurrying to the front.

For the next half hour they visited with Mr. Beasley between customers, updating him on their progress with the gas pump. Handing them each an ice cold bottle of root beer, he shared little nuggets of advice on dealing with customers and filling their tanks. When a car pulled up at one of the pumps, he invited them to observe as he lifted the front seat to reveal the gas tank underneath. He unscrewed the gas cap and inserted the pump nozzle, paying close attention to the sound of the gasoline as it gushed into the oblong tank. Livvy and Inez watched closely, inhaling the gasoline fumes.

"I guess your husband usually handles this for you," he said, his eyes on Inez.

"Oh, I'm not married."

"I'm a widower, myself. My wife died five years ago from cancer."

"I'm so sorry."

"Thank you kindly. Lucky for me, I've got three grown children who poke their noses into my business whenever the notion strikes 'em."

Inez and Livvy laughed.

Now Livvy understood why her sister dressed up this morning, her hair styled like she was meeting Charlie Chaplin. It wasn't the loan signing. And it wasn't the visit to the bank.

As they were preparing to leave, Livvy asked him the question she'd put to the bank cashier, this time claiming she'd heard a rumor. But she got the same reply. He'd never heard of an Englishman living in the vicinity and had certainly never met one.

After they said their farewells, Inez gave Livvy a suspicious glance. "When did you become the town gossip?"

Livvy was ready, though. "A customer said something about it one day. I didn't believe it but figured it wouldn't hurt to ask Mr. Beasley."

All the way home, she half listened as her sister talked about the improvements they would make at the store. She let Inez regale the family at supper about signing the loan agreement and driving to Kinston. Afterwards, as they all pitched in to water the cornfield again, her mind returned to the Englishman who insisted he lived in Kinston, insisted he'd been living there his whole life. She supposed it was possible he lived in the Kinston area without Mr. Beasley or the bank cashier ever hearing of him. But not likely. Although why would he lie? Furthermore, if he didn't live in Kinston, where did he live?

7

After another morning of cleaning and rearranging the store, Livvy returned to the house. When she stopped by the kitchen to find a bite to eat she was met with a panicked screech. It was Clara in the bathtub by the stove, a sheet hanging from the quilting frame for privacy.

"It's just me," Livvy said. "Grabbing a biscuit. Now I'm gone."

Once she changed clothes, she borrowed the wheelbarrow and her father's hatchet, and made her getaway, craving the tranquility of the woods.

With an image in mind, she searched for branches about half an inch in diameter. Most of them needed to be new growth so they'd be flexible. Using the hatchet, she chopped them from a variety of bushes, gathering some dead limbs as well. It took her most of the afternoon and repeated trips.

She cleared the spot where the boat would sit, about ten feet in front of the doorway. Next, she cut two-foot lengths of the dry branches until she had enough to create the hull of the craft. Positioning them about eighteen inches apart around what would be the perimeter of the vessel, she pounded them into the ground with the butt of the hatchet, creating the vertical studs to which the hull would be attached. It was about eight feet in length and about three feet across, the ends narrowing like a canoe.

She was exhausted and hungry as sunlight streamed through the canopy high above, deep shadows at ground level. She had tried not to hope Gordon would come but had been listening for his approach all afternoon.

Later, as she sat down for supper, the first thing she noticed was that Clara was all dolled up. Wearing her violet dress, her shiny dark hair fell in waves on her shoulders instead of being pulled back in her usual bun. The children kept giving their mother furtive glances, exchanging secret smiles. Ah, yes. Preston was coming home tonight.

It wasn't just Clara who looked pretty. Inez also had a certain glow about her. Although her hair was a little limp after a long day, there was warmth and humor in her eyes like there used to be when she was young.

Livvy grinned to herself as she helped her plate with Mama's chicken and dumplings, minus the chicken. Instead, it was loaded with beans, squash and onions and lots of dumplings.

Once they'd cleaned their plates, it was back to watering the cornfield. As darkness fell, they were putting everything away when headlights appeared in the distance, bouncing as the car traveled the last quarter of a mile down the road and into the yard. Nettie and Faye squealed, running to greet their father even before he pulled to a stop. Cecil and Vernon jogged from the barn, waiting their turn for their father's attention. He hugged the girls and slapped his boys on the shoulder. Then his eyes were drawn to the house as Clara stepped through the door, looking like she was ready for a photographer to take her picture.

"All right now, I've got to give your mama a hug," Preston said, disentangling himself.

He strode to the porch and took Clara in his arms. Cast in shadow by the lantern light streaming through the door behind them, they formed a silhouette of a man and a woman clinging to each other through thick and thin. A lump formed in Livvy's throat. Despite his questionable choices lately, she had to admit Preston was a loyal, loving husband.

Livvy drew Ruthie with her to their little bedroom, wanting to give Preston and his family time to themselves in the kitchen. Inez, Mama and Daddy sat on the porch, Daddy rolled a cigarette and enjoyed his evening smoke. Livvy and Ruthie lay on their beds, reading, the hum of voices rising and falling outside their window.

But then the conversation grew louder as Preston, Clara and the kids adjourned to the porch as well. Livvy and Ruthie wandered out of their room to join them. Daddy had given up his rocking chair for Clara. He and Preston sat on the edge of the porch.

"After listening to those saws roar all day long," Preston said, "I have to listen to the other men sawing logs in their sleep all night."

Everyone laughed.

"One of the men I bunk with remembers Hank," he continued, looking in Livvy's direction. "Says Hank was well liked, a good worker. But he says Hank was bucking for a promotion from his first day on the job, wanted a better wage. Says all the men thought he was too green to work anywhere near the head saw and never understood why the boss let him do it. They let him fill in for the blocksetter. He's the one who positions the log with a hook on the sliding platform, then drives a couple of stakes into it to hold it in place as it's pulled through the circular saw. He uses hand signals to alert the sawyer when to set the platform in motion. He says Hank was moving too fast, didn't have the log firmly braced, gave the sawyer the 'go' signal, then lost his balance and fell into the saw."

Livvy covered her face with her hands.

"Sorry," Preston whispered.

There was an uneasy silence as everyone exchanged uncomfortable glances.

Clara was the first to speak. "I hope you're not working near the big saw."

"Hauling logs, moving boards. That's all."

Livvy stepped off the porch, leaving the family behind. Trying to erase the grisly image from her mind, she let her gaze rise to the night sky. So many stars. Gordon said the Andromeda Galaxy was visible to the naked eye if you knew where to look. She skirted the pecan tree to get a better view. A smudge. That's what he said it looked like. She searched and searched but couldn't see it, not knowing where to look.

Later, lying on top of her bed in her coolest nightgown, she thought back to what Preston said. She'd never liked thinking about Hank's accident. Still, it didn't surprise her that he'd pushed for a better paying job. But she hadn't known until tonight that he'd been moved to a more dangerous position so quickly. The grief that overwhelmed her after Hank's death returned along with a sense of guilt that he'd been trying to make enough money for them to move to Athens so she could attend the university.

*

After working her shift Saturday, Livvy returned home to find Clara on the porch muttering under her breath as she rocked to and fro at a furious pace. How she could snap beans at the same time was a mystery. Livvy gave her a nod but knew better than to speak. If Clara was this upset, it meant the men had taken off for the still. Either that, or they had driven over to Athens for supplies.

She found Mama putting up pickled beets, Nettie and Faye flitting about the kitchen doing her bidding. Livvy swallowed her frustration. She'd planned to take a bath this afternoon to prepare for tonight's date with Coy. Obviously, Mama forgot.

She pitched in with the canning, trying to speed things up. When twenty jars were sealed and sitting on the sideboard to cool, she helped with clean up before boiling more water in the big canning pot. Dragging the tin tub over by the stove, she hung the sheet once again from the quilting frame.

Mama blotted sweat from her upper lip with her apron. "It's almost time to start cooking."

"I'll be quick as lightning. You sit down on the porch, have a glass of tea and cool off."

Mama and the girls cleared out as Livvy bathed in a couple inches of water, pretty sure it was the fastest bath on record. She was done in time for Mama to start peeling potatoes.

Once she was ready, she stood before the mirror in Mama's bedroom. With her new green dress, her low-heeled pumps, matching pocketbook and a touch of lipstick, she gave herself a small nod of approval.

She stopped by the kitchen to tell her mother Coy would be there shortly. Mama's eyes were so focused on the dress she didn't notice Livvy biting her lower lip.

"That cloth made up real nice," Mama said, flour smeared on her cheek. "Have a good time!"

Livvy stood on the porch to wait, thankful Clara had moved inside. She didn't have to wait long. Coy's Model A roared into the yard, causing Livvy to cough as dust filled her lungs. He hopped out and walked around to the passenger side, opening the door like a gentleman.

"You're looking mighty fine this evening," he said as she crossed the yard.

"So are you," she replied, as though going out on dates was old hat.

While she'd been tense before, she was on the verge of nausea now, realizing she looked like she was going to a barn dance in her new dress while he looked sophisticated enough in his summer suit and tie to be taking a lady to a formal restaurant.

He gestured at the car, taking no notice of her discomfort.

"Paid to have it washed and Simonized. That color, by the way, is called Andalusite Blue."

He closed the door once she was seated, patting the hood as he walked around to the driver's side like the car was his favorite hunting dog.

With her scarf tied securely in place, she thought her hair might withstand the drive to Athens. Whether her nerves would survive was another matter. Coy raced down those two-lane roads, not even slowing down for the curves. Livvy gripped the seat, hoping a farm wagon didn't pull out in front of them.

When at last he slowed to enter the city, her body relaxed. They parked near a favorite restaurant from his college days.

Thank goodness it wasn't as fancy as she feared. He ordered steak and french fries for them both.

The lumber mill was the first topic of conversation – how they were getting big orders from a paper company in Augusta and orders for building materials from an Atlanta company.

"Your big brother is a good worker. Smarter than the younger men. Knows how to stay safe."

It seemed an innocent remark, like he was making small talk. But she couldn't help but wonder if he might be making a veiled reference to Hank.

When the food was served, he slid a flask from his pocket and poured whiskey into his Coke.

"Want some?" he said.

She shook her head.

"I need to get more. Gotta contact my new supplier." He put the flask away, then took a drink. "I'm surprised you don't have a taste for it."

"Why does that surprise you?" she said, curious whether this might be another veiled comment.

"Most women I know wouldn't turn down a little nip now and then."

Wanting to change the subject – and maybe find some common ground between them – she asked if he'd attended many plays while he was in college. She thought she might share her enthusiasm at seeing a production of *Romeo and Juliet* while at Young Harris.

"Never did. But I went to a lot of football games."

He launched into descriptions of great plays he witnessed from the stands and the celebrations that followed big wins.

He was so animated, he seemed to lose track of time. He finally glanced at his watch, immediately calling for their check.

"The picture's about to start," he said. "It's a talkie, you know. A big, loud talkie!"

Hell's Angels was a war movie with realistic aerial dogfights during The Great War. It included terrible scenes of airplanes crashing into each other and bursting into flames, spiraling to the ground with black smoke trailing out from behind. Most of the film was in black and white but there were some scenes in color too. It was amazing and intense and Livvy found herself clutching her pocketbook tighter and tighter in her lap. As engrossed as she was, she still caught an occasional whiff of liquor, wondering how many times Coy pulled his flask from his pocket.

He held her hand walking back to the car. She wasn't ready for that just yet but didn't want to seem rude. On the drive home, he couldn't stop talking about the battle scenes and Jean Harlow, the platinum blonde actress with the sexy smile.

When they were almost to her house, he surprised her by pulling over in front of her store. Before she could say a word, he put the car in reverse and backed into the spot beside the store where the gasoline storage tank would be installed. Tucked so close to the building, they were sitting in near total darkness. When he turned the key, silencing the engine, she realized what he was up to.

"No offense, Coy, but I'd rather not."

"A little smooching wouldn't hurt, would it?"

"The dinner was nice and the movie was exciting. It was a fun date, but I'm ready to go home."

"You'd think someone like yourself wouldn't mind just one little kiss."

A not so subtle reminder that she'd been married at one time and was not new to kissing.

"I think we should get to know each other better," she said.

"Kissing is a pretty good way to do that."

"Coy…"

"Just one?" he whispered.

She chuckled like she found his behavior amusing. "No offense, but this reminds me of high school kids sneaking around."

"Well now, you might have a point."

He heaved a sigh and cranked the engine, lurching forward. When he reached her house, he left the engine running and turned toward her in the dark.

"Sorry, Livvy. I guess that picture just made my blood hot, if you know what I mean."

"Yeah, but I'm not Jean Harlow."

She let herself out and headed toward the house as he took off. Pulling the scarf from her hair, she sat down in the rocking chair hidden deep in shadow, avoiding the dim lamplight spilling from Mama and Daddy's bedroom window. She wanted to be alone with her thoughts.

Despite his expensive clothes, fancy car and impressive home, Coy Whitaker was not well acquainted with the social graces. Hank, despite his humble upbringing, used to open doors for her. If they'd ever gone to a picture show, he would've asked what she wanted to see. And he would've let her order her own meal if they'd gone to a restaurant. One thing Hank didn't do was drink liquor while they were together. It's possible he imbibed from time to time, but never in her presence. Coy must be used to flapper girls.

She rocked back and forth staring into the darkness, irritated that she hadn't enjoyed the evening. He loved to talk but apparently wasn't keen on listening. He'd made it pretty clear, though, that he found Livvy attractive. Which she had to admit was a nice feeling. So far, though, he didn't make her heart pound. Still, it made sense to give him a chance. He was the most eligible bachelor around. And he had eyes for *her*. It was also true that she didn't want to end up like Inez – single, lonesome, and living with her parents in middle age.

She was more attracted to Gordon who always seemed interested in what she had to say and what she was doing. But Gordon was undeniably out of reach so it was a waste of time wishing he might be more than just a friend.

The quiet was broken as a car rumbled down the road toward the farm. There was another set of headlights behind it. They turned into the driveway and parked along the edge of the field beyond the pecan tree. Livvy stopped rocking, sitting still in the deep shadows of the covered porch.

Preston and Vernon emerged from the car while Daddy and Cecil climbed out of the truck. Not wasting a minute, the boys crouched down to re-attach license plates to each of the vehicles. Then they started slowly across the yard, all four of them walking like their shoes were made of cast iron.

"Cecil," Preston said, "don't ask Vernon to tell you about the chase, you hear?"

"Yes sir."

"There's a lot of big ears in this family."

Livvy remained silent as the four of them quietly let themselves in, never looking her way hidden as she was in the darkness.

Not moving a muscle, she remained quiet as the door closed, then sat a little longer until the lamps were extinguished.

Just as she was about to turn in, more headlights appeared in the distance. A car drove slowly along the road, its motor puttering softly as it approached the driveway. When it came to a stop, Livvy held her breath. After a long moment, it continued down the road past the house.

*

After church on Sunday, Livvy made herself a tomato sandwich to eat in the woods. It was a relief to sit on the tree stump surrounded by her nature sculptures. It seemed ages since she'd been here. With her straw hat shading her face and her hair pulled into a ponytail, she soaked in the serenity.

As if he knew she was watching, a bright red cardinal landed on top of the fairy door, singing a few notes, ending with a trill. Seconds later, his mate flitted into view to perch on the bottom. The male swooped down, alighting beside her, both of them eyeing the forest through the opening in the doorway. It was almost as though they too were waiting for Gordon to ride into view. Then, without warning, the male flew through the door, disappearing into the trees beyond. The female hesitated, then flew toward Livvy, rising into the canopy.

If Grandma were sitting beside her, she would say it was a sign. Livvy smiled wistfully as she got to her feet. It was time to get to work.

Building the boat was kind of like making a basket. She used the green branches she had cut the week before to weave between the vertical sticks she'd driven into the ground. Although they were not quite as green now as they were the day she cut them, she was still able to bend them so they slid in front of one stud, then behind the next one. She pressed them down bit by bit, the second one sliding into place on top of the first one, and so on until she had that portion of the hull completed. Working section by section, she finished one side of the boat in about an hour. Then she weaved the other side the same way, section by section, until the hull was complete.

Her excitement grew as she stood back to view her latest creation. It actually looked like a canoe. Luckily, it didn't have to be seaworthy.

She needed oars. Scouting the area, she selected two dead limbs lying on the ground that branched out at the end and dragged them to the boat. After a bit of trimming, she laid one on either side of the canoe, the branched ends representing the wide end of the paddle. To keep them in place, she used vines to wrap the handle ends to the top of the hull on both sides.

She stepped inside the boat, sat on the ground and placed her hands on the paddles, imagining gliding through the doorway.

Pulling Grandma's embroidery scissors from her pocket, she undid her ponytail and snipped several long strands of hair, tying them around the top rail of the hull. As she finished, a tremor traveled through her body. The air was charged like a bolt of lightning was about to strike.

A sudden pounding of hooves drew her eyes to the north. There was a lurch in her stomach as Gordon raised his arm in greeting. When he dismounted, his eyes widened as he took in Livvy's latest creation.

"Is your canoe like a magic carpet? Does it take you through the air in an instant to your destination?"

She laughed as she rose and stepped from the boat.

"It's stupendous," he said. "And I see you crafted the tree nymph's partner." He moved forward, taking in the entire scene. "I must say, you've created much more than an enchanted doorway. You've created an enchanted woodland."

For all his enthusiasm, there was a trace of disappointment in his voice.

"I'm sorry I went ahead without you on the second tree nymph," she said. "When you didn't come, I assumed something important came up."

"But I did come. Or rather, I tried to. It was like before when…"

"…when Bailey couldn't find the way?"

"Indeed. No matter how far we rode, we couldn't find the path."

He looked so sincere.

"It's strange," he said. "We rode in the same direction but somehow Bailey took us down the wrong path so that we couldn't find this little section of the forest. Until today."

Did he realize how ridiculous he sounded? "You don't have to pretend you got lost if you were busy. I know you have your work, your family."

"Believe me, I'm not pretending. It's like this woodland exists one day and doesn't exist the next."

Now he was talking crazy. Which surprised her. He seemed like a rational, intelligent man.

"And I nearly didn't find it today," he went on. "Bailey and I have been riding back and forth. I was about to give up and return home when we saw the path."

How was she supposed to respond? Maybe he was taking some kind of medicine that clouded his mind.

"I can see your skepticism," he said. "What I'm saying may sound illogical. But it's true." He shook his head in frustration.

Maybe he fought in the Great War. She'd read that many soldiers returning from the battlefield suffered nightmares and delusions.

He seemed to read her thoughts.

"I assure you I am not of unsound mind. Nor do I suffer from wild phantasms. My poor cousin has had such problems ever since fighting on the battlefields in France, but I was too young to go to war."

As much as she liked him, and as much as she felt invigorated in his presence, she no longer felt she could believe everything he said.

"And there's something else," he said, pulling an envelope from his jacket pocket. "The pictures I took of your artworks are blank." He fanned them out for her to see. The photographs were completely white.

"An accident in the dark room?" she suggested.

"Perhaps."

Then Livvy cleared her throat. "I drove to the bank in Kinston the other day. The cashier and a store owner down the street told me they've never heard of you or anyone like you."

"That's not possible."

There was a skeptical expression on his face as if she were the one spouting nonsense. An uncomfortable silence ensued where the only sound was the loud song of the cicadas.

"What is that buzzing?" he asked.

"Cicadas."

"Cicadas," he whispered, twirling around in place, examining his surroundings, then looking up at the sky. "Strange, strange light."

He squinted, looking as though he was about to comment further but then changed the subject.

"How long have you been creating forest art? What inspired you?"

"Since I was eight years old. I used to walk through the woods with my grandmother who said the forest was a magical place. One day she pointed out some beautiful smooth stones lying among the yellow hickory leaves, telling me it looked like the fairies might've been here before us. Which made me want to create something too. So I gathered more stones and some hickory nuts and arranged them in the leaves in a starburst pattern like Grandma used for some of her quilts." She gazed around at her new creations, quiet for a moment. "She used to tell me magic happens all the time; we just have to look for it." She laughed. "Grandma always had a glint in her eye. It was like she saw things the rest of us couldn't see."

"You were lucky to have her."

She didn't tell him that soon afterwards she was mourning her grandmother's death.

"Rain's coming and it'll be dark soon. I better start back," he said, walking toward his handsome horse.

Livvy looked up at the hazy summer sky, no sign of rain clouds as far as the eye could see. If rain was on the way Daddy would've said something about it. It was Gordon's way of tactfully cutting their visit short.

"Hope to see you again soon," he said, waving as he rode away.

The contrast between Gordon's well-heeled style and her overalls and freckles couldn't have been more dramatic. He had the appearance of someone who had never had to sweat working in the field, someone who'd never worn a pair of hand-me-down shoes that hurt his feet. Her initial awareness of their differences had receded into the background as time went by. But after today's visit, the difference couldn't be ignored. There was also his bizarre behavior. She couldn't help but feel distrustful.

8

The highly anticipated installation occurred on Wednesday of that week.

"That is one fine-looking gas pump," Inez said, caressing the painted metal like it was one of her beloved hens.

She was right. The gas pump was a sight to behold. The main body was narrow but as tall as a man and painted bright red with a hand crank on one side. Atop that was a clear container so you could see the gasoline inside with markings to gauge how much it contained. On the very top was a round sign. It was red with the Texaco star in the center. No way drivers could miss seeing the colorful gas pump, that's for sure.

Inez spent the day staring through the newly cleaned windows at her prized possession. Unable to help herself, she strolled out front from time to time, wiping the red metal with a rag to remove the slightest bit of dust.

The following day, a truck pulled up to fill the big silver storage tank. Livvy and Inez both stood outside in the heat to watch.

"That right there is the smell of money," Inez said, breathing in a lungful of gasoline fumes.

After supper that evening, Daddy drove his truck to the store so Inez could practice. Because they didn't have electricity, the first thing she had to do was use the hand pump to deliver the fuel into the clear cylinder atop the body of the device so the customer – Daddy, in this case – could see how much fuel he was getting. Next she lifted the bench seat of his truck because that's where his tank was located. Then she unscrewed the cap on the gas tank and inserted the nozzle, letting gravity do the work of delivering the gasoline from the clear cylinder to his tank. Daddy shook Inez's hand when she was done as though he was pleased doing business with his elder daughter. She grinned.

On Friday, the pastor of their church stopped by. Livvy insisted on giving him a free fill-up. His tank was under the cowl on the hood of the car, which made for easier access. When she finished pumping the gas, Reverend Blackwood drove away with a satisfied smile.

When she got home that afternoon, Livvy saw her father, Cecil and Vernon squatting in the cornfield. She'd been so focused on the gas pump that she hadn't noticed when she walked down the driveway this morning that tiny seedlings had broken through the soil at last. She was on the verge of calling out 'praise be' like Grandma used to do when Daddy got to his feet and shook his head.

She approached the nearest row and leaned down. The small leaves were yellowed and curled inward which meant the soil was too dry. The men started toward the yard. Livvy waited for them.

"Tell your mama we're taking three rain barrels to the creek," Daddy called out. "Gotta haul some water."

They crowded into the small truck cab and took off.

Talk at the supper table that evening was about the grand opening of the Hopkins Filling Station the following week. Inez was beside herself at the prospect.

"Reverend Blackwood says he'll mention it from the pulpit on Sunday," she gushed.

As soon as they finished eating, everyone except Mama and Clara reported to the field for watering duty. Preston pulled into the yard when they were nearly finished.

*

As Livvy and Ruthie headed to the store Saturday morning, Daddy and Vernon took off for the creek again to refill the barrels. It was a more time-consuming chore since the lack of rain had decreased the water flow. The newspaper said drought had lowered river and lake levels too. But it didn't matter how tedious it was, he was determined to save the corn crop.

Mama made it clear one barrel had to be filled for the garden as well. She also told Daddy and Preston that the boys couldn't ignore their traps any longer. They needed some meat on the table sooner rather than later. It would be months before fall arrived when they could slaughter the hog.

Word was already getting around that Hopkins General Merchandise was now also a filling station. Daddy's brother, Uncle Tyrone, and two of his grandkids stopped by to get a fill-up, then came inside so he could buy the kids Moon Pies. It was a rare act of goodwill. Tyrone resented his mother leaving the store only to her granddaughters because he never had any daughters of his own to share in that inheritance.

Livvy was relieved when Inez arrived mid-morning. They had Ruthie remain behind the cash register while the two older sisters pumped gas and waited on customers. They made a point of asking them to spread the word to family and neighbors to come back next week to put their name in the jar for the prize drawing.

One thing they hadn't considered – they'd need two people at the store at all times from now on. If Livvy had to pump gas for a customer and someone else arrived and walked inside the store, she couldn't leave the pump to help the new customer. Which meant she wouldn't be able to keep her eyes out for would-be thieves either. Ruthie would only be available to spend all day at the store until September when school started. Then she could only come over after school. It looked like Livvy and Inez would both be working long days for the foreseeable future.

She may have been tired, but Inez was on top of the world that evening. Nettie and Faye enjoyed her stories about the rush of customers and how much gas they pumped. Daddy and Vernon were drained, focusing their energy on chewing their food. Preston and Cecil weren't home yet, leaving a cloud hanging over Clara's head once again.

Proof that there was no rest for the weary, the watering brigade resumed in the cornfield before their food had time to settle.

Preston and Cecil didn't get home until well after dark and everyone had gone inside. Listening through her bedroom window, Livvy heard the car pull slowly into the yard. Their footsteps sounded like bone-weary men too tired to speak.

The next morning, Daddy told Mama to go on to church without them. He and Preston left early for the creek, the boys in the back of the truck with the barrels. Livvy heard them talking low among themselves – they'd haul the barrels of water to the farm, leaving the watering for the evening, as usual, then drive over to the still to finish another batch of hooch.

Clara clenched her teeth so hard no one said a word to her when she refused to dress for church, disappearing into her bedroom.

Since Livvy was the only woman in the family who could drive, she got behind the wheel of Preston's car and drove Mama, Inez and the girls to the Sunday service. It was important they show up today so they could invite everyone to the store for cheap gas and a chance to win a prize.

When it was time for announcements, Inez rose shyly from her spot in the choir to extend an invitation to come by the store for a fill-up, or at least to put their name in the jar for the prize. When she sat down again, Reverend Blackwood turned to the congregation.

"Wanna thank the Hopkins sisters for filling my tank for free the other day," he said. "Mighty nice gesture to your pastor."

Inez beamed behind him.

Before the final hymn, the pastor prayed for rain, eliciting a hearty 'amen' from the congregation.

*

A car was already waiting by the pump when the sisters arrived at the store Monday morning. While Inez filled the tank, Livvy escorted their cousin Ronnie Hopkins inside to write his name on a slip of paper and slide it through the slot in the lid of a giant pickle jar.

Handmade signs were posted on the front door, by the cash register, on the jar, on the table and behind the table about the drawing. Only adults could enter. Only one entry was allowed per household. The sisters spent every day that week explaining the rules time and again, and tactfully preventing people from filling out more than one entry or having their children write their names on entry forms as well.

That was her first inkling the drawing might not be the fun and easy promotion they imagined. But boy, did it bring in the customers. After dropping their slips of paper into the jar, people wandered through the store contemplating what they'd use their winnings for. Unlike Inez's friend, Mr. Beasley, Livvy and Inez chose to award a first prize of five dollars' worth of merchandise and a second prize of two dollars' worth of merchandise. That way, the winners could choose anything on the shelves. Unfortunately, that meant not many people made purchases, hoping to win the drawing instead of spending what little cash they had in their billfolds. Still, they did make some sales, including staple items like sugar and coffee, as well as cold drinks and candy for the kids. And Inez was thrilled they sold a good many eggs.

Livvy and Inez took turns pumping gas, filling the tanks on a dozen cars by the end of the day. They made sure to point out the new "No Smoking" signs tacked onto the front of the building.

When closing time arrived, they sent Ruthie on home before locking the cash drawer and the over-sized pickle jar in the safe, which was hidden in the floor of the work room. It's not that they didn't trust Ruthie, but she was prone to blurt things out without thinking.

*

Saturday morning dawned dry and dusty, as usual. Customers began arriving about eleven-thirty, crowding around the table with the pickle jar.

As though she did public speaking every day, Inez announced the drawing was about to get underway a few minutes before noon. With great enthusiasm, she thanked everyone for coming and wished them good luck.

First came the explanation that she was dumping all the entries from the jar into a wash tub so they could be stirred around, not wanting to give the entries on top – those that had been added last – any advantage over entries submitted earlier in the week. Everyone watched closely as she deposited the contents of the big jar into the tub and used a long-handled kitchen spoon to stir the slips of paper around for a couple of minutes. Then she chose a little girl standing with her mother to reach into the tub to choose the first entry, thus selecting the second prize winner. In a clear voice, Inez read out the name and address so everyone could hear.

"Winner of the second prize – two dollars' worth of merchandise – is Betty Jean Hopkins, Route four, box seventeen."

A stout woman standing near the cash register gave a little hoot. She was the widow of Joe Hopkins, one of Daddy's distant cousins. The two men had shared a great-great-grandfather but their branches of the Hopkins clan didn't mix or mingle much.

"Congratulations, Mrs. Hopkins," Inez said. "I've forgotten your maiden name."

"Skinner."

"That's right," Inez replied, trying to make a point. "You're from the Skinner family. Well, once the drawing has concluded, we'll help you gather up your winning merchandise."

Livvy applauded, hoping others would follow her lead. Only a few did.

Inez asked a little boy if he would like to draw the grand prize entry from the tub. He nodded enthusiastically and dug through the bits of paper, pulling one from the bottom of the pile. Livvy's stomach churned as he handed it to Inez. If the first prize went to someone named Hopkins, they were in trouble. Inez smiled as she took the paper from the boy's hand and proceeded to announce the big winner.

"Okay, folks," she said, sounding like an experienced carnival barker, "the winner of our first-prize – five dollars' worth of merchandise from our store shelves – is Leroy Hall, Route two, box twenty-seven."

Livvy clapped loudly, relieved beyond measure that Leroy's last name wasn't Hopkins.

There were a lot of disgruntled customers and some crying children. Livvy grabbed a box of hard candy, making the rounds, handing out a piece of candy to every child in attendance.

It was hot and hazy as everyone cleared out. All except the two winners, that is. Through the window, she watched as Arlene walked slowly back to the wagon where her husband and little boys waited. If only Arlene's name had been called. Livvy resolved to pay her old friend another visit and take some groceries with her.

Coy had shown up just before the drawing began, smiling at everyone and shaking hands. He was still talking with stragglers when Livvy and Inez finished helping the winners make their choices. As Inez and Ruthie began cleaning up, Coy pulled Livvy aside, congratulating her on how well everything went.

"I think y'all did a great job! You've got yourselves a genuine filling station right here in Hopkinsville."

"Thank you, Coy."

"Hell, half the county turned out for the drawing! Now it's time to celebrate," he said, lowering his voice. "I know a speakeasy over toward Athens. You and me can go and have a couple of drinks."

"I don't know. I don't have the right kind of dress."

"My sister left a couple of flapper dresses at the house. You'd look damn good in one of them."

"That's thoughtful of you. But to tell the truth, I'm exhausted."

"You've got to celebrate, Livvy! Couple of drinks and you'll feel just fine."

"I do appreciate the offer, but…"

"You're turning me down?" There was a hint of indignation in his tone. "Maybe I should ask Inez instead. I bet she'd go with me."

She chuckled. "Guess I better help tidy up. Thanks so much for everything, Coy."

*

Not even the heat could dampen Inez's spirits as they walked home that evening.

"We actually made money this week! Even with the prizes we gave out, the store made a profit for the first time in a long time. That gas pump is the start of a whole new era for the Hopkins general store."

Ruthie whooped like a cowhand.

The three sisters were in a good humor when they sat down at the supper table. The men were running late, which was not unusual on a Saturday, so the women and Preston's daughters started without them. Inez couldn't stop babbling about the grand opening. Eventually Clara couldn't stand it another minute, rushing from the room like she had to pay an urgent visit to the outhouse.

Assuming they'd hear the car and truck any minute, Mama left the food on the table once the women and girls finished eating. But the evening wore on and there was no sign of Daddy, Preston and the boys. Clara sat knitting in a rocking chair on the porch as the sun went down, her shoulders stiff and her mouth locked in a deep frown. Eventually, Mama covered the food and had the girls wash the dirty dishes.

As darkness settled over the farm, the women rushed to the door when the truck puttered into the yard. They watched Daddy and Vernon trudge silently toward the house.

"Where's Preston and Cecil?" Clara demanded, leaping to her feet.

Vernon gave his grandpa a sorrowful look but said nothing.

"Don't know," Daddy admitted.

Clara threw her knitting needles and yarn onto the rocker.

"You don't know?" she cried.

"There was a chase," Daddy said, shaking his head in frustration. "We split up, me and Vernon veered over toward Rabbit Hollow. Preston and Cecil headed south. The sheriff followed their car. We waited an hour for them to find us at our usual meet-up place, but they never showed up."

Clara covered her mouth with her hand as Daddy continued.

"Don't worry, honey," Mama whispered to Clara. "They're just hiding out, that's all."

"This was bound to happen!" Clara shouted, glaring at her father-in-law. "We all knew it!"

She burst into tears and ran inside. When her daughters started to follow, Mama held them back.

"Believe she needs a little privacy right now," she said. "You can help me warm the food for Vernon and your grandpa."

Later that night, as the lamps were being snuffed out, Livvy heard a noise outside her window. Frozen in place on the side of her bed, she realized what she heard was footsteps in the yard. Forlorn footsteps. The hairs on her arms tingled as she thought of Grandma's stories about ghosts. With her heart pounding in her chest, she inched toward the window. A tremor passed through her body as she saw the shadow of a man crossing the yard toward the house. Then she recognized the exhausted gait of her brother. Even in the faint light of a crescent moon, it was plain he was weighed down with a deep sorrow. She grabbed the lamp and rushed through the door onto the porch.

9

Dirty from head to foot, face and arms scratched and his shirt ripped, Preston looked so pitiful, Livvy had the urge to hug him. Instead, she called out to let everyone know he was home.

Clara appeared first, barefoot, in her frayed nightgown. Ignoring the layer of filth, she threw her arms around her husband, a sob racking her body. He rubbed her back as the rest of the family appeared in their nightshirts.

"Cecil?" Clara whispered, her voice shaking.

"He's all right," Preston replied. "Sheriff hauled him off to jail."

She put her hand to her heart, another sob bursting forth.

Livvy hurried into the kitchen to warm a plate of food. Preston washed up at the pump and changed his clothes. In a matter of minutes they were gathered around the table.

He took a couple of bites before launching into his story. He said they were on their way to deliver a load over toward Athens when he spied the sheriff's car. Like Daddy told them earlier, the sheriff took off after Preston and Cecil when Daddy and Vernon split off.

"We tried to shake him but he was right on our tail. I could tell he wouldn't think twice about running us off the road. So

I told Cecil I was jumping out and for him to take over behind the wheel. That if I was arrested, there would be no paycheck from the sawmill, which might... well, it might do us in. But if *he* was arrested, we'd find a way to get him released one way or another."

Clara opened her mouth to speak but managed to hold her tongue.

"I slowed down after taking the Raeford curve. Cecil slid behind the wheel as I jumped out. I rolled down into the ditch, heard the sheriff barrel past me. I waited a minute before starting down the road after him. It took me fifteen, twenty minutes to find my car abandoned on the side of the road. The sheriff's car had come and gone. Cecil was gone too. I opened the trunk, lifted the false bottom and all the jars were still there."

"You let our boy be arrested?" Clara cried.

"If I'd stayed in the car, we'd have both been arrested. Then I wouldn't be getting a paycheck. Sheriff Teague has no evidence. I hauled all the crates from the car to a hiding place way off the road. I took the false bottom too. So when Teague comes back after sunup to get a better look, there'll be nothing to find."

Vernon and his two sisters watched helplessly as tears streamed down their mother's cheeks.

"He'll be all right," Preston insisted. "He knows what to say. He took his daddy's car for a joyride. When I talk with Teague, I'll let him know Cecil's in big trouble for taking my car without permission."

The next morning, Preston attended church with the family, saying he needed to show his face. Because they only had the truck, they left Ruthie and Preston's other three kids at home. Daddy drove, Mama up front beside him, while Preston, Clara, Inez and Livvy piled into the truck bed.

As usual, Mama played piano and Inez sang with the choir. When it came time for announcements, Reverend Blackwood allowed Inez to thank everyone who came out for the grand opening and those who took part in the drawing.

Livvy never looked directly at Sheriff Teague but she could feel his presence like heat from a fire. After the service she stayed three steps behind her family as they exited the sanctuary. They went through the motions, greeting relatives and neighbors as they slowly made their way to the dirt parking area. She sensed the sheriff moving in their direction before she saw him. He stopped directly in Preston's path, his Sunday hat shading his eyes.

"Need to have a word in private, Mr. Hopkins."

Preston patted Clara's arm and followed Teague a short distance away to a spot in the shade of a scraggly oak. Not far enough, though, that their conversation couldn't be heard by anyone with a mind to listen. Which Livvy found maddening, as if the sheriff wanted everyone to know their business.

"Got your oldest boy in a jail cell for running moonshine."

Preston's shocked reaction was genuine. He was certain he'd hidden all the liquor.

"Running moonshine?"

"Caught up with him last night driving that old Model T of yours like he was guilty of something."

"He was guilty of taking my car for a joyride, that's for sure. But he couldn't have had any alcohol in the car."

"He could and he did. Found a jar under the driver's seat. As you know, it's illegal to make, transport or sell alcohol."

"But it's not illegal to drink it." Everyone's head turned as Coy appeared beside Teague. He gave the sheriff a neighborly smile. "That's what most folks do with one jar of hooch. They drink it."

There were a few quiet chuckles from the men standing close by.

Livvy thought the sheriff might give Coy a dirty look, maybe tell him to butt out but Teague just raised his eyebrows like he was taking Coy's comment under consideration.

"When I was sixteen," Coy went on, giving Livvy a wink, "I remember sneaking a little nip now and then."

After a moment's hesitation, Sheriff Teague said that in spite of being a Sunday, Preston should come to the jail at three o'clock so they could discuss it further. Once the sheriff rejoined his wife, Preston turned to Coy.

"Much obliged, Mr. Whitaker."

"Mr. Teague and my daddy are old friends. He's almost like an uncle to me. So I can say things he might not take kindly if they were spoken by someone else. Of course, I don't know what he'll decide, but maybe he'll go a little easier on your boy."

"Thank you," Preston said, reaching out to shake hands.

Daddy shook Coy's hand too before the Hopkins family continued toward the truck as a wave of whispers swept through the crowd.

Coy nodded at Livvy.

"That was awfully generous of you," she said.

"I do recollect what it was like being sixteen – the urges, the longings, the thirst." He laughed and headed back to where his family was visiting with the pastor.

*

Although the moonshine business was no longer a big secret within the family, not one word was said during Sunday dinner about Cecil or Preston's car. Livvy still couldn't believe the sheriff had openly accused Cecil of wrongdoing right there in the church yard with everyone listening. And then Coy stepping forward like that in Cecil's defense. She was confident the gossip mill was already churning.

She ate a few bites and excused herself, anxious to flee to the woods and sweep the family worries from her mind, if only for a little while. It would be torture waiting at the house for Preston to have his meeting with the sheriff. Clara and Mama were already peevish and it would only get worse as the afternoon wore on.

She also missed the peace of the forest where she was surrounded by birds and critters that didn't need anything from her. She missed the rustling in the boughs of the trees above her. She missed creating her artworks.

When she reached the woodland she sat on her favorite log wearing dungarees and a shirt the boys had outgrown. Her creations were holding up nicely except the vine hammock, which had pretty much disintegrated. The tree nymphs looked as though they were happy to see her again.

She had no grand idea for a new sculpture, but a strong creative impulse had her wandering around the woodland under an azure sky. She gathered nuts, leaves and a few fallen bird feathers.

Where the hammock had been, she swept the dead vines aside, creating a space on the ground. She didn't know where the inspiration came from, working instinctively, arranging the leaves on the ground so they looked like mountains in the distance. She placed the nuts here and there as though they were large boulders that had tumbled down the mountains. She positioned the feathers so they appeared to be ravines cut into the mountainside, hidden streams within them. Then she searched for limbs in the underbrush, breaking them into small pieces and placing them here and there along the lower level of the mountains, giving the impression of trees on the lower elevations.

She smiled looking down at it. It resembled a painting of a scenic panorama, maybe somewhere in the Appalachians. The view made her feel for a moment like she might really travel one day and see such beauty with her own eyes. She pulled Grandma's old embroidery scissors from her bib pocket and trimmed a few strands of her hair, wrapping them around one of the feathers. When she set the feather down again, she experienced one of those vibrations, gooseflesh rising on her arms.

Her eyes were drawn to the doorway, a hint of a rainbow visible again just inside its periphery. Through it, she could see a darker sky in the distance. He was coming. She knew before she heard the sound of hoofbeats.

Horse and rider appeared through the trees as though she had conjured them. As before, he wore riding attire. She had seen a picture in one of Ruthie's magazines – an English actor riding a horse. The pants were called jodhpurs. They fit tightly into black knee-high boots and flared on the sides at thigh level. He wore a brown riding coat over a white shirt and small tie, a tan cap atop his head. It was a look she'd never seen until he appeared that first day. A look alien to her, but so natural on him.

He paused before walking slowly toward her, noticing her new design on the ground.

"A mountain vista. Amazing how you created such a grand illusion with detritus from the forest floor."

He pulled his camera from his saddle bag, asking if he could take more photographs.

"Of course. I should've taken some photos myself but I've been so busy lately." She didn't reveal that no one in her family owned a camera.

He snapped pictures as he asked what had been occupying her time.

"We had a gas pump and storage tank installed at our general store. Lots of preparation for our grand opening as a filling station this week. There was a prize drawing yesterday."

"You own a store?"

"With my two sisters."

"What's it called?"

"Hopkins General Merchandise. My grandmother left it to us."

"A businesswoman. Most impressive."

Which gave her the opening she'd been hoping for so she could ask without sounding too nosey.

"And you?" she said.

"I recently completed my law degree and I've begun further training with a local law firm."

Which simultaneously impressed her and deflated her. She knew he was educated, knew his social status was higher than hers. But this left no room for doubt for either of them.

On her walk home, she wondered again about his customary excuse for taking his leave – time to get home before it got dark. How far did he have to ride to reach home, for heaven's sake? Granted, it was a bit of a ride to Kinston, *if* he lived in Kinston. But not *that* long of a ride. And it begged the question, how could he be absent from work so much in the afternoon?

Something was a little bit off. It was probably just as well there were obstacles between them. Even if he was attractive and smart. Even if he was the one person she wished she could spend time with.

As was often the case, she stayed longer in the woods than she planned. When she reached the farm, she was just in time to see Preston's car drive into the yard. The passenger door opened and Cecil emerged. He and his father sauntered toward the house, Preston's arm draped over his son's shoulder. Clara, who had been waiting in one of the rockers, ran to embrace him.

After a celebratory supper during which the sheriff, the jail and the events of the night before were never mentioned, the men took Cecil and Vernon with them out by the pecan tree. They arranged chairs in a circle, keeping their voices down.

Not to be outsmarted, Livvy snuck out the other side of the house, making a wide circle until she reached Daddy's truck. Sitting on the running board on the far side, she caught snatches of conversation, including Daddy's confession that the corn crop was done for. Which put an end to daily trips to the creek and the drudgery of hand watering, but which also meant they now had two bank loans hanging over their heads and no crop coming in to pay off either one.

She also heard Preston's voice. "Have to be more careful, he'll be watching us like a hawk." Then she heard him say they had to find another route to the speakeasy, that the owner was offering good money for regular deliveries.

If the Hopkins women thought Cecil's close call might convince the men to call it quits as bootleggers, they were sadly mistaken.

10

By Thursday of that week, they'd filled the tanks of a dozen cars. Purchases inside the store were up a bit, but business wasn't exactly booming. At least not yet.

Livvy had just finished pumping gas for a neighbor when Coy walked in, white teeth gleaming in the bright morning sunshine.

"I knew a gas pump would do the trick," he said. Helping himself to a Coke from the drink barrel, he glanced through the front window to where Ruthie was sweeping the porch. "Now that you've had a chance to rest up from all the big doings, it's time to celebrate. Saturday night, we'll drive over to that speakeasy I told you about. They've got music and a nice little dance floor."

Using the opener on the wall, he popped the cap off the bottle and took a swig of his drink, sighing with contentment.

"I'm not sure I'd fit in, Coy. I don't drink, I don't know how to dance and I don't have anything to wear."

"They fix cocktails for the ladies with a little sugar. And like I said, you can wear one of my sister's dresses. As for dancing, I'll teach you. You need to put some fun in your life. One thing's for sure – it's not something high school kids do." He gave her a wink and took another slug of his Coke.

"I just…"

"You can't say no. I'm the man who came up with the idea for the gas pump and then loaned you the money to pay for it. Remember? And I hear Sheriff Teague let your nephew out of jail on Sunday. Believe I might deserve a little credit for that too. Now I'm offering you a fun night out. There's a lot to celebrate." He did a little twirl right there by the cash register like he was already on the dance floor, smiling from ear to ear. "How about it?"

So there was an obligation for Coy's good deeds. But urging the sheriff to let Cecil out of jail was truly appreciated. And while he might think it was his idea to get a gas pump, she and Inez had been wishing they could do that for some time. Still, it was true, both were acts of kindness. Who knows, maybe it would be fun, although it was hard to imagine herself dressing up and going out to a secret – and illegal – nightclub.

Ruthie stepped through the door, broom in hand, complaining about the heat.

"I'm getting me a cold drink," she said, heading for the barrel.

"Well?" Coy said, a playful grin on his face, ignoring Ruthie.

"All right," Livvy replied. "But don't say I didn't warn you. I'll stand out like a mule harnessed to a quarter horse."

He let loose with a belly laugh, then asked her to accompany him to his car. From the back seat, he pulled out a package wrapped in brown paper.

"Saturday! Pick you up at six. Takes a while to get there."

He handed her the package then drove off with a jaunty wave, dust rising up behind him.

At home that evening, she opened the package. Inside was a dress the likes of which she had never seen. Not in person anyway. It was made of a filmy blue material in the flapper style. She tried it on, studying her reflection. It had no waistline but dropped in a straight line nearly to the knee – a couple of inches shorter than the dresses she wore. At least the bodice wasn't low cut. There was a thin scarf attached around the neckline that covered her shoulders, for which she was thankful. Also in the package was a string of beads that hung nearly to her waist and a pair of evening slippers. She blushed imagining herself gussied up like that in public.

Knowing her appearance would cause quite a stir at home, she told the family Coy was taking her to a party in Athens thrown by one of his college friends. There was no way she could admit the truth.

That Saturday she took off from work mid-afternoon, leaving the store to Inez and Ruthie. She was a nervous wreck as she hurried home to take a bath. Once that was out of the way, a big part of getting ready was styling her wild red hair. Using hair pins, she arranged it close to her head in flat whorls. Then she twisted a black scarf Inez loaned her into a wide headband which she wrapped around her head, leaving some waves in front to frame her face and some fluffs on the crown of her head. Next she put on the sparkly earbobs that Hank had given her before they married. Once she was dressed, her hair done up and she'd added a touch of red lipstick, Livvy hardly recognized herself in the mirror.

What a big to-do she created when she emerged from her room as the family gathered for supper. Cecil and Vernon's eyes nearly popped out of their heads on their way from washing up at the pump. Preston and Daddy seemed rooted to the spot as they dried their hands on their pants.

"Lordamercy, Livvy," Daddy said. "What kind of party are you going to?"

Preston narrowed his eyes, suspicion written all over his face.

"Go on inside, boys," he said to his sons. As soon as they were through the door, he got right in Livvy's face. "I hope you're not going to that speakeasy."

"Going to a party. We're supposed to dress up like flappers."

Ruthie, Nettie and Faye appeared at the screen door, giggles erupting as they eyed Livvy's outfit.

"I hate to be the one to tell you," Ruthie said, "but I see what the movie stars are wearing in the magazines. And they don't wear those flapper dresses anymore."

"It takes longer for fashions to make their way to Hopkinsville," Livvy said.

Mama, Inez and Clara pushed through the girls and stood on the porch, judgmental eyes sizing her up.

"Goodness, Livvy," Mama said. "You look like you're from New York City."

"It's just for a party. I'm not turning into a flapper."

"I have to admit," Inez said, "if I were fifteen years younger, I'd be happy to dress up if Coy Whitaker came calling."

"And if I was five years older," Ruthie said, "I'd wear a flapper dress to go with Coy to a party, even if it *is* out of style."

"Everybody, stop your gawking," Daddy said. "I'm hungry."

They all followed the smell of food into the kitchen, all except for Preston.

"I'm serious, Livvy. If Coy Whitaker takes you to a speakeasy, you're just asking for trouble."

"Spoken like someone who knows what he's talking about."

His eyes sparked with anger. "I'm trying to save the farm, to save the family from ruination. What are *you* trying to do?"

"Well I could hardly turn him down after he got Cecil out of jail."

That shut him up. With a pained expression, he walked past her, joining the rest of the family. No one stood by her to tell her to have a good time or to shake hands with Coy when he arrived. No one was there to admire how he was dressed to the nines in a dark pinstripe suit, his hair brilliantined into place, glistening in the evening sunlight.

"I knew it! I knew it!" Coy wagged his finger at her, a wily grin on his face. "You're gonna be the belle of the ball!"

*

It was nearly dark by the time they parked on a side street at the edge of town. They walked a short block to a nondescript building with "R. S. Warehouse" in faded paint on the brick exterior. There were two cars close to a side door.

"Where is it?" Livvy said.

"Tucked away where the revenuers can't find it."

He led her around back to another door and knocked two times, waited, and knocked twice again, glancing around them. A man's voice called out from inside.

"Delivery or pick up?"

"Pick up," Coy replied.

What looked like a knot in the wooden door slid to one side at eye level.

"Whatcha picking up?" the man said.

"A load of ice."

There was a loud click, followed by two more clicks and the door swung open. A brawny man dressed in dark clothing ushered them inside, locking the door behind them.

"You know the way," he said to Coy, gesturing with his head.

They walked through a bare room with a concrete floor and a single light bulb hanging above them.

Livvy's stomach was in knots, wondering what she'd gotten herself into.

They passed through an interior door that opened onto a staircase descending to the basement. At the bottom Coy pushed another door open and escorted her into a room about the size of the church sanctuary. One wall was brick, the others were made of wood planks. Light fixtures hung from the ceiling and there were tables and chairs lining the long walls, about half of them occupied. There was a wooden bar at the other end of the room. Music played softly from a phonograph and two couples were slow dancing in the center of the room.

Livvy had read about speakeasies up north but this was not what she expected. Despite the laughter and buzz of friendly conversation, this was the most uninviting room she'd ever been in.

Several ceiling fans rotated lazily above them, but it was still too warm. It was also too smoky. And it wasn't just men smoking. Most of the women had cigarettes too. Everyone had a drink.

Without warning, Livvy felt Coy's hand slip around her waist as he guided her across the room, pausing at tables to shake hands with friends and give the women a flirtatious smile.

"This is my girl, Livvy," he said to a man named Joe. No last names were mentioned.

"Your girl?" Livvy said, raising her eyebrow at him to make her point but keeping her voice playful.

He laughed and pulled her toward a table where four young women were having a high old time, laughing and talking. Besides Livvy, they were the only ladies in the room wearing flapper dresses and hairdos. And, although it was still early, all four of them were half drunk. Maybe two thirds drunk.

"Hey, Coy!" a dark-haired girl sing-songed, ignoring Livvy. "I need a light." She waved a cigarette in the air.

"Looking good, Jessie!" he said, pulling a matchbox from his pocket and lighting her cigarette.

"Coy's always got a match," Jessie said, giggling as she blew smoke in Livvy's direction. "And he's a damn good dancer."

Coy winked at her and they continued on to the bar, where he ordered a whiskey for himself and a Lady's Cocktail for Livvy.

"Shipment arrive on time?" he asked the bartender.

"Ahead of time. The new fellas came last night."

Coy nodded his approval before placing his hand on Livvy's elbow as they made the rounds. There was plenty of back slapping, flirting, tall tale telling and lots of comments about the quality of the hooch. It seemed like everyone was making a point of complimenting Coy, as if he, himself, had made the whiskey they were drinking.

When he noticed Livvy's glass was still full, he insisted she drink up, reminding her they were here to celebrate.

"I'm pretty sure it'll make me sick."

"Hell, Livvy, you're a grown woman, not a school girl."

She set her glass on a table and shrugged. Her refusal seemed to irritate him.

When he recognized a popular tune on the phonograph, he guided her onto the dance floor.

"This is the Fox Trot. Easy as pie. Just follow me."

He held her close, one hand on her waist, the other holding her right hand. They glided around the floor which was filled now with sweaty bodies. He was right – there was nothing hard about it. Although the room was too crowded, too smoky and reeked of body odor, she rather enjoyed the dancing despite having to remove his hand from her butt a couple of times and re-position it on her waist. She also had to work at keeping some space between their bodies as he continued to tug her closer.

After a few dances, Jessie, the dark-haired flapper with eyes for Coy, appeared beside them.

"You owe me a dance, big fella," she said, her speech slurred.

He hesitated but Livvy said she needed to rest her feet, wandering off to sit in a chair along the wall. She watched with interest as Jessie wrapped herself around him. He responded by squeezing her butt, pulling her hard against him and laughing.

When the song ended, Jessie yelled out for everyone to hear: "Let's do the Charleston!"

The crowd responded with a cheer as someone put a new record on. Fast Charleston music filled the room and everyone swung into frenzied motion, including Jessie and Coy, who waved at Livvy to join them on the dance floor. But she forced a small laugh and shook her head as if that was beyond her ability.

The music was cranked up louder and the dancers laughed as they stepped forward and backward, kicking their legs and swinging their arms, the young women's beads flapping as they danced.

There was so much noise, no one noticed at first that a man was shouting from the stairs door. Livvy turned in time to see him unplug the record player, silencing the music. There was a communal groan of frustration but he yelled at the top of his lungs for everyone to clear out.

"Revenuers are coming! Close the bar down! Skedaddle!"

Everybody flew into action, women screaming and men cursing. Coy and several other men joined the bartender to slide a wooden wall into place in front of the bar, making it appear there was a bare wall on that end of the room. Doors opened that she hadn't noticed before so guests could flee the basement by three different sets of stairs. Coy grabbed her arm and hustled her up the stairs they had arrived by, charging through the room to the exterior door and bursting through the doorway. People scattered in all directions. Heart pounding, she struggled to keep up with him as they retraced their steps to his car a block away. Right after he cranked the car, they heard the screeching of tires in the distance behind them and men's urgent voices.

She thought he would floor it but he lit a cigarette before driving slowly along the side street, his arm dangling out the window like they were returning from seeing a picture show.

"Damn, that was fun," he said, chuckling softly and puffing on his cigarette.

She stared at him in wonder.

"Never gets old – fooling the revenuers. Just like the Georgia Bulldogs, our team is better staffed and better coached than our rivals. Good defense and good offense."

It hit her then.

"You own the speakeasy," she said.

"Shh," he said, glancing in her direction with a sideways grin.

It was after midnight when they reached Hopkinsville. She was desperate for a tall glass of water and her bed. So when he turned right instead of left toward her house, she told him he was going the wrong way.

"I just need to stop by my sister's house for a minute," he said.

"How about dropping me off first."

"Won't take a second."

He parked in the driveway next to a nice brick home. The house was dark with no cars parked outside.

Cutting the engine, he walked around to her side of the car and opened the door.

"Sis said I could use the house while they're in Atlanta this weekend."

She knew what he had in mind.

"I'm not going inside your sister's house. I've had enough excitement for one night."

"Come on, Livvy," he said, a teasing tone in his voice.

"I want to go home."

"To your mama and daddy's home, you mean. You said you didn't want us to act like high school kids. But that's what you're doing. You wouldn't even take a sip of that good liquor tonight. Even your sixteen-year-old nephew drinks moonshine. You need to loosen up a little."

She didn't move.

"There's nothing wrong with a grown man and a grown woman sitting together on a comfortable sofa while the man presses his lips onto the woman's soft, velvety neck," he went on. "Nothing wrong if they stroll down the hallway to the guest bedroom so they can lie down together to get a little more sociable. Especially when they're a perfect match like you and me."

It was too dark to see his face clearly, but his voice was soft and inviting. Did he honestly believe they were a perfect match?

There was a time when she would've dismissed any man who made his living selling illegal booze. But she'd been humbled. Her own father, her brother and his two sons helped support the family as bootleggers. Preston argued that if *they* didn't run the still and deliver the moonshine, someone else would. She knew he was right. So who was she to judge Coy Whitaker?

Truth be told, she missed male companionship. She could do a lot worse than this handsome man, who for some odd reason had set his sights on her.

She averted her eyes, struggling with how to respond, struggling with whether she was ready for what would begin as necking and escalate into something a lot more steamy.

"Besides," he went on, "it's not like any of this is new to you. You lost your virginity a long time ago. Come on, Livvy. I've got what you need."

She'd been on the verge of going along with him but her body went rigid. It was only with extreme effort that she managed to keep her voice from quivering in fury when she spoke.

"Coy, please take me home."

"Come on," he said, taking her hand and tugging gently.

When he tightened his grip, she yanked her hand free.

He loomed over her in the darkness and for an instant she feared he might try to force himself on her. Instead, he slammed the car door, returned to the driver's seat and tore off toward her house, dropping her off without another word.

11

Church was out of the question Sunday morning. Livvy had no desire whatsoever to see Coy's starched white shirt and sparkling smile. Claiming she didn't feel well made her family suspect she'd been drinking the night before. She retreated to her room to avoid the disapproval in their eyes.

"Hope you feel better," Ruthie said on her way out, a mocking tone in her voice.

Inez appeared, stepping inside the younger sisters' humble quarters – something she never did.

"I got drunk once when I was young," she said, shaking her head. "There was this boy named Willis Monroe – I thought he hung the moon. Anyway, he thought if he got me liquored up, I'd fall for his charms, if you know what I mean. He was right about that. I was ready and willing."

Livvy sat up on the side of her bed.

"Preston found us behind the barn and threatened Willis within an inch of his life," Inez continued. "Saved my honor, you might say. Next thing I knew, Willis had taken up with Thelma Butler. She was pregnant when they married. They moved to Atlanta before the baby came. Nowadays, he's a

Georgia Power lineman. I've always wondered how things might've turned out if my brother hadn't *saved* me."

Livvy was stunned to hear the real story behind Inez's broken heart. It wasn't quite the romantic tale she'd always imagined.

The truck sputtered to life and Mama called out for Inez to come on or they'd be late. Inez shrugged and headed off to join the family.

Was her bossy, church going, choir singing older sister warning her that if she was too principled she'd regret it for the rest of her life? Was she suggesting that going to bed with Coy might be a good thing? Livvy was flabbergasted.

Alone at the house, she carefully washed the borrowed flapper dress and hung it up in her room to dry. She would return it tomorrow while Coy wasn't home. She didn't want to keep it one more minute than she had to.

Shortly before the family was due home, she wrapped a couple of boiled eggs in cheesecloth and escaped to the woods. She didn't have an art project in mind. She just wanted to breathe the fresh air and sit beneath the trees. There was also a nugget of hope that Gordon might come riding through the forest.

She sat on her log and ate lunch, surveying the woodland. What she needed was some inspiration for a new artwork. But her mind kept flitting to places she'd rather avoid, like that damned speakeasy. Coy thought it was fun escaping from the revenuers just in the nick of time. What if they'd been caught? What if they'd been hauled off to jail?

Then it hit her – she needed to focus on a path. Her own path. Here in the forest, what better way to do that than create a path like you might find in a fancy garden. Of course, hers would be a much humbler version.

She started by clearing the ground between the boat and the doorway, using her hands and feet to sweep limbs, pinecones and nuts aside. Then she gathered pine straw, scooping it up in her arms and spreading it along the pathway, which was about two feet wide and eight feet long. Once she completed the ground cover, she rounded up pinecones to place along both sides. It wasn't nearly as elaborate as her other creations but she liked it. It seemed natural that there was a pathway between the boat and the doorway. From a certain vantage point it looked like a river upon which the boat was gliding.

Using her little scissors, she cut a few strands of her hair and wound them around one of the pinecones. The trembling began in her spine as soon as she returned the pinecone to its spot, followed by a pounding she could feel through the ground where she sat – rhythmic hoofbeats. In the distance she noticed the darkened sky beyond the trees as the striking grey horse came into view, his master in the saddle.

If she ever told a soul about any of this, they'd say she was out of her mind like they used to talk about Grandma. She'd heard the neighbors laugh about old Miz Birdie Hopkins and her ghost stories. She'd heard them poke fun at Grandma's interpretations of signs, like a hornets' nest built high on a tree meant a hard winter was on the way. Unlike Grandma, Livvy would keep her secrets to herself.

Gordon laughed as he dismounted.

"Aha! You think Bailey and I are in need of a marked path to follow so we won't get lost."

She chuckled self-consciously, wondering whether that might've played a part in her choice.

"You recall I took more photographs last Sunday?" he said, withdrawing an envelope from his jacket.

"I hope they turned out this time."

"Quite the opposite. These pictures are the same as the first ones – blank."

He fanned the pictures out for her to see.

"Maybe there's something wrong with your camera," she said.

"I suspected as much myself. So I had a photographer friend examine it. He says it's in good working order. I loaded a fresh roll of film and took more photos at my home, then had the film developed. The photographs came out fine."

He put the blank pictures away and pulled out a single photo. She stepped closer to study the black and white image of a large house. It was made of bricks and large stones, ivy covering part of the front wall, with carefully trimmed hedges and a grass lawn in the foreground.

"Is that your home?" she asked.

"It's my family's home."

She almost blurted "you're rich!" but bit her tongue.

"It's beautiful," she said.

"Thank you. But the question remains: why did the photos I shot here in the woodland not develop correctly? I wanted to capture some of your works of art."

"Very odd."

"What's odd is the light in this woodland. It's always brighter here." He stared at the sunlight glinting through the trees.

She was half listening, imagining what he would think if she showed him a picture of her family's home.

He cleared his throat, tucking the photo back in his pocket.

"I wondered if next Saturday afternoon you might let me take you to the Ice Cream Emporium."

His invitation was so unexpected. He had to be as conscious as she was of the differences in their backgrounds and social standing. She'd given up any real hope of him ever inviting her out.

"The Ice Cream Emporium?" she said.

"In Kinston."

"I didn't know Kinston had an ice cream shop besides the soda fountain at the pharmacy."

"It's on Perth Street next door to the haberdasher."

She didn't recall a Perth Street although she didn't know Kinston like the locals did. Still, she was feeling as fizzy as a Coke float.

"I can pick you up around two," he said.

That wouldn't do. If he laid eyes on the farmhouse she called home, he'd do a U-turn and escape back to his mansion and she'd never see him again.

"I have to drive into Kinston next Saturday anyway," she lied. "I can meet you there."

"Why, of course. I can see how that might suit you better."

They stood smiling at each other for a moment until he broke the silence.

"I must be going now," he said. "We're having guests for dinner and I have to dress."

Watching him disappear into the distance, little crinkles formed at the corners of her mouth and eyes. He would not have invited her for ice cream if he didn't like her. It was confirmation that she had not imagined the sparkle in his eyes when he looked at her. It was confirmation that it wasn't just her artworks that drew him back to the woodland. A quiet blush rose from her neck to her cheeks. It went without saying she would wear her new green dress.

On her walk home, she couldn't help but imagine the table where Gordon and his family would entertain company. Was it polished mahogany? Would they eat on fine China? When he said he had to dress for dinner, did that mean a well-cut suit and tie? Surely it didn't mean a tuxedo. Whatever sophisticated styles the well-to-do ladies wore at the Collins' dinner, Livvy was certain she would never fit in, not in a million years.

*

Although they weren't overly busy at the store early in the week, they had more business than they used to before they started selling gasoline. They rang up seven fuel purchases by noon Wednesday.

Inez rode with Daddy to the bank that afternoon, both of them making deposits, intent on saving enough money to make their loan payments.

Livvy hadn't seen hide nor hair of Coy, which was fine with her. But his fancy blue Ford pulled up at the pump shortly after Inez left. She dashed out the door, instructing Ruthie to stay behind the cash register.

"Fill 'er up!" Coy said, leaning against the car door. "Business good?"

"It's picked up a bit." She hand-pumped gas into the clear cylinder, then removed his gas cap and inserted the nozzle.

"Thanks for returning the dress, by the way."

She nodded, keeping her eyes on the pump, listening as the gasoline streamed into his tank, gauging when to release the handle so it wouldn't overflow. She could feel his eyes on her.

"Came up with a good plan for Saturday," he said. "Maybe something more like what you're used to. I know a shady spot along the river where we can spread a blanket for a nice picnic. I'll have our maid fix us a basket, including a homemade peach pie."

She let go of the handle, then hung the nozzle on its hook.

"Sorry, Coy. I'm visiting a friend Saturday. Come on inside so I can ring you up."

"Who you visiting?"

"An old girlfriend."

She started toward the door. He followed.

"You'd choose an old girlfriend over me?" he said.

She laughed.

"How about Sunday then?"

She stopped, turned and looked up into his face. No time like the present to say what she had to say.

"Coy, I don't think I'm your kind of girl."

"Sure you are."

"You and I have different interests."

"I'm planning on asking about the plays you've seen. Maybe we could go see one together."

"There are lots of pretty girls who'd be happy to have your attention."

"But you're the one I want."

She opened the door, motioning Ruthie out of the way as she hurried around the counter to ring up his purchase. She was flustered that he wouldn't take no for an answer.

He followed, facing her across the cash register as he dropped a bill on the countertop.

"Thank you," she whispered.

"Think on it some more. You need to give me a chance, Livvy."

As soon as he was out the door Ruthie started in on her.

"Did you say no to the best-looking man in Burgess County?"

Livvy gave her a stern look.

"Holy moly, Livvy! You're a bird brain!"

"You need to mind your own business."

"I know, I know. I'm only fourteen years old. But even I understand you should be finding yourself a husband! Inez is right. A woman is like a fresh tomato. Once it ripens, it's only good for a few days before it gets all soft and mushy and moldy. Inez says we haven't got all the time in the world to find a man. She agrees with me that Coy Whitaker is the best husband material we've got in all of Hopkinsville."

"Leave it be, Ruthie! And don't you be gossiping about my business. You hear?"

But gossip she did. Starting with the family that evening at supper. Livvy hadn't even taken her second bite of rabbit stew when Ruthie spilled the beans.

"Y'all won't believe this, but Livvy told Coy Whitaker to go jump in the lake today."

"Ruthie Hopkins! I did not say that!" Livvy cried. "You have the biggest mouth of anyone I've ever met. And one day it's going to get you in a heap of trouble."

"Well, it's the truth. They had words in front of the store this afternoon. Then when they came inside Coy asked Livvy to give him a chance."

"All right, Ruthie," Mama said. "I think you need to button your lip."

Inez raised her eyebrows at Livvy while Clara gave her four children a motherly glance that said they should keep their noses out of it.

"Sure is good to have more meat on the table again," Clara said to Cecil and Vernon, whose rabbit boxes had provided the main course for tonight's meal.

"Amen to that," Daddy said, scooping another spoonful into his mouth, hungry after a long day with his grandsons at the still that nobody ever mentioned.

No more was said about Coy. But Livvy knew Mama would have a private word with her later. She also knew Inez would wait until they were alone at the store to pry into her business. Clara wouldn't ask at all, having more important things to worry about than her sister-in-law's love life.

When the dishes were done and the evening had cooled a bit, Mama sent Ruthie, Nettie and Faye to water the garden while she sat down at her beloved piano, launching into "Silver Threads Among the Gold." The boys disappeared to tend to their traps before it got dark and Clara patched a pair of pants on the porch as Inez sat nearby straining to read a book in the fading light, both of them slapping at mosquitoes.

Livvy was in her room examining her new green dress to make sure it was ready for her date with Gordon when she heard a car approach. Peeking through the window, she recognized Preston's Model T turning into the yard. What in the world? It was Wednesday evening. He only came home on Friday nights.

Stepping onto the porch as Clara set her sewing aside, she watched Preston drag his lean frame from the car. He lifted his tattered travel bag from the seat and started toward the house.

The screen door slammed as Daddy came out to see what was going on. The music ended and Mama appeared on the porch. The girls trotted around the corner of the house with watering cans in their hands.

Preston stopped a few feet from the porch, sighed heavily and locked eyes with his wife.

"I was fired."

No one spoke as the impact of his words sank in. Losing that paycheck pushed them that much closer to financial disaster.

Clara reached out to him. He stepped up onto the porch, took her hand and followed her inside, leaving the rest of the family to wonder what happened.

An hour after Preston's arrival, Mama served a big breakfast for him – scrambled eggs, a bowl of grits and warmed up buttered biscuits. She knew he needed food in his belly.

Cecil and Vernon arrived with two rabbits in their bag, washing up before joining the family at the table. They waited patiently while their father ate by lamplight, washing the food down with a cup of coffee. Finally, he pushed back from the table.

"Jack McCord left right after lunch today saying he was sick at his stomach. He's the blocksetter who gets the logs into place on the platform before they're moved down the line to the circular saw. I was out in the yard stacking boards for a shipment to Augusta when Willy, the foreman, yelled for me to come see him. There was a funny look on his face when he told me I needed to report to the main cutting room. He said they needed me to fill in for Jack. I told him I'd never done the blocksetter's job, that nobody had ever trained me. He said I'd seen it done enough to know the basics and for me to get on over there. I stared at him a minute, trying to figure out why they'd pick me to fill in for Jack. I told him Charlie, Isaac and Henry had a lot more experience than me. He said they had other work so I should do as I was told. I was cogitating on it, knowing full well that being near the big saw is dangerous." He looked at Livvy then. "That's the same job that killed Hank.

"But I considered how much we need the money, knowing we might lose the farm. I thought about all of that. I also thought about Clara." He glanced at his wife, reaching for her hand. "And I thought about my children. I decided I wasn't going to risk my life doing a job I'm not ready for. So I told him that. I said it quiet-like. But I made it clear where I stood. He told me to report to Mr. Whitaker's office. He's nothing like his son. Acts like he's King George and the rest of us should bow down and lick his boots. He's always reminding people his name is Jefferson Davis Whitaker, named after the president of the Confederacy. Anyhow, he said if I didn't do as I was told, I would be terminated immediately. I told him I was sorry, but that I didn't have any training and could get myself killed. He told me to get my things and clear out, to stop by the paymaster's office for my final pay."

His story made Livvy shiver like a cold wind had brushed against her neck. She couldn't help but wonder about the circumstances surrounding Hank's death. Was he forced to take on that dangerous job? But Preston's co-workers said Hank *wanted* the promotion, wanted to make more money.

"You did the right thing," Clara said.

"Yeah, Pa," Vernon said.

Cecil nodded enthusiastically beside him. Nettie and Faye jumped up and ran around the table, squeezing in on either side of him to give him a hug. So Preston could have some privacy with his wife and children, Mama stood, signaling for the rest of them to follow her.

They all wandered out onto the porch. Then Mama slipped her arm through Daddy's and they walked out toward the pecan tree, just the two of them – a sight Livvy hadn't seen in a long time. She, Inez and Ruthie stood silently, each of them lost in her own thoughts. Now the success of their general store was more essential than ever, as was the men's not so secret family business.

12

After a long day Thursday, they heard a car pull up in the driveway. Daddy rose from the table, telling everyone to stay put while he went outside to greet the unexpected visitor. Livvy and the family listened intently, the clink of silverware coming to a halt. She recognized Coy's booming voice.

"Preston," Mama said, "why don't you see what's going on."

He wiped his mouth and walked outside while the rest of the family took the last couple of bites of food on their plates and the girls started stacking dishes by the wash tub. Livvy was dying to peek through the window but stifled her curiosity. If Coy was here to speak with her, someone would've called her name by now.

Cecil and Vernon left by the back door to make their rounds of the rabbit boxes while the women cleaned up. Wasn't long before they heard an engine crank and a car drive away.

After a few minutes, the two men returned, Daddy gesturing for Preston to speak.

"That was Coy Whitaker. He says I've got my job back."

No one knew how to react, especially Clara. She hated the sawmill job, dreading bad news every day. But she also knew the family was in dire straits. Her eyes teared up but she held herself together.

"He says he told his daddy I was right refusing to do the blocksetter's job without being taught how to do it properly. He says I'll get full pay for this week, but I can have tomorrow off and come back to work on Monday."

Inez spoke up then. "Coy seems like a decent fellow."

Which Livvy knew was meant for *her* ears.

"Handsome too," Ruthie said, nodding at Inez.

*

Friday morning Coy strolled into the store dressed in a suit and tie. Ruthie was right. He was a good-looking man. But Livvy wished he hadn't come. She was focused on her ice cream date with Gordon tomorrow. Daddy was letting her borrow the truck and Inez and Ruthie would run the store so she could take the afternoon off. But here he was, looking like the successful businessman he was.

"Morning, Livvy! Morning Ruthie! How are the pretty Hopkins sisters this fine morning?"

Ruthie giggled as she restocked the drink barrel.

"Doing just fine," she replied. "Especially after your visit to our house last night."

"Well, your big brother did the right thing. Smart man. Good worker. Daddy just took it the wrong way I guess. But he came round. Now, I need an ice cold root beer and a Baby Ruth for my trip over to Athens. Like to have a little snack while I'm driving."

Ruthie hopped to it, pulling a root beer from the ice, drying it off with a towel, then getting the candy bar. She set both beside the cash register with a smile, then returned to her work.

He laid some coins on the counter and opened his soft drink on the bottle opener by the door. "I'm going to have some homemade lemonade for our Sunday picnic. Not taking my flask along. Just good old-fashioned lemonade."

"But, Coy..." Livvy said.

"No buts. I'll give you time to change out of your church clothes before I pick you up."

He marched out the door before she had time to say another word. She almost ran after him to call the whole thing off but since he'd gotten Preston's job back, there was this growing feeling of obligation. How many times had he helped her family now?

"Dammit," she muttered under her breath.

Big-eared Ruthie heard.

"Now you're cussing because Coy Whitaker is a good deed doer?"

Livvy finished up at the store at noon, hurried home, washed up and changed into her pretty green dress. She styled her hair with more care than usual and applied a little lipstick. The mirror told her she was dressed just right for an informal date at the Ice Cream Emporium. With a scarf on her head, she got Daddy's keys and took off for Kinston.

When Daddy and the rest of the family had asked why she had to go to Kinston, she told them a girlfriend from college asked her to meet for a visit, that the invitation arrived in the mail at the store. She could only imagine their skepticism if she revealed the truth – that she was going on a date with a man she met in the woods.

She'd managed to calm down about the picnic with Coy by filing it away in that little corner of her mind where she stored things she would deal with later. Including what the newspaper was calling an economic recession and the never-ending drought. She wasn't going to think about those things today. Instead, she was going to have fun sharing ice cream with a man whose company raised her spirits and whose praise made her feel special.

It was a perfect day for ice cream. Hot and humid. She was relieved when she left the dirt roads of Hopkinsville where you could see someone coming in the distance by the cloud of dust rising from the road as they drove along. She picked up speed when she reached the paved highway, arriving in Kinston about a quarter till two.

The town wasn't very big, so finding the ice cream shop would be easy. She drove in on Main Street, watching the street signs as she drove. No Perth Street. And there was no ice cream parlor on Main Street. Turning left, she spotted Mr. Beasley's general store. He knew the town like the back of his hand.

When she entered the store he was busy helping a dark-haired woman in her thirties. She was dressed like a picture in Ruthie's magazines in a fancy dress and hat with expensive shoes and pocketbook. Livvy wandered around the aisles but couldn't help overhearing their conversation.

"I guess you heard my husband is now vice president," the woman said.

"I did hear that. That's good news, especially in these tough times," Mr. Beasley replied. "I read that a bank in Atlanta went out of business last week."

"Poor management, I'm sure. My husband is an expert at managing our bank's assets. He has a degree in business management."

"That's good to know. That'll be one dollar and seventy-four cents, Mrs. Buchanan."

The cash register jangled as the drawer opened, then closed. Mr. Beasley thanked Mrs. Buchanan who took her leave, high heels clicking as she crossed the wooden floor.

When she was gone, Mr. Beasley called out to Livvy.

"Aren't you Inez Hopkins' sister?" he said.

"You have a good memory. Livvy Sloan. Good to see you again."

"Is Inez with you?"

"No, I'm by myself today. Actually, I stopped in to ask if you could tell me where the Ice Cream Emporium is. I was invited by a friend to have ice cream there this afternoon but I can't find Perth Street."

"Perth Street?"

"That's the address I was given. I was told it was right in the middle of downtown but I can't find it."

"I hate to be the bearer of bad tidings, Miz Sloan, but there is no Perth Street in Kinston, downtown, uptown or around town. And there's no ice cream emporium. The only place you can sit down for an ice cream around here is the soda fountain at Denton's Pharmacy."

She wanted to burst out crying. Either that or stamp her feet in anger. Maybe both. It was not like she could drive to Gordon's house to find him. Mr. Beasley had already told her he knew no one by that name. Nor did he know anyone with an English accent. Here she was making a fool of herself.

"Well, I must've misunderstood my friend. We were talking on the telephone. And you know how that can be sometimes – there was some static on the line. I thought she was talking about Kinston, but she must've been referring to some other town."

"Can I get you a cold drink? You look a mite overheated."

"That would be nice," she admitted, pulling a nickel out of her purse. "I'll take a Coke."

He dried the dripping bottle and opened it for her.

"Thank you, Mr. Beasley. I better get going."

"By the way, how's the store doing with the gas pump?"

"We're getting more customers than we were. We do a pretty good business pumping gas."

"Glad to hear it. Please say hello to Inez for me. Bring her with you next time you head this way."

"You should drive over to Hopkinsville and stop in our store sometime. I'm sure she would enjoy giving you a little tour."

"I might just do that!"

She started toward the door but stopped. "If you don't mind my asking, is that lady who was in here related to the Whitakers who live in the Hopkinsville area?"

"Sure enough. She's Jefferson Whitaker's daughter. The Whitaker family has come a long way in the last twenty years. Connections in high places these days, not like when they could barely put food on the table. She married well, that's for sure. Now her husband is vice president of the bank. She usually sends her maid to shop but gave her the afternoon off."

It was hard to imagine the prim and proper banker's wife in a flapper dress.

All the way home, Livvy fought to keep tears from welling up. She'd been imagining the little ice cream social with Gordon all week. She wanted him to see her as something other than an oddity. But why would he tell her there was an ice cream parlor in Kinston if it wasn't true? He seemed so normal. But there were moments when he didn't make sense. She shouldn't be angry with him. He wouldn't mislead her intentionally. Something was definitely amiss.

Maybe it was just as well that she was going on that infernal picnic with Coy. Maybe Ruthie was right – he was the man she should have her eye on. Mama and Inez thought so too. He had come to the aid of her family now several times in dramatic fashion. She didn't know why she wasn't attracted to him. There was just something about him that she couldn't explain. Part of it had to do with his professed attraction toward her. There were so many pretty women who would suit him better. Women who liked drinking and dancing. Women who liked hanging on a handsome man's arm at a football game. Looking at it logically, Coy Whitaker should find Livvy boring. But she wasn't a man. She supposed there were some things she would never understand.

When Mama asked why she was back so soon, she told her the truth, except for changing the identity of her friend from Gordon Collins to Gloria Hancock. That there was no Ice Cream Emporium in Kinston and Gloria must've been thinking of some other town when she sent Livvy the letter.

Inez blushed when Livvy told her Mr. Beasley asked about her.

*

Upon arriving home from church on Sunday Livvy changed into her hand-me-down dungarees and a plaid, short-sleeved shirt, pulling her hair into a ponytail. Mama, Inez and Ruthie all gave her disapproving looks. But she wanted to make it clear she was not the prissy kind of girl Coy was naturally drawn to. By the expression on his face when he got out of his car, she had succeeded.

As usual, he looked like a model in a men's clothing advertisement wearing creased khaki trousers, a pale blue button up shirt and polished leather shoes.

He quickly regained his composure, though, snickering as he commented on what a practical woman she was.

They spread the blanket beneath a stand of pines close to the bank overlooking a section of the river with small rapids that sluiced around a series of rocks. When he unpacked the picnic basket it was clear that someone – probably Mae Glover – had gone to a lot of work. There was fried chicken, deviled eggs, pickled cucumbers, a ripe tomato – thick slices arranged on a plate – the homemade peach pie he'd promised and a big jug of sweet lemonade.

She reminded herself several times on the drive over that she should do her best to give Coy another chance. One thing was clear – he was doing *his* best.

While they ate, he asked her about her experience at Young Harris College, asked why she liked theater. Asked if she wanted to be an actress.

"Acting? No. I just like seeing a drama acted out on the stage right in front of me."

"And you saw *Romeo and Juliet*? What's that about?"

Even if he wasn't into theater, she thought everyone knew the basic story of one of Shakespeare's most famous plays.

"A boy and a girl from two feuding families make the mistake of falling in love. Which eventually leads to the deaths of both of them."

"Feuding families – like when a rich family looks down its nose at a poor family."

He kept steering the conversation back to her, refusing to talk about himself even when she gave him an opening. In fact, it was like he was rushing through a checklist, giving her time to answer before asking another question. She did manage to tell him about seeing his sister at Beasley's General Store.

"I didn't know she was your sister until after she was gone. Mr. Beasley said she was Jefferson Whitaker's daughter. She's very pretty."

"The boys used to follow Janie Whitaker around like she was Fay Wray. But she was very particular. Married Merle Buchanan, whose daddy was president of the bank back then. Now that he's bank vice president, we've got a big shot in the family."

Livvy said they should save the pie for a bit, suggesting they wade in the shallows to cool off. She rolled up the cuffs on her jeans and took off her shoes. Putting the straw hat she'd brought atop her head, she stepped carefully into one of the small pools, enjoying the sensation of cool water eddying around her feet and ankles. He followed her lead.

"You know what we oughta do," he said. "We oughta go skinny dipping. There's a secret spot about half a mile down river. I've got a couple of towels in the trunk."

She hooted with laughter.

"Don't tell me you've never done it before," he said.

"I guess it's not my style."

"Come on, Livvy. Loosen up a little."

She stepped from the water onto a dry rock.

"You act like you've never been with a man. But we all know that's not true."

"I'm sure you know some girls who'd be happy to go skinny dipping with you. Why don't you ask them?"

"Because I'm asking you."

"Sorry, Coy."

He shook his head in frustration.

They returned to the blanket to have a piece of pie. After which, Livvy was ready to leave. But he moved closer, taking her hand in his.

"You were right," he said. "We needed to get to know each other better."

Then he leaned even closer, intent on giving her a kiss, but she withdrew her hand from his and got to her feet.

"I enjoyed the picnic."

"Livvy, I think you owe me a little appreciation. I'm pretty sure I've proven I'm a generous man." His tone was reasonable, calm, friendly. "I've said it before and I'll say it again – you and me, we're the perfect couple. That being the case, I'm able to help your family from time to time."

"I do appreciate you helping my family. Very much."

"Not to mention the interest-free loan for the gas pump."

"That too. We're grateful. Truly, we are. But if we're not suited to be sweethearts we can still be friends."

"Friends," he grumbled.

His signature smile vanished and they repacked the basket in silence. The smile didn't reappear as he drove her home. But she couldn't force herself to feel attracted to him. She had tried and failed. And although she didn't want to end up alone, there were worse fates. Like being married to someone you didn't love, someone you didn't trust.

She thanked him again as she got out of the car but he didn't respond, just gunned the motor, raising dust as his car fishtailed across the yard toward the road.

Because she was in no mood to answer questions, she borrowed a wheelbarrow and disappeared into the woods before anyone noticed she was home.

Anger boiled over with every step. She was furious with Coy, thinking she should become "his girl" because he helped her family. It riled her that he viewed his good deeds as requiring payment in the form of giving her body to him. Because no matter how nice a man Mama, Inez and Ruthie thought he was, and no matter how good looking and successful he was, there was something about him that left her cold. She had almost convinced herself she should overlook that feeling in her gut. But no more. She would be civil. She would be friendly. And she would make sure she and Inez made their loan payments on time. But she wasn't going out with Coy Whitaker again. That would just be leading him on.

There was also her frustration over her wasted trip to Kinston. She didn't believe for a minute that Gordon would intentionally mislead her. But now she was convinced he had some kind of mental problem. It was possible the picture he'd shown her wasn't his house. It was possible he hadn't finished law school and wasn't really starting a career as a lawyer. It was possible that sometimes he couldn't find his way to the woodland. Maybe he had good days and bad days. In her heart, she thought he was a good man. But she also now believed something wasn't quite right about Gordon and she had to reconsider her feelings for him. She didn't think he would ever hurt her. Still, she had to be careful his confusion didn't cause her to do something that would be unwise. Like agree to meet him at an ice cream shop that didn't exist.

She could continue to make her art creations in the forest. And if he visited from time to time, she would be friendly. But that's all. She needed to focus on making the store a success so she could help the family regain some financial stability. She didn't want Daddy, Preston and the boys to end up going to prison for bootlegging.

In addition, if they were going to make the farm a success, they had to find a way to irrigate the crops. Maybe they should pay a visit to Uncle Tyrone and see if he might soften his stance on allowing Daddy access to the stream. Maybe she could help make peace between them. At the very least, she should try.

Right now though, all she wanted was to commune with the forest. By the time she arrived, she realized she had picked enough flowers along the way to make a small artwork. She braided together some of the vines that had fallen from the hammock, interlacing the flowers inside and outside so it was quite literally a flower basket. She hung it from a twig protruding from the doorway and added her signature – a few strands of hair.

At the same time she felt the vibration in her back, there was a pounding beneath her feet. She recognized the sensation – it was a horse galloping toward her. But Gordon never came this late. She was startled at the sight of him.

There was no friendly wave or smile of greeting. He dismounted and strode toward her looking more than a little annoyed.

"You didn't come," he said, a look of accusation in his eyes.

"I did come. But I couldn't find Perth Street or the Ice Cream Emporium. There's no ice cream parlor of any kind in Kinston."

His eyebrows shot up. "I don't mean to be disagreeable, but there most certainly is a Perth Street and an Ice Cream Emporium. I sat at a table waiting for you for over an hour."

She wasn't sure what to say. If he suffered delusions, maybe she shouldn't argue with him. It dawned on her then that when he mentioned a cousin who developed mental problems because of his battlefield experiences in France that it might not have been a cousin at all. Maybe he'd been talking about himself.

"I'm sorry, Gordon. I did drive to Kinston and tried to find the Ice Cream Emporium. I was disappointed too."

His forehead wrinkled in confusion.

"Something has always troubled me about our encounters," he said. "Sometimes it seems we're great friends. Other times it seems you're suspicious about who I am and why I'm here. We even have conflicting observations about the time and weather. I rode over here in the dark."

Which drew his attention to the sky.

"Why is there so much light here? Night has fallen at my house."

There it was. Another delusion. He had always said the light here was strange. And he always said he had to hurry home before it got dark even though it was the middle of the afternoon.

Scanning the area, he noticed the little flower basket she'd created. He strolled to the doorway to take a closer look.

"It's almost like you're a magical creature," he said to her over his shoulder.

He reached up to touch the little basket but gasped, yanking his hand back like he'd burned his fingers.

"What's wrong?" she said.

When he turned toward her, there was fear in his eyes.

"Preternatural," he whispered.

His behavior convinced her he must be suffering some kind of neurosis.

He turned back toward the doorway, lifting his arm slowly to extend it through the opening. Then he swung his arm from side to side as if to knock her artwork from its moorings.

"Gordon!" she cried.

But instead of hitting the woven twigs and vines that made up the door, his arm passed through them like it didn't exist.

Her mouth fell open as she tried to comprehend what her eyes were seeing. Moving quickly, he strode to the boat and walked right through it like it wasn't there. There was no sound of crunching twigs, no movement in the boat's hull.

She thought of Grandma's story about seeing her granddaddy's ghost when she was a girl. She said his spirit walked around the outside of the house some nights like he was guarding it. But Livvy had never put much stock in her stories, figuring there was always a rational explanation behind even the strangest events. Now she wasn't so sure, feeling an uncomfortable prickle on the back of her neck. Should she run?

"All of this looks so real," he said, his voice uneasy. "And you – you look so real."

"I *am* real. You're the one who just walked through my canoe."

"I always thought this place was ethereal, but..." he muttered, no longer speaking to her.

He started for his horse, looking over his shoulder as if to make sure he wasn't being followed. Saddling up, he gave Livvy a disturbed glance as he galloped away.

She watched as he rode toward the dense trees in the distance. The sky was dark beyond him like a violent thunderstorm was pounding the earth with a torrential downpour.

She found it hard to breathe, unable to make sense of what she'd witnessed. Ironic that she'd been concerned about him suffering delusions when he wasn't even real. There was no denying what she'd seen with her own eyes. But he didn't fit the bill for any ghostly sightings Grandma had shared. Yet she couldn't think of another explanation. He used the word preternatural. She knew what that word meant: existing outside of nature. She couldn't argue with that.

Although Grandma said her granddaddy patrolled outside the house after he died, he never spoke. He certainly never struck up a conversation with anyone. And there was nothing scary or ghostly about Gordon. Nothing otherworldly. He seemed very much alive. She had to admit there were things about him that were troubling. His claim that he lived in Kinston. And all that nonsense about being unable to find his way to the woods. Still, the only explanation for a man passing through a solid object was that he was a spirit.

But if he were truly a ghost, why would a dead Englishman visit her as she created nature sculptures in the woods of northeast Georgia? Grandma would know what it meant. But she was gone. And if her spirit still abided in Burgess County, she'd never shown herself.

Despite the warm afternoon sunshine, Livvy was as spooked as if a goblin were chasing her through the forest at midnight.

13

After staying awake half the night, dreaming of ghosts under the branches of the pecan tree, jumping at the least little noise, Livvy was bleary-eyed Monday morning. She had almost talked with Mama about what she'd seen. Each time, she held back, knowing how Mama felt about spirits. She'd always made it clear that, despite all her good qualities, she thought her mother-in-law was a little touched in the head. Besides, that's all Mama needed was something else to worry about. In this case, Livvy's sanity.

Livvy, herself, was filled with self-doubt. But if Gordon Collins wasn't a ghost, then what was he? A figment of her imagination? Maybe *she* was the one suffering delusions. Maybe *she* was the one with some kind of neurosis.

Grandma had always seemed like an enchanting old lady to her, with her spooky stories, her predictions and her signs. That's one of the reasons Livvy loved her so – she was interesting, she was different, she was fun. And those ghost stories were part of the fun. She could imagine her grandmother as a little girl peeking through the window to see her old granddaddy guarding the house. Was that little girl scared? In her old age, she never sounded like it had frightened her. Of course she'd grown up in a family that thought spirits were a part of the natural world, a world filled with mysteries.

Right now, Livvy wished she could emulate her grandmother's calm. But it was easier said than done. Watching Gordon's hand slide through the vines and sticks that made up the doorway had shaken her. It was like he didn't exist, like he was an apparition. Because she knew for certain the doorway was solid to the touch. She'd created it with her own two hands. And yet, he had accused *her* of not being real!

She was lost in her confusing thoughts as she dressed for the day. She was about to join the family at the breakfast table when she heard a car approach, its motor humming quietly. That was a sure sign it belonged to a man of means. What well-to-do man would be stopping by their house at seven-thirty on a Monday morning? Giving her hair a quick brush, she smoothed her dress and stepped onto the porch in time to see a middle-aged man in a suit exit his car, walk to the edge of the parched cornfield and survey the damage. He pulled a pad from his leather briefcase and made a quick note before making his way to the house.

"Good morning," he said to her. "The name is Harold Williams. May I speak with Mr. Leon Hopkins?"

"I'll tell him you're here." She left him on the porch while she hurried into the kitchen. Daddy was eating scrambled eggs surrounded by the family, except for Preston who had driven back to the lumber mill the night before. The buzz of conversation had kept them from hearing the guest arrive in his fancy car.

"Daddy, there's a Mr. Harold Williams here to see you."

There was a look of recognition in his eyes and a frown on his face as he set his fork down and took a gulp of coffee.

"I'll talk with him outside," he said.

Livvy sat down for a minute but popped back up, too jittery to eat. She had a bad feeling about that Mr. Williams. Before anyone could stop her, she tip-toed into Mama and Daddy's room, staying in the shadows as she peered through the window. In a flash, Ruthie was by her side. They watched as Daddy and Mr. Williams strolled toward the field talking quietly. When they reached the edge of the yard Mr. Williams gestured at the dead seedlings and shook his head as he said something with a serious expression on his face. Then he withdrew a long white envelope from his briefcase, handed it to Daddy, shook hands and walked back to his car. Daddy didn't open the envelope, just stood there gazing over the ruined cornfield as Mr. Williams drove away.

The table had been cleared and everyone was ready for the day by the time Daddy returned. He set the unopened envelope on the table in front of him. Mama poured him another cup of coffee and sat down beside him in Livvy's chair. Although it was time for Livvy and Inez to go to the store, they both waited with the others to find out what was in that envelope.

Daddy took a couple of sips of coffee and drummed his fingers on the table.

"Mr. Williams is with the bank. They've denied my request for an extension to pay back the loan I took out in the spring to pay for cotton seed and other supplies. The loan is due in full by the end of next week. He says since the corn crop failed as well, there won't be any chance of an extension on that loan, which is due September thirtieth – four weeks from tomorrow. If we default on either loan, we forfeit the farm."

"You've always paid your loans in the past," Mama said. "Why, all of a sudden, are they treating you like a bad customer?"

Daddy shook his head. "He said they got word we'd had two failed crops in a row and he was sent out here to have a look-see."

"Got word?" Livvy said.

"Right now we need to get to work. Tonight we'll add up all the money we've saved – what's in the bank and what'll be going in the bank – and we'll figure it all out. Inez, I'd appreciate it if you and Livvy would see how much you can spare from the store."

With that, he rose from the table, leading the way as they all headed to their workday destinations.

*

Livvy was surprised to find Mae Glover standing in front of the store when they arrived, her egg basket on her arm. Knowing how territorial Inez was about her eggs, Mae normally didn't come when Inez was there. Inez gave her a disapproving glance before unlocking the door and going inside. Guessing Mae would rather keep their conversation private, Livvy waited with her out front while Inez set up the cash register.

"Morning, Mae. Haven't seen you lately. Everything all right?"

"I don't need to trade for anything this morning. I brought these eggs for you to take to your friend, Arlene White." She handed Livvy the basket.

"For Arlene?"

"I saw her last evening as I passed by her house. From the look of things, they're worse off than me and mine. Anyway, she said she needed to speak with you about something but her husband can't drive her to the store. I told her I'd give you the message. Now I've got to get on to work. Mrs. Whitaker gets right angry if I'm late."

"Thank you, Mae. Very kind of you."

Mae hurried off, walking as fast as her legs would carry her.

Inez calmed down when Livvy told her the eggs were for Arlene. As soon as Ruthie arrived for her afternoon shift, Livvy walked over to Arlene's to deliver them, paying Inez for a can of coffee, a bottle of milk and two penny candies to take as well.

Livvy wore a straw hat, knowing it would be a long hot walk with little shade. She had worked up a good sweat by the time she made it to the driveway that turned off the main highway. She was struck by how rundown the small house appeared. The glass in one of the front windows was gone, the window covered by a threadbare sheet. The front steps were rickety and she found the front door standing wide open.

"Arlene?" she called out, knocking on the door frame.

There was no answer from within but she heard children's voices from the back yard and wandered around the house, her bare legs switched by knee-high weeds. She found Arlene hanging diapers on a clothesline strung between two trees, her two little boys playing in the dirt nearby.

"Arlene!"

Her friend whirled around in surprise.

"Livvy!"

"Mae Glover asked me to bring you these eggs." She held the basket out. "And I brought a couple of other groceries."

"Come in, come in."

Arlene wiped her hands on her apron. She left the clothes basket on the ground, leading the way to the back door, through the kitchen to a dark living room, the boys tagging along behind.

Livvy took a seat on a worn sofa and set her grocery bag on a bushel basket turned upside down to use as a table.

"I brought milk, coffee and treats for the boys, if that's all right."

Arlene was clearly uncomfortable having Livvy visit her shabby home. But the boys grinned eagerly, waiting for their mother to give her approval. When she nodded, Livvy handed each of them a piece of hard candy. They popped them in their mouths and ran toward the back of the house.

"Don't wake your sister," their mother called after them softly, then turned to Livvy. "Thank you. "I don't know how I can repay you."

"No need. I know you'd do the same for me."

Arlene stared at her fidgeting hands. "You're going to think I'm terrible when I tell you my news. But I wanted you to hear it from me first." She paused to gather herself. "As you know, Wade has been without work for a long time. He's been taking odd jobs here and there and my family helps us when they can. But now he's gotten a job offer that will mean a decent paycheck for a while."

"That's good news! Jobs are so hard to come by right now."

Arlene shook her head in frustration. "The problem is, he's been hired by Coy Whitaker to build a store right there at the Hopkinsville crossroads."

"A store?"

"A hardware store catty-corner from your store."

"Coy is building a hardware store?"

"He pulled up in front of the house late yesterday afternoon. He and Wade stood in the yard and talked. When Wade came inside he said Coy knew he was a good carpenter and wanted him to help build his new store. A load of wood will be delivered later this week."

Livvy was dumbfounded. That the man who loaned her and Inez money to install a gas pump to boost business would now build a competing store across the street was beyond comprehension. While theirs was a general store, a good many customers bought hardware from them – small items like screw drivers and buckets and more expensive items like ladders and fencing wire. A hardware store would siphon off a lot of business.

She knew in her gut this was aimed directly at her for refusing to be his girl.

"I'm so sorry," Arlene said.

"It's not your fault. It's not your husband's fault either. I don't hold it against either of you. Times are hard. You and me – we'll always be friends."

"You're awful kind to me, Livvy. I appreciate it more than you know. I have to tell you I'm not surprised about Coy. My brother Lonnie is the same age. He used to talk about what a mean rascal Coy was. He's the one who told me Coy swore he was gonna marry you as soon as he got rich."

The trip home from Arlene's house was even hotter than the walk over there. Livvy fanned herself with her hat as she trudged alongside the highway, steaming from a combination of heat and fury.

What kind of person would take revenge like this? She had never made him think she had romantic feelings for him.

She'd never done anything unkind to him or his family, had she? Was it possible all those years ago in school that she'd said something he'd construed as being mean? She didn't even remember talking with Coy when they were children. He was just another one of the little boys playing hide and seek and running around bothering the girls. When she moved up to Kinston High School she didn't even remember seeing him. No, she would never have been mean to Coy. Or any of the other younger kids. She was busy with her own friends, her own activities.

Then Daddy's words from this morning came back to her. He told the family the bank *got word* they'd had two crop failures in a row which is why Mr. Williams came out to the farm to see for himself. Was it possible the bank got word from Coy? That maybe he called his sister yesterday afternoon after the picnic didn't go the way he planned? She recalled his sister's conversation with Mr. Beasley that day. Her husband was now vice president of the bank. Which meant the Whitakers had a big shot in the family. A big shot Coy could call on to take revenge on Livvy Hopkins and her family? But it was so hard to believe.

And now she had to tell Inez. She would also have to tell Mama and Daddy. Of course, everyone would know soon enough when construction began.

When she reached the store, she kept walking. She wasn't ready yet to tell anyone what she'd learned. Refusing to look across the road at the corner lot where the hardware store would go, she kicked a stone lying on the dirt in front of her.

*

Daddy's chair was empty when they sat down for supper. But Vernon and Cecil were there. Daddy had dropped them off in the early afternoon and driven to the sawmill to speak with Preston, saying he'd talk with the family about the loans when he got home.

It was after nine when his truck rumbled into the yard. Mama had a plate of food waiting. The adults sat down with him for the family meeting.

"Talked with Preston," he began. "We agreed the time has come for me to sell my truck. *If* we can find a buyer. His car is more useful to us. So he's spreading the word with the other workers. Inez, you and Livvy can put up a sign in the store tomorrow advertising the truck for sale. Here's the particulars." He slid a wrinkled slip of paper across the table to her. "We think with money from the truck, Preston's paycheck and a couple of deliveries we'll be making this weekend, we should have enough money to pay off the first loan."

He was looking a good bit older these days, Livvy thought as she watched him eat.

"We'll help you as much as we possibly can," Inez said. "Wonder if Coy might give us an extension on the loan," she said, shifting her eyes to Livvy. "Maybe he'd be willing to delay our first payment by a month or two? That might free up more cash we could use to help with the farm loans."

"Worth a try," Daddy said, nodding slowly.

"There's not a chance in hell of that happening," Livvy said.

All eyes turned toward her in bewilderment at the message and her language.

"Coy Whitaker is about to build a hardware store right across the street from our store," she said.

"What?" Inez cried. "That can't be true. He just loaned us the money to turn our store into a filling station. He said it would be good for the community."

Livvy told them about her visit with Arlene, how Arlene's husband had already been hired to help with construction.

"But why would he do that?" Mama asked.

"I'll tell you why," Livvy said, bitterness overflowing. "To put it politely, he thinks I should have conjugal relations with him. But I refuse. He tried again yesterday but I asked him to take me home. He must've driven directly over to Arlene's house after he dropped me off to ask her husband to help build his new store."

"Coy helped get Cecil out of jail," Inez said.

Clara shook her head. "I've always had a bad feeling about him."

"He also got Preston rehired at the sawmill," Inez replied.

Clara grunted softly.

Daddy set his fork down and silence descended on the table. It didn't last long.

"I wouldn't be surprised if the bank *got word* about our two failed crops from Coy," Livvy said. "His sister is married to the bank vice president. What a coincidence that the bank man turned up *this* morning to tell you your extension request was denied."

Daddy leaned back in his chair folding his arms across his chest.

"I don't know about all that," he said. "What I do know is that we've got to work hard to pay off the first loan. I'll visit the bank again tomorrow to ask them to reconsider an extension on the second loan. I'll tell them we're working on raising the money."

"But Daddy," Inez said, "it's not like we've got some rich relations we can lean on. How are we supposed to come up with more cash?"

"Tyrone and his boys have had their eye on my acreage for a while now. I could sell some of the land."

"Might as well sell them *all* the land if you can't water your crops," Livvy said.

"Livvy!" Mama said, surprised by her daughter's harsh comment.

"Well, it's true. If you're going to sell him some land, sell it to get your water rights back."

Daddy pushed back from the table and left the room, so tired he was barely able to put one foot in front of the other.

"Livvy," Inez said, "you and I need to have a talk with Coy."

"That would just stir up more trouble. If he learns we've already heard the news, he could figure out who told us, knowing me and Arlene are old friends. A vengeful man might fire Arlene's husband to retaliate. I wouldn't put it past him. And don't mention any of this to Ruthie. Sometimes she talks too much."

14

As soon as they arrived at the store the next morning a handmade sign went up on the front door advertising Daddy's truck for sale, just in time for several customers to see it.

More customers were coming in compared with earlier in the summer. Hopefully, it was a sign the economy was improving, although there would have to be a lot of improvement for their store to benefit. Especially considering they had that loan hanging over their head as Coy prepared to open a competing store.

Mid-morning they had a pleasant surprise when Mr. Beasley walked through the door. Inez's eyes positively sparkled when she saw him.

"Gib!" she cried. "Good to see you again!"

"My son is filling in for me this morning. Thought I'd drop by and see how business is coming along at the Hopkins General Store, especially since Livvy invited me when she stopped by my place Saturday."

Inez flashed her sister an appreciative grin, then gave him a little tour of the premises, including the gas pump and storage tank. Livvy couldn't help but notice how animated her sister was. It was easy to see that Mr. Beasley hadn't come to tour their humble country store. He was here to visit Inez. Which was like a much-needed slow rain on the parched soil of their lives.

He didn't stay long but by the time he drove away, Inez had been smiling steadily for thirty minutes. The smile lingered even after he was gone. It was amazing how that smile transformed not only her sister's face, but also her voice and the way she moved. Livvy thought about all the times she'd been told she didn't want to end up like Inez. And look at her now.

But the happy interlude was brief.

A few minutes after noon, Livvy spotted Coy standing with another man on the bare piece of property on the opposite corner. There was lots of gesturing and pointing and measuring going on. She called Inez over to take a look-see.

They moved back from the window when they saw Coy shake the other man's hand and turn to cross the street in their direction. He strolled through the front door like he was the governor of Georgia.

"Hope business is booming at Hopkins General Merchandise!"

"Hello, Coy," Livvy said, doing her level best to sound friendly and natural. "What can we do for you today?"

He chuckled softly. "I'm not here to buy anything. Just wanted to let you ladies know I'm opening a hardware store on the vacant corner over there." He gestured with his chin toward the window.

"You're opening a store right across the street?" Livvy said, playing dumb.

"I think our community has grown big enough to support two stores. Besides, it'll be a hardware store. I won't be selling all the stuff you ladies sell. Won't be a filling station either. You don't have any objections, do you?"

Livvy paused, weighing her words. "We sell a lot of hardware items."

"Well, you can shift your attention to other things, maybe stock more food, magazines, pretty things women and girls like to buy. You know, perfume, lipstick, scarves and such."

Inez couldn't hold her tongue a minute longer.

"You'll put us out of business."

"I'm the man who gave you the interest-free loan! Why would I want to run you out of business?"

Livvy wanted to yell the question right back in his face. Did he really want to put them out of business because she refused him? But she didn't dare say a word. It could make things worse. Much worse.

The look in his eyes said it all. The only way he would back off was for her to give in. He flashed her one of his big toothy grins and sauntered back across the street to where his car was parked. He revved his engine, then raced off down the road.

"Mama told me years ago that Jefferson Whitaker was quite taken with her back in the day," Inez said.

Livvy listened, staring blankly through the window.

"She went out with him once, but she had her heart set on Daddy. Mr. Whitaker ended up marrying a pretty girl named Mildred Taylor."

"I didn't know he was one of Mama's admirers back then," Livvy said.

"Big difference though. Mr. Whitaker retaliated by marrying another girl, not harassing Mama's family."

Livvy and Inez agreed they'd have to be careful what they said about Coy's plans when customers brought it up. And they were sure to bring it up. They agreed to pretend it was no big deal. If they said anything critical, there would likely be repercussions.

Ruthie was late getting to work, explaining she ran into a girlfriend from school on her walk from the house. She apologized for letting time get away. Since she'd started helping at the store, she'd been punctual and reliable. So her sisters didn't give her a hard time about it.

It was after three when Livvy got home. Although she was tired and hungry, she was also filled with a deep anxiety that made her tense and restless. She longed to escape the real world, longed to be in the woods immersing herself in creating a new design. But the prospect of seeing Gordon made her hesitate. Still, it occurred to her that he had been at least as frightened as she'd been, maybe more so. Which meant that it was extremely unlikely he would return. She'd seen it in his eyes – he thought *she* was a ghost. She was pretty sure she'd have the forest to herself. And if he did make an appearance, she didn't believe she'd be in any danger. If Gordon was a spirit, he was most certainly not an evil spirit.

*

She took her time hiking through the trees, filling the wooden wheelbarrow as she went with vines and twigs, confident that inspiration would come. When she arrived in the woodland, she was drawn to the large boulder Grandma had perched on that day after pointing out the pretty river rocks on the golden carpet of hickory leaves. From there, Livvy looked toward the brook off to the right where the trees grew more closely together.

The view reminded her of gazing through a window. Yes, she would create a window overlooking the brook.

It didn't take her long to figure out how to brace the structure. She would build a stick platform anchored to two trees, then use those same trees to install the casing so that the window was about four feet above ground level.

First came the foundation, then, bit by bit, she wove sticks and vines together to create lengths of the casing, attaching them to the trees. She used braided vines to hang the top of the casing from higher branches, a feeling of satisfaction growing as the exterior took shape. Then she created what looked like windowpanes with sticks to divide the window into four sections. Afterwards came the decorative touches – lengths of braided vines that streamed out from the periphery. The vines also helped stabilize it, attaching it more firmly to the tree limbs and the foundation. She was completely absorbed in the process, pushing all of her frustrations into some other realm. She didn't realize that dusk had settled until she paused to step back so she could evaluate her new artwork.

There was a mystical quality to it – the vines streaming out from the edges, disappearing into the trees, making it look like some otherworldly force made it hover in the air. She smiled to herself, invigorated, feeling as though she might actually look through the window and see something extraordinary on the other side.

She reached for Grandma's tiny scissors so she could add a few strands of her hair. But what sounded like the snapping of a twig nearby stilled her hand. She held her breath, listening. She was used to the sounds of woodland critters scurrying about. This was a heavier step.

Another twig snapped. The sound was coming from her left, maybe twenty feet away. Was it a spirit? But this wasn't

Gordon's style. He always galloped toward her astride his horse, making a grand entrance. No, someone or something was hiding, watching her. She could feel it now. A bear? Or was it a man?

She bolted toward the farm, moving fast. There were footsteps close behind her. This was no bear charging after her on four legs. This was a man chasing her. She racked her brain trying to think of somewhere to hide if she could get enough distance between them. Daddy's words came back to her – "your hair's so red I can spot you a mile away." It would have to be a well concealed spot to elude her pursuer. What if he had a weapon?

Her heart thundered in her chest as she raced through the trees. There was a stitch in her left side that hurt more with each step. She panted from the strain but realized the footsteps were not as close as they had been. She raced up a small rise, spotting a dense thicket of bushes when she topped the hill. A hiding place. She sprinted for it, scooted around to the far side, then threw herself onto the ground, rolling under the bushes. She pulled her knees up to her stomach, lying on her side, holding her arms over her head to cover her hair. The challenge now was to quiet her breathing so he wouldn't hear her.

The footsteps drew closer accompanied by panting. Then a figure darted past. Livvy caught sight of bare legs beneath a knee-length floral dress. A dress she recognized immediately. It was the dress Ruthie wore to work that day, a dress Mama sewed her last year with pink and blue flowers.

"Ruthie Hopkins! Why are you chasing me through the woods?" Livvy yelled at the top of her lungs.

Ruthie came to a halt and turned around, searching for the source of the angry voice.

Livvy rolled out from beneath the dense bushes and got to her feet, brushing dirt, leaves and pine straw from her hair and clothes.

"Lord, Livvy!" Ruthie panted, leaning over, hands on her knees. "You'd think you were being chased by a haint!"

"Answer me: why are you chasing me through the woods? You scared the bejesus out of me!"

The normally self-confident Ruthie, the girl most likely to never be at a loss for words, couldn't come up with an answer. She pulled herself upright, gulping for air.

"Well…"

"Answer me!" Livvy cried.

"Well…"

"Ruthie!"

"Well…"

"If you say 'well' one more time, I'll wrestle you to the ground and sit on your stomach until you answer my question."

"I just wanted to see where you go when you run off into the woods. That's all."

"You're a good talker, Ruthie, and you can exaggerate with the best of them. But when it comes to lying, you stink!"

Although the sun had set, they were both coated with a sheen of perspiration. Ruthie used the sleeve of her dress to wipe sweat from her face, refusing to meet Livvy's eyes.

"Why were you spying on me?" Livvy demanded.

As soon as the question was out of her mouth, she knew the answer.

"Well…"

"Spit it out!"

"All right, all right. It was Coy."

Livvy knew it. "Go on."

"He stopped me on my way to the store today – which is the real reason I was late – and he was just chatting about this and that. He asked me if you've been seeing some other man. I told him not that I know of, that the only thing you do besides work at the store and boss me around is to run out into the woods to do some kind of strange sculptures or something. He laughed like he thought that was stupid. He asked if I'd seen any of them. I told him no, but that Cecil and Vernon had. So, finally, he said he had a proposition for me. He said he'd give me ten dollars if I'd follow you next time you went into the woods and find out what you're doing. He thinks you're meeting up with a man out here."

If she'd been angry before, Livvy was now enraged.

"I honestly can't believe you let Coy Whitaker pay you to spy on your own sister. That is so low-down and dirty! Shame on you! You turned on your own sister for ten lousy dollars!"

"I was going to give the money to Daddy to help pay the loan."

Livvy looked to the heavens for answers. What was happening to her family? Daddy, Preston and the boys had turned into bootleggers to make a living. She, herself, had agreed to go out with Coy, feeling she had to thank him for his generosity. Now Ruthie was spying on her sister to earn a few dollars for the loan payment. What next?

"I'm sorry. I knew you wouldn't be having secret meetings with a man out in the woods. Cecil and Vernon came on your sculptures while baiting their rabbit boxes. They both said you have a talent. And they're right. I've never seen anything like that strange window you built. Anyway, I figured I'd just follow you so I could tell Coy you're not dating another man. I'd get the money and that would be that."

"And what if I *had* been meeting a man in the woods? Would you have told him?"

"Well..."

"It's none of his business what I do. It's none of his business that I create art from sticks and vines. And if I *were* meeting a man in the woods, that would also be none of his business! So when you report back to that son of a gun, don't tell him anything about what I do. You just say you followed me and didn't see a man."

Ruthie nodded her head.

"And if Coy ever asks you to do something – anything – again, you say no. He's not the nice guy he pretends to be."

"Yeah, Inez told me about him opening a store across the street."

As drained as she was from the wild chase and the unpleasant talking-to she'd given her little sister, Livvy told Ruthie to go on home while she retrieved the wheelbarrow. Every little thing counted these days. They couldn't afford to lose the wheelbarrow. So it was dark by the time she reached the farm.

Livvy stopped at the edge of the trees when she saw the sheriff's car in the drive. There was movement in the deep shadows of the pecan tree and men's low voices. Then she spotted the tiny hot ember of a cigarette. What was going on now?

Leaving the wheelbarrow, she got down on hands and knees, crawling slowly along the edge of the field. When she was close enough to make out their words, she flattened to the ground.

"That's how it works, Leon. Five bucks a week."

"But we can't afford it," Daddy said.

"I gave you time to build up your business. Now I get my share. Otherwise..."

He didn't have to finish the sentence. The sheriff was demanding a bribe. All this time Livvy had naively thought the sheriff didn't know. She thought the Hopkins men were operating the still and delivering the liquor in secret. It had never been a secret. Daddy and Preston had been just as gullible as she was, not grasping how things worked in Burgess County.

"Don't bring money to the office. After church on Sunday is a good time, starting this Sunday. We shake hands, you slip me the cash. Don't try anything sneaky. I know where the still is. I can arrest you anytime. Or I can report you to state revenuers."

The talking ceased, followed by the closing of a car door and the cranking of an engine. Livvy lifted her head to watch as the sheriff pulled out of their yard onto the road.

It occurred to her that the ten dollars Coy promised Ruthie to spy on her sister might come in handy.

15

She found Daddy in his rocker. Although she couldn't see his face in the dark, she sensed the gloom hanging over him.

"I heard what the sheriff said," she whispered.

He took a drag on his cigarette.

"I've been a right proper fool. Teague said they *chose* me to replace Singletary knowing how bad off we were, making me think it was my idea."

Livvy cursed under her breath.

"Now we're in so deep, I don't know how we'll ever get out. You and Bess were right from the get-go. Trying to save the farm by running moonshine was a lame-brained idea. Arresting Cecil was just part of the dog and pony show to make us think we outsmarted them."

He sounded on the verge of tears, something she hadn't heard in his voice since her brother Garnett was killed in the war.

"We'll figure something out," she said softly.

"We need a miracle."

"First things first. Why don't you and I go talk with Uncle Tyrone?"

He groaned in frustration.

"If we can make those payments," she went on, "then we can work on a plan to quit the bootlegging business."

He stubbed his cigarette out in a can of dirt and leaned forward, burying his face in his hands.

*

After working it out with her sisters to let her have the following morning off, Livvy hopped in the passenger seat of Daddy's truck for the drive to Uncle Tyrone's farm. She could tell how much it cost Daddy's pride to lower himself before his brother. But they had run out of options.

They arrived unannounced, finding Uncle Tyrone and his three sons in the field. Aunt Maude sent one of the grandsons to get her husband, serving Leon and Livvy a glass of tea on the porch while they waited. Tyrone arrived about fifteen minutes later with his oldest son John who was about Preston's age. Aunt Maude brought them iced tea as well, then disappeared inside the house.

"So," Uncle Tyrone began, "the rumor must be true. You're about to lose the farm."

"The bank won't give me an extension to repay my loans," Daddy said.

"And you want *me* to lend you money?"

"No. I came to ask if you're still interested in buying some of my land."

"Interested? Yup. But I won't have any money until my soybeans are harvested this fall. Times are hard for everyone, Leon."

Livvy kept her mouth shut. She and Daddy had talked on the drive over about this possibility.

"I'm thinking the bank might accept a bill of sale for a future date, which would prove I could pay that amount when the sale of the parcel of land is final," Daddy said. "We could agree on the acreage and a price and sign an agreement for me to show the bank."

Uncle Tyrone took a big swallow of tea.

"It'd have to be a good deal. Course, I'd want to talk with my lawyer. One thing's for sure, I could only do it if I get a good crop. If my crop ain't up to snuff, why then I couldn't afford to pay you."

"That's right. You have a lawyer." Livvy said.

"Same one as before."

Out of the corner of her eye Livvy glimpsed John give his father a cautionary glance. He clearly didn't want Uncle Tyrone talking about that.

"Do lawyers work for a cut of the profits?" she went on. "Is that how they get paid?"

"Unless you have a friend."

John rose from his chair, cutting his father off. "Daddy, let's you and me talk about this tonight. Right now we need to get back to work."

Uncle Tyrone stood as well. "Good idea, son. I'll let you know in a couple of days, Leon. Money's tight."

Daddy grumbled under his breath as they pulled onto the road for the drive home. He dropped Livvy off at the store before driving to the bank. He would tell them he was in talks with his brother to sell some of his land to prove he could make good on repaying the loan.

The unpleasant family meeting was on Livvy's mind all afternoon as she and Ruthie worked together at the store. Her cousin John didn't want his father to tell them about the lawyer. Which only piqued her curiosity.

Ruthie was on her best behavior after their set-to in the woods the night before. She took it upon herself to stock the shelves with some new items that had been delivered.

That evening, as the boys headed out to the woods and the girls skipped out to the barn to milk the cow, Livvy joined her parents, Inez and Clara on the porch.

Daddy said the banker told him they'd have to see the sales agreement before committing to a loan extension. The banker said it wasn't likely to change their decision but said it would depend on the particulars. Daddy said he would drive back over on Friday to talk again with Tyrone.

Livvy took the opportunity to ask some questions that had been rolling around in her head all day.

"Daddy, who were Uncle Tyrone's friends growing up?"

"Jefferson Whitaker was a buddy of his."

Mama grunted at that.

"Your mama didn't like Jefferson," Daddy explained, giving her an amused grin.

"Didn't you tell me once that you went on a date with him?" Inez asked.

"Big mistake," Mama replied. "He was very pushy."

Inez pumped her eyebrows at Livvy, letting her know what 'pushy' meant.

"Who else was Uncle Tyrone friends with?" Livvy asked.

"He and Jefferson spent a lot of time with Billy Teague."

"Sheriff Teague?"

"One and the same. And the three of them were friends with a boy named Lester Thompson."

"Lester Thompson," Livvy said, exchanging a look with Inez. "He's the Whitaker family attorney who drew up the papers for the loan Coy gave us."

Daddy nodded his head slowly, realization dawning.

"All four of them buddied around in school," he said.

"Sounds like they *still* buddy around."

Clara hadn't spoken the entire time, sitting quietly, mending her husband's shirts. But she broke her silence then.

"Sometimes when boys come together, they're like a pack of wild dogs, following the strongest one down the meanest path."

Everyone turned in her direction, a little surprised she'd spoken, and maybe by her insight.

*

Daddy insisted on visiting his brother by himself when he went again on Friday. So Livvy went on to work with Ruthie that morning. When Inez arrived midday, she told Livvy Uncle Tyrone refused to write out any kind of sales agreement. He said if he had a good soybean crop in the fall, only then would he consider buying some of Daddy's land.

"He knows full well the bank may foreclose on it before then," Inez said. "I guess he figures he can get the land real cheap if he bides his time."

"His lawyer probably advised him," Livvy said.

Not long after Inez left for home, a big truck pulled up across the street with a shipment of lumber. Arlene's husband and two other men were there to unload it. Construction on the hardware store would get underway without delay.

When the sisters got home, Daddy, Cecil and Vernon weren't there. Mama and Clara were both jumpy, turning to listen at the least little noise in the yard while Nettie and Faye chattered on about a girlfriend they were going to visit the next day.

Darkness had fallen when they heard Preston's car. A lot had happened while he was working at the sawmill this week.

He had just sat down to eat, Clara by his side, when Daddy and the boys arrived, stomachs growling. Mama, Inez and Livvy joined them at the table, telling Ruthie to keep Nettie and Faye occupied so the adults could talk. Daddy filled Preston in on the banker's visit about rescinding the loan extension, about the sheriff's demand for bribes and about his unsuccessful attempt to get Uncle Tyrone to commit to buying some acreage. Preston took the news hard. Like his father, he now realized they were in much deeper than either had suspected.

"I have news too," Preston said. "First, my roommate Charlie says he'll buy your truck. He can pay half the cash up front, then he'll have the rest in a couple of days."

"That's a relief," Daddy said.

Livvy immediately worried that her brother's friend might not be able to pay the full amount.

"And," Preston continued, pausing to look at Clara. "I quit my job this afternoon. They let me collect my wages before I left but there won't be any more money from the sawmill."

"What happened?" Daddy asked.

"It's kind of like the situation with the sheriff. I was set up. Charlie told me they made the blocksetter go home the day they tried to force me in there. Charlie said the foreman was doing as he was told by Mr. Whitaker. But Charlie says they knew I would refuse which would give them a reason to fire me. Charlie says he thinks it was all staged so Coy could step forward and pretend to talk his daddy into hiring me back. And the only reason for him to do that was so Coy could act like a big shot do-gooder to impress Livvy."

Livvy slammed her fist down on the table in anger, startling everyone.

"Charlie says the Whitakers are touched in the head," Preston went on. "That it was Coy who told his daddy six years ago to let Hank do that dangerous job. Don't know why Mr. Whitaker would've listened to his son. He was just a college boy back then."

"Why?" Livvy asked. "What did Hank ever do to Coy?"

"My guess? He married you."

It was so hard to believe that Coy wanted Hank dead so he could court her. After Hank's death, the Whitakers had been kind – paying her the death benefit, sending flowers to the funeral, bringing food to the house. But Coy was off at college and she hardly saw him for four years. And when she did see him, it was a quick exchange of small talk at the store. It wasn't until this year that he'd shown any interest.

"Are you sure Charlie knows what he's talking about?" she asked.

"He keeps his ears open. He and some of the other guys wish they could quit too, but they've got families to feed and no other way to make a living. Charlie says it was a good place to work until the Whitakers took over. Now it's gone to hell. They have injuries every week. A man's life means nothing to them as long as they can deliver the wood they've promised to those big companies. And to think Mr. Whitaker would allow his son to endanger men's lives for his own purposes makes me sick." He paused, glancing at his father before continuing. "Of course, when I told them I was leaving this afternoon I didn't know about the sheriff's demands. It didn't dawn on me that he knows all about our business."

With perfect timing Ruthie strolled in, handing her father a ten-dollar bill.

"This is to help pay the loan, Daddy."

"Where'd you get that much money?" he asked.

"I've been saving up." She peeked at Livvy out of the corner of her eye before turning on her heel to leave the room as quickly as she'd arrived.

*

Livvy assumed Coy wouldn't show his face in their store again. She was wrong. As though purposely rubbing salt in the wound, he walked in Saturday morning to buy hammers and nails so his construction crew could get to work across the street.

"More supplies will be delivered soon but I want my men to get started right away. I'll take three hammers and ten pounds of nails."

"I'll let you get your nails. I'll get the hammers."

She brought three hammers to the register while he chose the nails he wanted, bringing them to the counter in a box. She weighed the box and rang up his purchase.

"Keep the change," he said, handing her the cash. "Before I go, I wanted to give you one last chance to help your family."

She raised her eyebrows, suspicious of anything he said at this point.

"If you become Mrs. Coy Whitaker, you and your family would never have to worry about finances again."

Ironic that he didn't resemble the devil. Because that's what he was. She wanted to scream at the top of her lungs for him to go straight to hell where he came from. It was all she could do not to shout that she would never, ever consider marrying a man who made her skin crawl. She barely managed to keep a lid on her emotions but knew if she didn't, he could make things so much harder for them.

"No offense, Coy. But I think we both know by now that we're not suited for each other."

"You're making a mistake, Livvy. A big mistake."

He carried his purchases across the street to where his men were already sawing boards.

16

Livvy stalked home, her feet pounding the dirt, her arms swinging like she was itching for a fight. Coy's smug face deserved to be slapped and slapped hard. It had been all she could do to stifle the urge to deliver that slap. The nerve of him showing up at the store to buy hammers and nails to begin construction on his confounded hardware store. On top of that, he had the gall to tell her she could protect her family by marrying him. She was seething. Not just because he was so cocksure, but also because his words were not just an idle threat.

Her family was caught in a trap. Like the rabbits Cecil and Vernon brought home from the woods, the Hopkins family had been suckered into a rabbit box by some tempting bait. Now it was just a matter of time until the trapper arrived to slit their throats.

Arriving home, her bedroom seemed to have shrunk, the walls closing in on her. Making sure to avoid Mama, Clara and the girls, she changed out of her dress into dungarees and a shirt. Then she swiped a yellow squash from the garden and took off for the woods.

In the week since that unsettling experience with Gordon, she had concluded that despite all of Grandma's stories, she couldn't worry about ghosts. If Grandma was right, then they were more to be pitied than feared. Besides, Livvy wanted to understand whatever transpired that day. Thinking back on it, she realized Gordon had leapt onto his horse and galloped away like *she* was a spirit come to haunt *him*. Grandma never told any tales about ghosts who acted like that. Apparition or not, she wanted to see him again.

There was also the window she'd been working on when Ruthie scared her half to death. She needed to put the finishing touches on it.

She breathed in the fragrant air as she made her way through the trees, the peace of the forest enveloping her. The deeper she went into the woods and the more distance she put between herself and the frustrating trials of everyday life, the calmer she became. When she reached the brook, the sound of the water flowing through reeds and around the smooth rocks was like a balm for her weary soul.

Sitting on the ground a short distance away, she viewed her latest artwork, captivated with how the vines streamed up and away as if it were being held aloft by a miraculous force. Maybe what she was looking at was a window into the beyond.

She thought she felt Grandma's presence as though her spirit had settled here, becoming one with the forest. She heaved a big sigh wishing her grandmother could come back to her, at least for a little while. She reached for Grandma's little scissors and clipped several strands of her hair. Moving closer, she wrapped the hair around the center point of the windowpanes.

As she tucked the scissors back in her pocket, she felt the familiar vibration travel through her body. Then came the thundering of a horse approaching through the dense forest. Gordon appeared on the far side of the stream, pulling on the reins as he approached, splashing across the brook before stopping on the near bank.

There was no broad smile this time. Instead, his expression was wary. She suspected she looked the same.

She wasn't afraid of him exactly but couldn't keep her heart from hammering in her chest as he dismounted.

The horse whinnied as though nudging them to speak.

"I'm not a ghost," he blurted.

"Neither am I."

They seemed uncertain what should come next.

"I'd like to do an experiment," he said, withdrawing a key from his pocket. "I'm going to hand you this key." He held it out to her.

She extended her hand, palm up. But when he dropped it into her hand, it fell to the ground, passing through her hand as though she wasn't made of flesh and bone.

She responded with a shrill yelp.

"See if you can pick it up," he said.

She squatted down and tried to pluck it from the ground but couldn't get a grip on it. In fact, she couldn't feel the dark metal at all.

He leaned down and retrieved it.

"As I suspected," he said, returning the key to his pocket. "I cannot feel your world and you cannot feel mine."

"Let's shake hands," she suggested.

They both reached out but watched in amazement as their hands passed through each other's as though they were mere shadows.

"It's like we're not on the same plane," he whispered.

"The same plane?"

"It's like we're both standing on the same ladder but on different rungs."

"That doesn't make any sense."

"Tell me where you are."

"I'm right here in the woods, same as you."

"No, tell me what your address is. Your complete address."

"Rural Route fourteen, Box twenty-two."

"What's the rest of your address?"

"Hopkinsville, Georgia."

"Georgia?"

"Yes, the state of Georgia."

"In America?"

"Of course."

"Well, I'm in England. Kinston, England."

Thus, the English accent. Thus, all the confusion about Kinston and the non-existent ice cream shop.

"But that's absurd! How on earth can you be in England and me right here in Georgia, and yet we can see and hear each other?"

"I wish I knew. That first evening when I came upon you after you created the doorway, I had been on a ride, enjoying the evening. But a strange feeling came over me, as though I was being drawn in this direction. And each time I've visited you in your woodland, I've felt drawn by something inside me that I don't understand. Curiously, I believe I had the same experience when I was a boy. I used to think it was a dream but now I believe I visited you when we were children. I remember the ginger girl doing something on the ground and an old woman standing with her arms outstretched. It looked very much like this place."

"It *was* this place. And the old woman was Grandma. That's when I made my first forest artwork. That's when she told me that magic happens all the time."

"Magic."

There was a look of wonderment in his eyes.

"Is it getting dark where you are?" she asked.

"Yes. I could never understand why the light was so strange, so bright, when I visited you. It's because England is five hours ahead of you. There have been times when I felt the pull of the woodland late at night but couldn't saddle up and ride over here in the dark. That must've been when you came in the evening."

"I suppose that's why your photos were blank."

"Ah, yes. My camera couldn't record images here."

"I was so frustrated that you sent me on a wild goose chase to the ice cream parlor."

"And I was irritated you stood me up."

They exchanged a smile, but then turned serious.

"How can this be?" she said.

He shook his head, pacing slowly among the woodland artworks. "I've never believed in phantoms. But I'm having a difficult time coming up with a rational explanation."

"You mentioned different planes."

"Just grasping at straws. I've read about other planes besides the physical plane such as the astral plane. It's supposedly a different level of existence that includes spirits, dreams and mystical events. I've always thought it was a bunch of rubbish."

"What if there is no rational explanation?" she said.

He nodded slowly. "This means we can never have dinner together at a restaurant. Which is where I wanted to invite you next time. There's an ocean between us. But perhaps we could share a picnic. I'll bring food and you can bring food. We can sit together on blankets."

Her real life came rushing back to her – all the challenges her family was facing, the very real possibility that they would soon lose the farm. Then they'd be looked down upon even by their country neighbors. She had feared from the beginning that there could never be a real relationship between her and Gordon. Her background was much too humble and would soon be even more so. But she wasn't ready to face the inevitable just yet. She accepted his invitation. It was her artworks and her friendship with Gordon that had given her hope here in the same woodland Grandma introduced her to so long ago.

Ironic that both Gordon and Coy invited her on a picnic. But her feelings about this one contrasted sharply with the picnic by the river with Coy.

"Tomorrow," he said. "We have much to talk about. Perhaps we might begin to understand how this magic works."

He mounted up and rode back across the brook, disappearing into the forest.

She felt a bit like a child with an imaginary friend, a friend only she could see, a friend who could never be part of her real life. Although she was glad they would have their strange little picnic, she knew her friendship with Gordon would fade, whatever the explanation was, assuming there *was* an explanation. They would each have their own separate lives. There was also the possibility that all of this was some kind of delusion – that she was escaping the unpleasantness of her real life by creating the ideal man in her mind. If that were true, she had a vivid imagination, as she'd been told often enough.

Dreading her return to reality, she strolled through her creations, admiring them anew. The doorway seemed more enchanted than ever now that she knew she and Gordon had been meeting by means of some sort of supernatural connection. But now she realized it was really the woodland that was enchanted. It was already a magical place when she was a child, long before she created the doorway. It was here that they had been brought together across thousands of miles by some inexplicable force.

With dusk settling over the forest, the shadows deepened and she headed for home. But she didn't have any desire to sit at the table with her family and partake of the dread they all shared about what lay ahead. She didn't want to think about a future so bleak it drained her of enthusiasm for life.

It was full dark by the time she arrived at the farm. Preston's friend had come and taken Daddy's truck, leaving them with only Preston's car. But his car wasn't there, presumably in use making deliveries.

*

Livvy was relieved she didn't have to go to church the next morning – there wasn't enough room for everyone in the car. She, Cecil and Vernon stayed home while the rest of the family squeezed in and headed off for Sunday worship.

The boys headed to the river for a swim. They used to spend time with friends. But this summer they'd been forced to work seven days a week, doing jobs around the farm, working at the still and helping with deliveries. They'd had precious little time for themselves and seemed relieved the car was too small for all of them.

189

Alone at the house, Livvy fixed herself a sandwich and washed a tomato from the garden. She poured sweet tea into a canning jar. Her picnic lunch ready, she made up her mind to wear the new green dress, the one she'd worn when they were supposed to meet at the ice cream parlor. Besides her lunch, she packed the dress in a bag so she could change into it before Gordon arrived.

She left shortly before the family got home, which meant she'd reach their meeting place slightly before Gordon did. He would be eating supper, she realized, while she had lunch. It was all so fantastical. She was still trying to get used to the idea that two people who lived on opposite sides of the Atlantic Ocean were somehow able to come together in her little woodland. Despite thinking of nothing else since their conversation yesterday, she still didn't understand how it was possible. His suggestion that they were on different planes didn't explain how it worked. She supposed some mysteries of nature were beyond human comprehension.

Regardless, she was eager to sit down with him, to get to know him. She felt like she was going on a first date and didn't want to throw cold water on her feelings by admitting it could never lead to anything more. She changed into her dress in a dense thicket of bushes halfway there, excited about him seeing her in something besides overalls and dungarees.

Like a hostess waiting for guests to arrive, Livvy chose a nice spot where they could spread their blankets, a location with a view of her artworks. She laid her blanket on the ground near the canoe, leaving space for Gordon to spread his beside hers. Then she spent a few minutes tidying her art installations, tucking loose twigs and bits of vine back into the doorway and picking stray leaves from the tree nymph and her handsome lover, all the while waiting to hear the sound of a horse approaching. She removed some twigs that had fallen on her spiral rock design – the design that Gordon said reminded him of the Andromeda Galaxy. Noticing that her flower basket had shriveled and turned brown, she removed it from where it was hanging and returned it to the forest floor.

Still no sound of hoofbeats. She gazed in the direction Gordon always came from beyond the doorway. But there was no movement. The sky looked as bright in that direction as it did above her. Had Bailey lost his way again? She chuckled remembering how she used to think that was an excuse for him having more important things to do. There had been times when he told her he would come and then never appeared. She didn't believe that would happen today, of all days, when *he* had suggested they have their picnic. He would certainly find his way today.

He said yesterday he felt drawn here by something inside him, that he sometimes had that sensation at night when it was too late to saddle his horse and ride this way in the dark. What was it that triggered that feeling? Why was it that sometimes he felt it and sometimes he didn't?

She remembered inviting him to help her build the companion for the tree nymph. He'd seemed as excited as she was that they would work on it together. But he never came. She was positive he wanted to. He said so later, claiming he lost his way – blaming it on Bailey for not finding the path. She thought about when he *had* appeared. It dawned on her then that he always arrived as she completed one of her creations. When she added strands of her hair, the tingling sensation swept through her body and Gordon appeared atop his noble steed. Every time it happened, it seemed like she was stepping into a fairy tale. Which sounded ridiculous. Still, that's how she felt when she looked up to see horse and rider approaching. There had been times when she completed a creation and added her hair and he did *not* show up. Now she realized those were in the evening when she had lost track of time and it was nearly dark. Which would've been in the middle of the night where he was. The trigger that drew him here had to be adding her hair!

She panicked. It was too late to build something. It would take hours. Her eyes began to sting, understanding that he couldn't come unless she *called* him. She looked at the rock spiral and had a sudden inspiration.

Moving quickly, she grabbed three of the large smooth grey stones and three of the smaller light-colored rocks. She patted down a patch of pine straw beside the spiral and set the three larger stones in a triangular formation, their sides touching. Then she placed a smaller, lighter colored stone atop each of the bigger rocks, their sides touching as well. Grabbing one more small stone from the original artwork, she placed it atop the little mound she had just created. It was certainly not a masterwork, but it was a creation of her own. She hadn't brought her small scissors with her this time, not expecting to need them, so she separated several strands of hair atop her head and yanked them out, wincing in pain. Then she coiled the hairs together and pushed them between the newly positioned rocks.

The hoped-for quiver traveled down her back. Then she felt the ground tremble beneath her feet. Twirling around, she could see the sky had darkened in the distance and heard a horse racing toward her through the trees. He was coming!

Gordon had an anxious look on his face as he approached.

"I couldn't find my way," he called out. "I don't understand why that happens."

When he dismounted, she gave him a victorious smile.

"I must say, you look lovely," he said before she had time to speak. "It's the first time I've seen you in a dress."

She laughed. "I had to prove I don't always look like a field hand."

"I've never thought you looked like a field hand, Livvy." Said with what could only be described as an avid gleam in his eye.

"And you – I've never seen you look so casual. Where's your coat and tie?"

He was wearing a pair of slacks and a pale blue shirt, sleeves rolled to the elbows.

"Riding attire seemed a bit much for a picnic."

He unfurled a blanket next to hers and they sat down, unpacking their food and drink. He had a sandwich wrapped in wax paper, a tin of beans and a jug of water. She was surprised at how humble his spread was.

As they ate, she explained how their picnic nearly didn't happen.

"After I thought back to the times you came before, I figured out that you only show up when I add some of my hair to the artwork. So I quickly made this tiny creation here." She pointed to the little rock mound. "Sure enough, when I added strands of my hair, I heard you and Bailey approaching."

He was fascinated that it was embedding some small part of herself that opened the door between them, as he put it.

"The first time you created something – that time with your grandmother – did you add hair to that design as well?"

"She's the one who suggested it. She said Mother Nature supplied the materials, so I should contribute something of myself. She used her embroidery scissors to cut several strands and I placed them under one of the pretty stones."

"That must be why I saw you when we were children. Adding your hair drew me here. I didn't know I was anywhere besides the woods near my home. But it really was you and your grandmother I saw that day."

With her new dress spread carefully around her, Livvy asked questions about his family and his life. She was saddened to learn he had lost a brother in the Great War just as she had. She was not surprised that his family was well off financially, although that's not how he put it. His father invested in an automobile manufacturing plant some years back, which had turned out to be an excellent investment with the growing popularity of autos. He admitted his parents hoped he would become attached to the daughter of one of his father's business associates. But he found the young lady to be uninteresting, a little too prim and proper. Livvy tried not to show how much this pleased her. She did let her pleasure show when he said he began going for rides nearly every evening after he found her the day she completed the doorway.

He inquired about her life too. She tried to give him honest answers without revealing how awful things had become. She did tell him she'd been married when she was younger, that her husband was killed in a sawmill accident. He expressed heartfelt sympathy, visibly astonished that she was a young widow. She also told him she'd planned to continue her art education after she married but Hank's death and the passage of time had created too many obstacles to overcome.

They talked longer than they intended and she understood when he announced that it was time for him to be on his way.

"When can we do this again?" he said.

"Unfortunately, I can't come to the woods as often as I used to. Now that our store is also a filling station my sisters and I are working six days a week. But maybe next Sunday?"

"That would be lovely," he replied.

He waved as he rode away, leaving her with a warm feeling. It was a welcome respite from the stress in her life. The connection she felt between them seemed much more than friendship. Although she didn't understand how it worked and wasn't entirely certain that it was real, she would cherish every minute of their time together.

Finding a secluded spot, she changed from her pretty dress into her jeans and shirt. She tucked the dress and her Sunday shoes into her bag, pulling on her clunky work shoes. The closer she got to the farm, the heavier her heart became. By the time she walked through the door to her bedroom, the lightness she'd experienced with Gordon had evaporated, replaced by a bushel of woe.

She carefully hung the dress in the wardrobe thinking Ruthie was in the kitchen helping get supper ready. She nearly jumped out of her skin when her little sister swept through the door, almost catching her putting it away.

"Guess what!" Ruthie blurted. "Next Saturday I'm spending the night at Nancy's house. She's got a crank Victrola and some new records. She's going to show me some new dance steps!"

"That sounds like fun." It was a struggle for Livvy not to look like she'd been caught committing a crime.

"Yes sirree Bob!" Ruthie sat down on her bed to change shoes. "I just wish we could have a radio. When will we ever get electric wires in Hopkinsville?"

"Lord only knows."

"Were you back in the woods building more windows and such today?"

"Yep. I'll show you my new artwork sometime if you're interested."

"No offense, but I don't like hiking through the woods, thank you very much."

Getting to her feet, Ruthie hurried out of the room. Their brief interchange left Livvy's stomach in knots. If Ruthie had arrived a moment earlier, she would've seen her putting the dress away. Livvy could only imagine the suspicions that would've aroused.

During supper Cecil and Vernon talked about swimming in the river that morning, clearly trying to lighten the mood. But uneasiness hung over the table like a sagging roof that could give way at any moment. During a break in the conversation Livvy asked whether Preston's friend Charlie had brought the rest of the money for the truck.

"He'll bring the money on Tuesday," Preston said.

She looked from Preston to Daddy, knowing they needed that cash.

"Not to worry," Preston said. "Charlie's good for it. He's getting the money from his brother Tuesday afternoon. He'll drive directly over here and pay Daddy the balance."

"Inez and I are going to the bank tomorrow," Daddy said. "We both need to deposit some cash. While I'm there, I'll set up an appointment for Wednesday morning to pay off the loan."

17

As Livvy and Ruthie approached the crossroads Monday morning, the pounding of hammers greeted them. Arlene's husband Wade and his small construction crew had made a good start on the hardware store Saturday. It was obvious now that it would easily be twice the size of Hopkins General Merchandise. The front of the building was set back from the road by a good twenty feet, which made Livvy suspicious about Coy's denial of any intention to add gas pumps out front. She was grinding her teeth as she unlocked the door, starting the day in a foul mood.

Inez and Daddy were on their way to Kinston. With today's deposit, Daddy would have enough to pay off the big farm loan. He and Preston said they had some deliveries coming up in the next couple of weeks that might be nearly enough to pay off the second loan along with the sale of Daddy's truck, the hog and Mama's beloved piano. Mama's the one who offered to sell it, holding back tears. She said better to lose the piano than to lose the farm.

So while there was still hope, it wasn't the kind of hope that made anyone jump for joy. If they could just pay those two loans off, then they could figure out what came next.

When Inez reported for work a little after one, they let Ruthie go home and the two older sisters spent the afternoon together. Which gave them a chance to talk.

Inez said Daddy was relieved to get his cash in the bank, not feeling comfortable keeping it at home. He set up an appointment for Wednesday morning to pay off the loan. After they left the bank, she talked him into stopping by Mr. Beasley's general store to celebrate with a soft drink. Inez turned positively pink telling Livvy that while Daddy looked around, she and Mr. Beasley had a brief private conversation.

"Gib wants to take me out to eat Saturday night," she said. "To a little restaurant there in town."

"My, my!"

"I guess you were right about him being partial to me. It's a funny feeling after all these years to be going out on a date!"

The expression on Inez's face was pure bliss.

On Tuesday afternoon, as promised, Preston's friend Charlie brought the rest of the cash over to pay the balance on Daddy's truck. Preston had never been concerned about it but Daddy and the rest of the family were greatly relieved when the money was actually in hand.

After spreading the word at church on Sunday that she was selling her piano, the music director of a church one county over stopped in that afternoon as well, cash in hand and a man with him to cart the piano out to their truck. Mama hid in the bedroom for the rest of the afternoon, leaving Clara, Ruthie, Nettie and Faye to get supper on the table. Daddy tried to talk her into eating with them, but she said she wasn't hungry and didn't show her face all evening.

Because a man was supposed to come for the hog Wednesday morning, Preston stayed home while Daddy went to the bank to pay the loan. Deciding he shouldn't have to go alone, Livvy accompanied him. Driving Preston's car and wearing his Sunday best, he was anxious to get this bank visit behind him.

"We're going to be all right, Livvy," he said, eyes on the road.

She gave him a pat on the arm. She might be able to muster a smidgen of optimism once both loans were paid. Even then, more challenges faced them than she cared to contemplate.

As they drove down Main Street, they discovered there were no parking spaces to be had. Every spot was taken, something she hadn't seen since just before Christmas two years ago. The hairs on her arms prickled as she noticed a crowd overflowing the sidewalk into the street in front of the bank.

"What in tarnation?" Daddy said.

He took the next right onto a side street and found a place to park a block away. By the time they walked back to Main Street, the crowd had grown. Everyone was talking at once. Livvy stood on tip toes trying to see the front door. Oddly, it was locked up like it was Sunday with a sign posted that she couldn't make out.

"What's going on?" Daddy asked a man as they approached.

"Damn bank is closed."

"Can't be. I've got an appointment."

Livvy's stomach turned sour remembering Mr. Beasley mentioning an Atlanta bank going out of business when Coy's sister was in the store that day.

Her father continued peppering bystanders with questions, but no one had any answers. Then she spotted Mr. Beasley.

"Let's see if Mr. Beasley knows anything," she said, tugging on her father's arm.

"I'll miss my appointment."

"The bank is closed, Daddy. Come on!"

When they got closer, they could hear Mr. Beasley's voice.

"First word I got was yesterday afternoon. A customer came in and said there was a line at the bank, people trying to withdraw their money. I rushed over to see what was going on but they'd already closed the doors."

"It's our money!" a lady cried. "They have to give us our money!"

"I read in the paper that banks are failing," Mr. Beasley said, shaking his head. "They don't have enough in the vault to pay all the account holders."

The lady started to cry. "Every bit of our money is in that bank."

"We're all in the same boat," Mr. Beasley said. "I've been trying to call some bank people but their lines are busy. Can't get through."

Livvy waved her hand in the air, trying to catch his attention. He moved in their direction.

"Is Inez with you?" he said.

"No, Daddy and I came into town to pay off a farm loan." She introduced him to her father.

Mr. Beasley was as shaken as the rest of the crowd. "If those bank officials won't answer their phones, maybe the editor at the newspaper might be able to tell us what's going on. I think I'll walk down the street and see if I can find him."

"We'll go with you."

The Kinston Bulletin was located in a small building a block away. It was a weekly that published every Thursday and would hit the stands tomorrow. Mr. Beasley was confident that if anyone had the lowdown on the bank, it would be Tabor Phillips, the editor and main reporter.

A bell jangled as they walked through the door into a messy room with two desks, a black telephone atop each of them. A heavy man with salt and pepper hair and a short-sleeve white shirt sat at the desk on the left. He was typing away on a big typewriter, the loud clickety-clack filling the room.

"Tabor?" Mr. Beasley began.

"I'm busy, Gib," he said, barely looking up.

"But we need to know what's happening."

"Bank failed, simple as that. Talked with Mr. Hilliard, the bank president. He says there were some large withdrawals that depleted the bank's cash reserves. Customers crowded in demanding their money and by the end of the day, the vault was cleaned out."

"But what about all of us who had our life savings in the bank?"

"Doesn't look good. Trying to get more information from Mr. Hilliard. Everything I know will be in the paper tomorrow. I'm no different than the rest of you. My money was in that bank too."

Livvy and her father exchanged a panic-stricken look.

"What about the bank loans?" Livvy asked.

"Hilliard said the loans were bought up by a new company."

"What does that mean?"

"It means if you had a loan with the bank, you still have a loan payment. You'll just make it to the new company instead of the bank."

Daddy found his tongue then.

"Are you telling me the money I had in my account is gone but I still have to pay the farm loan I took out?"

"I'm no expert but I expect that's the way of it."

"That can't be!"

The drive home was silent except for the hot wind blasting through the open windows. Daddy focused on the road and Livvy stared at the sky, both of them in a state of shock. When they drove into the yard, neither made a move to get out of the car. The full impact of the day's news had sunk in. The farm loans still had to be paid but all of Daddy's hard-earned money was gone. And while she and Inez had some time before their first loan payment for the gas pump, they would have to sell a lot of gas and a lot of merchandise to have enough money to make that payment since their money had disappeared too. But if nearly everyone who had their money in the bank had just lost it all, who would have any cash to spend at the store?

At length, Nettie and Faye came running, spotting the two of them sitting in their father's automobile.

"Grandpa! Aunt Livvy!" Faye cried. "Why don't you get out of the car?"

Daddy groaned as he pushed his door open, taking his time getting to his feet. Livvy forced herself to do the same.

"Are y'all okay?" Nettie asked, looking first at her grandfather, then at Livvy.

Daddy couldn't find his voice. Livvy couldn't either. They trudged toward the house, both of them drained.

The two little girls ran ahead of them, the screen door slamming behind them as they rushed inside. "Granny!" they called out over and over.

Mama appeared at the door, holding it open for them. But Daddy collapsed into his rocking chair. Livvy settled onto a ladderback chair by his side.

"What is it?" Mama said.

"Something wrong?" Preston called out, trotting toward the porch from the barn.

Livvy looked at Daddy, waiting for him to speak, but he closed his eyes, squeezing the bridge of his nose with his fingers.

"I'll get you a cool glass of water," Mama said, rushing into the kitchen.

"Can one of you please explain what happened?" Preston said.

Daddy buried his face in his hands. Which forced Livvy to do the talking.

"The bank has failed."

"What?"

"The bank closed its doors. Mr. Phillips, the editor of the newspaper, says all the cash in the vault has been withdrawn. There's none left. Which means all of the money we had in the bank is gone."

"Our money can't be gone."

Livvy sighed. "Mr. Beasley said the same thing happened at a bank in Atlanta."

"Our money can't just disappear," Preston said. "It's *our* money, not the bank's money."

"There'll be an article in tomorrow's *Bulletin* that'll explain it a lot better than I can. I expect there'll be articles in the Athens paper and the Atlanta papers in the next few days."

"How can this be?" Mama said, standing by the door holding two glasses of water.

"I don't know, Mama," Livvy replied. "Unfortunately, there's even more bad news."

"More bad news?" Preston said.

"Before the bank closed, it sold its loans to a new company. So Daddy's farm loans still have to be paid even though there's not one thin dime in his bank account."

Mama dropped the glasses which shattered on the floor splashing water and shards of glass everywhere.

Clara stepped through the door behind her. Seeing the broken glass, she hurried to the kitchen to get a broom and dustpan.

Livvy dreaded having to repeat it all when Inez and Ruthie got home. As it turned out, there was no need. They heard the story from several customers who stopped by to spread the news. Ruthie said nobody bought anything all day, which confirmed Livvy's fears about the impact the bank closure would have on the store.

Livvy did tell Inez that it was Gib Beasley who led them to the newspaper office to find out what happened. Mr. Beasley had asked Livvy to tell Inez he would be in touch soon, but they'd have to postpone their restaurant outing for a while. Inez understood that his money was gone too, but she couldn't hide her disappointment.

*

The next morning, Preston drove Livvy and Ruthie to the store, knowing the newspaper would be waiting. They found a stack tied with string by the front door. Preston took a copy home, leaving his sisters to open for business. They'd barely gotten inside when the first customer popped in. He didn't want gas and he didn't want any merchandise. All he wanted was a copy of *The Kinston Bulletin*. Every last newspaper was gone by noon. That's the only thing they sold that morning – newspapers.

Hearing sawing and hammering across the street, Livvy was surprised to see Arlene's husband and his two workers on the job again. She'd expected construction on the new hardware store to come to a halt. The Whitakers were well off, but she assumed the bank failure would impact them as well. Maybe it did, but apparently not to the extent it hurt average folks who struggled to make ends meet.

By early afternoon a stack of newspapers arrived from Athens. Which brought in more customers. The article in the Athens paper didn't have any more information than the Kinston paper did, but it sold quickly too with folks hungry for news about the bank. Both papers reported the new company that had taken over some of the bank loans was called Chason Loans which would send letters to borrowers in the coming days.

One of those who stopped by for a paper was Mae Glover.

"Mrs. Whitaker told me to get her a copy of the Athens newspaper," she said, setting a coin on the counter. "Said for me not to dawdle or she'd dock my pay."

Livvy handed her a copy, expecting her to hurry out. But Mae glanced around the store, noticing Ruthie stocking shelves in the back.

"Need to talk with you, Miss Livvy," she whispered. "I'll be fishing at the bend on Sweet Creek about seven-thirty this evening. You might want to bring a fishing pole and join me. A hat to cover your red hair would be a good idea."

She turned and left without a good-bye. Livvy watched her trot across the street and charge full steam up the road leading to the Whitaker home. Whatever Mae had to tell her must be mighty important for her to set up a secret meeting like this.

Inez relieved Ruthie at two, but unlike every day since the gas pump was installed, there was no need for two people at the store. Nobody bought gas. Besides the newspapers, nobody bought anything. Neither of them was in the mood to talk so it was a long afternoon, both of them hoping that somehow the bank would reopen. It was impossible to believe their money had just up and disappeared. How could that happen?

When they got home supper was on the table. But Livvy had no appetite and declined to join the family. Besides, she needed to get ready for her mysterious fishing expedition. She slipped on a shirt and overalls, then wound her hair into a bun on top of her head, covering it with a misshapen straw hat that Daddy used to wear. Stopping by the shed, she borrowed one of the boys' fishing poles, a small tin for worms and a pail, then snuck off through the trees.

She reached the bend on Sweet Creek in time to dig some worms along the bank. She chose a good spot that allowed her to keep her eye on the water and on the woods around her. Then she baited her hook and cast her line into the middle of the stream and waited. From a distance, she could've passed for a young man. Close up was a different story. Mae was right to warn her to hide her hair.

While she wasn't interested in catching fish, it wasn't long before she felt a tug on her line, reeling in a small crappie. She placed it in the pail, which she'd filled with water and cast her line again. Just as she was settling in to wait, she heard someone approach. It was Mae.

She was wearing what Livvy guessed were her late husband's dungarees and a shirt with a dark hat on her head. Without a word, she baited her hook and cast her line, sitting down beside Livvy. She glanced around cautiously before speaking.

"Can't stay long. Mama's watching the kids. If somebody comes, I'll get up and leave, telling you I'm sorry I took your spot."

Livvy nodded.

"Mama always said I have good ears," Mae began. "And the Whitakers talk loud. So sometimes I overhear things. Last week their daughter Jane and her husband came for dinner. After supper, the men went into the library to talk and smoke a while. The women settled in the parlor for coffee and sweet tarts. I was clearing the table, going back and forth in the hallway from the dining room to the kitchen." She paused to scan their surroundings before continuing. "I heard young Mr. Whitaker say, 'So if we withdraw all our money, the bank would fail?' I couldn't help myself – I stopped to listen and heard Jane's husband say, 'That's right. If your family and my family transferred our funds elsewhere, the bank would have to close its doors.' Then I heard footsteps so I headed on down the hallway. When I returned to load up the cart again I heard Mr. Buchanan say, 'We can buy the loans from the bank this week, then move our funds.' I read that article walking back to the Whitakers' house this afternoon. I believe the Whitakers and Mr. Buchanan made the bank fail on purpose."

Livvy could hardly breathe. "Why would they do that?"

"The Whitakers and that son-in-law are in league with the devil. That's why."

"Besides being immoral, it's also illegal."

"They're rich and powerful. The rich and powerful always get away with it."

"But what if you told your story to…"

"I'm not telling anybody anything. Besides you, that is. No one would listen to a poor Negro woman. If I opened my mouth, I'd be found hanging from a tree the next day just like my husband was. He was lynched for being 'insolent.' I'd be hanged for telling lies about good white people. I have three little children. I'm already taking a chance talking to you right now. You have to swear on the Bible not to tell anyone how you learned what I just told you."

Livvy studied her for a moment realizing Mae was right.

"I swear."

18

After Mae left, Livvy stayed a while longer. Might not hurt to bring some fish home. She also needed time to think about what Mae heard. Why would the Whitakers want the bank to fail? Surely it couldn't be to hurt Livvy and her family. The majority of the people in three counties had just lost every penny they had. Even if Mae was right, that the Whitakers were in league with the devil, they'd have to be out of their minds to want to ruin so many families. People without money couldn't spend money – at a general store, a hardware store or anywhere else. Companies might have to lay off workers. Surely, Coy and his father didn't want to cause that kind of damage to their community. That would be insanity.

When it was nearly too dark to see, she had three small crappies and one catfish. She dumped some of the water out of the bucket, so it wouldn't be too heavy. She walked home with the pail in one hand and the fishing pole perched on her shoulder.

As she approached the yard, the house looked normal, lantern light streaming through the windows. But then she heard men talking. It was Daddy and Preston, their voices coming from the deep shadows beneath the pecan tree. There was something strange about their speech. They didn't sound like themselves.

She called out, not wanting to startle them.

"The older you get, the more peculiar you get, Livvy," Daddy said, his words slurred. "Just like my mama, God rest her soul. She was always traipsing through the woods by herself, just like you."

Livvy eyed her father and brother sitting in a couple of chairs, the burning embers of their cigarettes visible in the dark. Then the smell of alcohol hit her nostrils.

"What you got there, Livvy?" Preston said.

"Caught some fish."

"We figured you were out in the woods building stick horses or some such."

Preston laughed a drunken laugh. Daddy laughed with him, then raised a jar of moonshine to his mouth and took a swig. She'd never known Daddy to take a drop of liquor, so it was jarring to find him like this. Thankfully, it was too dark to see more than his silhouette. She didn't want to look into his bloodshot eyes.

"I hate to sound like a nag," she said.

"Then don't!" Preston barked. "Go clean your fish and put 'em in the ice box and leave us be."

So that's what she did, biting her tongue and leaving them to their whiskey and cigarettes.

Sleep was hard to come by with the bank failure and Mae's revelations weighing on her mind. Not to mention Daddy and Preston getting drunk. A sure sign that they had lost hope. Which worried her something fierce. What was life without hope?

*

The house smelled of fried fish the next morning. Mama had cooked Livvy's meager catch to go with the scrambled eggs, prompting Clara to remark that maybe she, Nettie and Faye might do a little fishing to put some extra food on the table.

There were four men, not three, working on Coy's hardware store that morning. Which made Livvy want to march across the street and demand the return of the hammers and nails she'd sold him last week. What Mae said must be true – the Whitakers and Mr. Buchanan had withdrawn their money, triggering the bank failure and causing misery for so many others while *their* money was safe and sound in some other bank.

Once again she and Ruthie didn't have anything to do when the newspapers were sold. Then, right about noon, a young man entered the store looking for some food. He was the new man on the construction site, middling height, brown hair, tanned from working outdoors.

"You're Livvy Hopkins," he said. "I mean, Livvy Sloan."

"Do I know you?"

"I'm Arlene's little brother Lonnie."

"I remember you. Good to see you again, Lonnie. What can I get for you?"

He chose an RC Cola, soda crackers and a Moon Pie, placing his coins on the counter.

"Coy hired me to help build his new hardware store." He scrunched his face up in embarrassment. "I wouldn't have taken the job but I need the money."

"Believe me, I understand."

He gestured with his head for her to step out front with him like he had a secret to share. She followed, leaving Ruthie inside.

"Just wanted you to know it took me a while when I was a kid to understand how mean Coy was. You probably didn't know he was head over heels for you back then. When you and Hank were engaged, Coy got drunk one night and said he was going to kill Hank. He said you were meant to become Mrs. Coy Whitaker."

Livvy took a deep breath, a crease wrinkling her forehead.

"Next thing you know, you and Hank were married. I thought the threat he made was just a drunk man talking, you know. But when Hank was killed, I remembered what he said."

"Do you have any idea why Coy took a fancy to *me*? I would've thought he'd have gone after the prettiest girls at school. Like Elizabeth Carter or Becky what's her name."

"I take your meaning. But I don't know."

He started across the street as Livvy headed back inside. But then he called out to her.

"I do know he thought the Hopkins were a little snooty. I don't think he ever liked it that this whole area was named after your family."

As she turned away a truck pulled up. The driver climbed out, grabbed a stack of newspapers and handed them to her rather than tossing them on the porch.

"Big news on the front page," he said, then hopped back in his truck and drove off.

She carried the papers inside, untying the string that bound them together. There on the front page was a big headline: "Second bank fails in northeast Georgia."

"Oh no," Livvy whispered.

"What is it?" Ruthie asked, looking over her shoulder.

The article said the failure of the Kinston bank appeared to have triggered a run on cash at a small bank in Thomasburg, forcing the bank to close. The article said account holders panicked after hearing what happened in Kinston, causing so many to drain their accounts that the vault was emptied out and the bank was unable to honor any more withdrawal requests.

"The world has turned upside down," Livvy said.

When Inez arrived, she was just as shaken by the news. She insisted both Livvy and Ruthie take the afternoon off, expecting to sell newspapers and nothing else. Livvy also suspected her older sister was feeling blue about the cancellation of her dinner date with Gib Beasley and preferred to be alone.

*

Saturday was the same as Friday. No customers all morning. When Livvy returned home in the early afternoon, she found Ruthie singing up a storm. Livvy changed into her overalls while her sister serenaded her with "My Blue Heaven," prancing around their bedroom brushing her long tresses. She'd taken a bath and washed her hair that morning, excited about spending the night at her girlfriend's house. Learning some new dances before starting high school was important for someone who'd been fantasizing about dating boys since she was twelve.

Livvy's mind was focused on creating a new artwork which she could finish up quickly tomorrow so Gordon could join her for their second picnic. She wasn't entirely certain she would be good company considering all that had happened this week, but she was determined to show up.

"Have fun with Nancy!" she said, heading for the door.

"That's what I plan to do!"

First stop was the barn to get the wheelbarrow. She wasn't sure yet what she wanted to make today. Something different. But whatever it was, she would need supplies. Often the trek through the woods provided her with inspiration.

She had made it past the withered cornfield when she remembered her pocketknife. It was either on the chest of drawers or in the pocket of her dungarees. Leaving the wheelbarrow on the path, she trotted back to the house. She could hear Ruthie belting out "Makin' Whoopee," which caused Livvy to smile. Maybe she should warn her to keep her voice down. Mama might not be keen on her fourteen-year-old daughter singing about making whoopee.

When she opened the door to their room, Ruthie's back was to her. Because she was singing, she wasn't aware someone had opened the door. She was holding a dress up in front of her, admiring it, wiggling her hips as she sang, "another season, another reason for making whoopee." Livvy stopped cold when she realized it was a flapper dress made from a shimmering fabric of black and gold with fringe along the hem. On Ruthie's bed was a pair of dressy black heels.

"You never planned on spending the night with Nancy," Livvy said.

Ruthie whirled around, hiding the dress behind her.

"Of course I'm spending the night with Nancy. I told you she's going to show me some new dances. She's wearing a fancy dress too. We'll be playing some of her records and…"

"We both know that's a lie."

Ruthie changed tactics, going on the offensive.

"It's actually none of your business where I'm going tonight."

"You're fourteen, Ruthie! Not twenty-four."

A screen door slammed and Mama appeared behind Livvy, squeezing by her into the girls' room. "What's all this about?"

"Show Mama the flapper dress," she said to Ruthie. "And tell her where you were really planning on going tonight."

"It's none of your business!" Ruthie shouted.

"Flapper dress?" Mama said.

"There was never any plan to spend the night with Nancy. I guarantee her real destination is a certain speakeasy near Athens with Coy Whitaker."

"Coy?" Mama said.

Ruthie's anger boiled over then, her eyes shooting daggers at Livvy.

"Coy says I'm beautiful. He says he can imagine me becoming Mrs. Coy Whitaker."

"Coy doesn't have feelings for you, Ruthie," Livvy said, softening her tone.

There were footsteps on the porch. It was Clara and her daughters, attracted by the ruckus.

"You're mean to him," Ruthie cried. "You look down your nose at him. I'm not like that. And he treats me like I'm special."

Mama was still trying to sort everything out in her mind. "He was going to take you to a speakeasy?"

"He knows I want to go dancing. He said we could have a good time even if we don't have a drop of Daddy's whiskey."

Livvy's jaw tightened hearing Ruthie describe how Coy casually mentioned Daddy's moonshine. Daddy and Preston were, no doubt, his suppliers. She could imagine Ruthie telling everyone at the nightclub that they were drinking her daddy's liquor. Lord.

"And you're wrong, Livvy. Coy loves me. He told me so."

"I hope that you and Coy haven't…" Livvy couldn't bring herself to say the words with Mama in the room.

"I let him kiss me. He asked me like a gentleman."

Livvy was afraid to contemplate whether Ruthie might give him permission to go further.

"Give me that dress," Mama said, her voice red hot.

"But Mama!"

"Give. Me. That. Dress!"

She extended her arm and Ruthie reluctantly dropped it in her hand, her mouth twisting into a pout.

"I have to give it back to him. It belongs to…"

"His sister," Livvy said.

"You're just mad because he wants me, not you!"

Livvy knew otherwise but it would be a waste of her breath to try to explain Coy's true motive. Flirting with Ruthie was Coy's way of punishing Livvy. She was beginning to think the man was deranged.

Crossing the room to the chest of drawers, she picked up her knife and marched from the room. Clara and her girls moved back as she burst through the door onto the porch, their eyes wide. She jogged across the yard to where she'd left the wheelbarrow along the edge of the field and set a fast pace as she disappeared into the woods, desperate to leave the farm behind.

The creative enthusiasm that had welled up inside her a short time ago had evaporated. Yet now more than ever she wanted to lose herself in her art. Dwelling on the unpleasantness of real life would only wear her down. It wasn't Ruthie's fault she'd been so easily manipulated. Coy was a master of manipulation. Still, Ruthie's words hurt. And now there would be a wall of resentment between them.

19

Livvy's meandering route through the forest slowed her heartbeat. She ended up standing before the window she'd created by the brook, listening as the current burbled over the mossy rocks. It wasn't as big as Sweet Creek where she'd fished with Mae Glover. The only fish that swam here were small minnows, their silvery scales reflecting the sunlight that filtered through the trees. That was her inspiration for the artwork she would create. A fish.

She gathered clumps of moss along the bank and rounded up small twigs and reeds. Constructing a frame by weaving the reeds with the twigs, she created the shape of a fish with fins on the tail, the top and sides. She carefully applied clumps of damp moss to the exterior so that when she was done, she'd created a shape that resembled a bass you might reel in along the river. She placed him on the pine straw walkway between the canoe and the doorway so it looked like the fish was swimming ahead of the boat, perhaps leading the way.

When she arrived home that night, Ruthie had moved her bed and chest of drawers out of their room to crowd in with Inez, Nettie and Faye. Livvy's clothes that had been in the chest were dumped in a messy pile on the floor. But there was room in the half-empty wardrobe for them now.

Sunday morning Ruthie refused to say a word to her and swapped chairs with Faye at the table so she wouldn't have to sit next to Livvy.

With everyone at the table Preston cleared his throat and made an announcement.

"Me and Daddy and the boys are leaving right after breakfast. We've got business to attend to. So we won't be driving to church this morning. If you want my opinion, I think it's a good idea for everyone to stay home and pray for our family. Pray that we can somehow get our money back from the bank."

"Amen," Daddy said.

*

Normally, Livvy was filled with anticipation at spending time with Gordon. It was something that lifted her spirits and allowed her to forget her troubles, at least for a while. But today was different. A deep foreboding clung to her like a swarm of mosquitoes on a sweltering summer evening.

The picnic now seemed boneheaded. Here she was walking to the woods to have a picnic with a man who said he was real but who might as well not be, because they were worlds apart, physically and socially. It was like she was a little girl playing pretend. *Pretend like I meet a handsome man from England who falls in love with me. Pretend like we meet in the woods year after year having picnics while I show him my nature artworks. Pretend like we talk about stars and galaxies.* Pretend, pretend, pretend. What good would all that pretending do? It was a make-believe escape from reality. It could never lead to anything more.

When she arrived in her outdoor museum, she studied the moss-covered fish. Gordon would like it. But so what? All she had to do was snip a few hairs from her head, entwine them with one of the fins and he would come galloping through the forest. Maybe she should put an end to this. Now that she understood what drew him here, she could leave Grandma's scissors at home from now on. No more cutting strands of hair from her head and working the strange bit of hocus-pocus that summoned him. Maybe it would be best if they never met again, if she focused on solving the difficult challenges her family faced and maybe, just maybe, leaving Burgess County to build a life elsewhere. And there was still her dream of studying art, even if it wasn't in the form of college classes that she would never be able to afford. Regardless, she should concentrate on building her future.

All of that sounded so rational. But if she put an end to her forest artworks and her rendezvous with the strange Englishman, she would be turning her back on happiness. Because there were only two things that brought her joy: creating her woodland art and the company of Gordon Collins.

So she found a thicket to hide in and changed from her overalls into her best work dress – the blue floral one she sewed a couple of years back. She slipped on her Sunday shoes, hid her other clothes in the wheelbarrow and returned to the canoe. Cutting him out of her life would hurt too much. Besides, she couldn't stop seeing him without some kind of explanation. Clipping a few strands of hair, she wrapped them around the fish's tail fin and tucked the scissors in her dress pocket.

A quivering seized her back, then she heard hoofbeats. Turning to watch him approach, she realized her heart was racing. Her heart had not been listening to her brain, regardless of how rational her thoughts might've been.

"Moss!" he gushed upon dismounting. "How very ingenious. If there were a way to preserve it, it would make a lovely work of art for my home."

As always, his compliment made her feel special, as though she possessed a rare talent worthy of praise. Of course, there was no way he could even touch the fish, much less take it home.

He took a moment to remove a raincoat and hat that were both dripping wet.

"I was afraid our picnic might be spoilt," he said, shaking them to remove the water. "We were getting quite the drencher at my house. But I remembered I had only seen rain clouds here once, so I put my Mackintosh on before Bailey and I took off like a pair of lunatics into the deluge."

"You're right. We're having an awful drought. Lack of rain killed our corn crop after boll weevils and drought together killed our cotton crop. It's been a terrible year."

She surprised herself by choking up. She hadn't planned on sharing the trials and tribulations of the Hopkins family. She had certainly not planned to lose control with a cascade of tears.

He instinctively stepped forward to embrace her but his arms passed through her body without the slightest sensation, unnerving them both.

"I'm so very sorry, Livvy," he said, heat rising in his cheeks.

She wiped her eyes, struggling to regain control.

"It's just that it's been one thing after another. And now our bank has failed and we've lost all the money we were saving to pay off two farm loans. But the loans must still be paid."

He withdrew a handkerchief from his pocket and then quickly returned it, realizing he couldn't hand it to her.

"If the bank failed, who owns the loans?" he said.

"A loan company bought them before the bank closed."

She took a deep breath, bringing her tears under control.

"That sounds rather dodgy," he said, "as though someone knew the bank was about to fail. Do you know anything about the loan company?"

"The newspaper said it's called Chason Loans."

"If you visit the company's offices, surely they'll give your family more time to repay the loans considering the circumstances."

"You think so?"

"It would be good business practice to do so. It would be in that company's best interests for the customer to repay what he borrowed."

She wiped her eyes with the backs of her hands.

"You should find out where the company is located, who owns it and how to contact the loan officer."

"The newspaper reported that it's a new company and the editor doesn't know who owns it."

"Suspicious, I must say. In fact, it makes me wonder if it's a front company created for the purpose of hiding its true ownership."

Livvy carefully considered his words.

They sat down then and began to eat. Calmer now, she related her family's struggles, and how every time she thought things couldn't get any worse, that's exactly what happened, one calamity unfolding on top of another. She told him about

Coy, about him pressuring her to become his wife, about how he had tricked her into believing he was helping her family. She poured out her story to him, even going so far as to reveal that her father, brother and his two sons had become bootleggers as a way of keeping the family afloat. She also told him the sheriff was demanding bribes and their growing fear that there might be no way to quit the business without serving time in prison.

He listened intently, never raising a judgmental brow. But now he knew that her family was nothing like his.

When she finished her story, she breathed a great sigh of relief, glad he knew the truth. She didn't want to pretend with him anymore. She wasn't just some Georgia girl with flaming red hair who led a charmed country life creating unusual nature sculptures in the woods. She was a poor young widow whose family was sinking under the strain of a string of crises, some dished out by Mother Nature, some by the recession, and still others by a man hell-bent on punishing her family because Livvy refused his advances.

Before long it was time for him to go. They rose to say good-bye and he stepped closer, close enough to touch her if that were possible. Looking down into her face, he shared words of encouragement, his eyes filled with tenderness.

"Find out who owns that company. Hopefully, the owners will give your family more time. Don't despair. Everything will get sorted out."

"Thank you for your kindness, Gordon."

"Shall we plan to meet again next Sunday?"

She nodded, doing her best to smile.

He held up his right hand, palm facing her, entreating her with his eyes to do the same. She extended her left hand, palm facing his until their hands looked like they were touching. Except there was no contact, no heat. The gesture made her ache for the wall between them to be breached.

With the sun sinking in the west, he donned his big raincoat and rode off toward the darkened sky, leaving her with a slender thread of hope.

*

Preston let her drive his car into town Monday morning. She had to visit Mr. Phillips at the newspaper office. He was on the telephone when she arrived. When he hung up, he greeted her as though he wasn't pleased at being interrupted.

She asked if he'd be checking into who owned the new loan company that took over the Hopkins farm loans.

"Honestly, it'll be all I can do to keep the paper going. I'm a one-man band now. Until last Thursday I had one reporter but I had to let him go. I had a secretary but I let her go too. I had two men who delivered papers every Thursday. Now I have one. I don't have the luxury of working on news stories that require an investment of time."

"But Mr. Phillips, don't you think the bank failure was suspicious?"

"I have no idea. The bigger newspapers will have to investigate that along with the bank regulators."

"But your readers…"

"Miz Sloan, I lost all my money too. Now my advertisers are calling me to cancel their ads."

She was wasting her breath.

"Call the Athens," he said. "Maybe a couple of the Atlanta papers."

She was about to thank him and take her leave when it occurred to her that he might have the names and addresses she needed. There was no way she could afford to place long distance phone calls to three newspaper offices. Thankfully, he obliged, providing her with the names and addresses of the news editors.

"Can you spare a few sheets of paper and envelopes?" she asked.

He hesitated, then nodded toward the vacant desk on the other side of the room. He also agreed to let her sit and write her letters there.

Abandoning her flowing cursive, she printed her sentences, aiming for a masculine look, avoiding round letters that looked feminine. She understood that a letter from a man would be taken more seriously than a letter from a woman.

She laid out the details she knew to the news editors of all three papers, pointing out that the creation of Chason Loans just days before the bank failure suggested that certain people knew ahead of time the bank would be closing. She said reporters should find out who owned this new company. She also said it might be worth investigating whose loans the company bought. She explained she'd heard that Coy Whitaker, his father Jefferson Whitaker and bank Vice President Merle Buchanan withdrew large sums of money the day before the bank run, likely sparking the panic and the closure of the bank. She explained that she could not reveal her own name or the name of her source for fear of retaliation. She signed it "a Burgess County resident."

She wrote out three identical letters and addressed them, with no return address. Then she walked to the post office and bought three stamps, dropping the envelopes in the mailbox as she exited the building. The letters should be delivered by Wednesday. She just hoped they would be read and taken seriously.

Inez had asked her to stop in at Beasley's General Store. Like their own store, Mr. Beasley's shop had no customers. His greeting was not as warm as usual, the stress of the financial crisis showing in the set of his shoulders.

"I've had one customer this morning," he said. "A neighbor of yours, Coy Whitaker, stopped in to buy a couple of saws."

Naturally, Coy would visit Mr. Beasley's store rather than give the Hopkins sisters any business.

"All we're selling is newspapers," she said.

"Yeah, I sell out as soon as they're delivered. This is a real mess. Don't know how folks are going to survive. The dress shop down the street is closed. No one's got the money to buy. Expect more bad news in the coming days."

"Well, I better get on home. Inez is minding the store. She'll need a break soon."

"Please tell her I hope to see her again before too long."

*

That afternoon after Inez went home, Livvy noticed someone approaching the store. It was Mae Glover, who glanced around to see if anyone else was there before speaking.

"Afternoon, Miss Livvy. Are you by yourself today?"

Livvy nodded. "Not enough business for two of us here. Everything all right?"

"Wanted to let you know me and my family are moving up north to Pittsburgh. Taking my little ones and my mama to live with my aunt until we can get a place of our own."

"I don't blame you one bit."

"Things have always been bad here, but now Mister Coy has made it plain that to keep my job, he wants to have his way with me."

"I'm so sorry, Mae. What a beast. I wish I had some money to help you a little, but with the bank failure we can hardly put two nickels together."

"Don't you worry. My money was under the mattress, not in the bank. And I've been saving up for a while now. Just wanted to stop by to say good-bye and thank you for your kindness."

Livvy considered asking how to reach her at her aunt's house, thinking there might come a time when Mae's testimony could help nail the Whitakers for driving the bank into the ground. But Mae was right – it would be dangerous for a Black woman to speak up about some well-to-do white men in Georgia. She stepped around the counter and gave her friend a quick hug.

"You take care."

Later that afternoon, as Livvy was reorganizing the cookware for something to do, she was startled when she heard the voice of the devil himself behind her.

"Looks like Hopkins General Merchandise has fallen on hard times."

She stood slowly and turned to meet his jeering eyes.

"Lord, Livvy, you could've saved yourself a lot of grief if you'd just admitted from the get-go that we were made for each other."

Choosing to keep her mouth shut was the wisest thing she could do at this point. If she started talking, it would turn into shouting in no time. And nothing good would come of that.

"Of course, there's still time," he said. "The offer is still on the table. You accept my proposal and I'll help dig your pitiful family out of the quicksand y'all have sunk into."

"What proposal is that?"

"Why, to become Mrs. Coy Whitaker, of course."

He helped himself to a pack of chewing gum, opened a piece and put it in his mouth.

"Thanks, but no thanks," she said, ready to get back to work.

"Well, if I can't get you to be my wife, I can easily get Ruthie to say yes. She's a fine filly, already got the body of a woman even if she is a little young."

He grinned, chewing his gum with gusto.

Livvy was on the very precipice of losing control. She sucked air into her lungs, aching for him to know just how intensely she hated him. But she paused for a moment, considering. When she did speak, her voice was calm, but dead serious.

"Stay away from my little sister, Coy, or you'll regret it."

"You know where to find me if you change your mind!" He laughed as he slapped a penny on the counter for the gum and walked out.

Watching him through the window, she was overwhelmed with a violent urge she'd never experienced before. There was a primitive impulse deep inside her that wanted to hurt him. In that moment she was glad she didn't keep a gun at the store. Because if she did, she was afraid the temptation to shoot that miserable excuse for a human being might be too much to resist.

20

When the men got home Tuesday evening a letter was waiting for Daddy on the sideboard. It was from Chason Loans. Daddy picked it up, studied it, then set it down again before taking his seat at the head of the table.

Normally, there would be a good deal of conversation at supper, but not tonight. Not with that envelope staring at them.

When they finished eating, Daddy retrieved it, slid it into his shirt pocket and headed outside, taking a chair with him to sit beneath the pecan tree. Preston grabbed another chair and followed.

Mama directed Ruthie, Nettie and Faye to clear the table and wash dishes, suggesting that Cecil and Vernon take care of some chores. Then she headed after the men.

"We're coming too, Leon," she called out to her husband, motioning for Inez, Livvy and Clara to join her.

A chair was brought for Mama to sit in. The rest of them stood in a circle.

After a moment, Daddy ripped the envelope open, pulling out a letter on white paper. Unfolding it, he read it silently, heaving a tired sigh before sharing the news.

"They're only giving us a couple of extra weeks on both loans. The cotton loan is due in full September thirtieth – two weeks from today. The corn loan is due October fourteenth."

Mama burst into tears, prompting Inez to hug her shoulder.

Livvy didn't wait for the men to comment, speaking just loud enough for them to hear without letting the girls eavesdrop from the house.

"A real loan company would allow borrowers extra time to repay a loan if a bank failure robbed them of their money. It would be in the company's best interest for a customer to repay what he borrowed," she said, remembering Gordon's words. "That would be good business practice. This is not good business practice. This is the action of someone who wants to do our family harm."

It was plain that Preston agreed and knew who she was referring to. But before he could speak, Livvy continued.

"I drove into town this morning and tried to get the editor of the *Kinston Bulletin* to find out who owns that company. He says he has no employees anymore and can't do a story on it. He suggested I contact the Athens paper and a couple of papers in Atlanta. So that's what I did. I wrote anonymous letters telling their news editors about this loan company that was created right before the bank closed. I suggested they investigate who owns it, that it might be what I'm told is sometimes called a *front* company to hide its ownership. I also told them they should investigate any large money transfers that took place in the days leading up to the bank closing. I'm a hundred percent certain the bank failure was no accident. As hard as it is to believe, I think it was planned for the purpose of stealing our money and keeping us from paying the farm loans."

"That's the most far-fetched tale I've ever heard," Mama cried. "Who would do such a thing?"

Livvy looked toward the house to make sure nobody was peeking through the window.

"Coy Whitaker, his father and his brother-in-law, the vice president of the bank."

"What makes you think so?" Mama said.

"Let's just say a little frog whispered in my ear." That's as much as Livvy was going to share about her conversation with Mae Glover. "Coy had the gall to come into our store today to tell me if I marry him he'll save my family. Then he went on to say if he can't get *me* to marry him, then he'll marry Ruthie, giving me the distinct impression that Ruthie would be more than happy to accept his proposal."

Even Preston, who had always been suspicious of Coy, was floored. He clapped his hands together angrily and cursed under his breath.

"As it stands right now," Inez said, "we can't prove anything."

"True," Livvy admitted. "But we know that Coy would steal Ruthie away if given half the chance. He threatened to do so to my face."

"We need to sit down and talk with her," Mama said, "explain to her what Coy is doing."

"She won't believe us. She was mad as a hornet when I saw her with that flapper dress and put a stop to her going to the speakeasy with him. She blames me for ruining her big chance. She thinks Coy loves her."

"You and me and Daddy will talk with her as soon as they're done in the kitchen," Mama said.

"We also need to keep her safe," Daddy added.

"She'll start riding the bus to Kinston High School in two weeks," Mama said.

"So will Cecil and Vernon," Preston said as if they could protect her.

Mama led the way to the kitchen, Daddy and Livvy following behind.

"Nettie, you and Faye run along," Mama said. "We'll finish up."

Ruthie looked irritated she hadn't been relieved of duty as well.

"We need to have a little talk, honey," Mama said, gesturing for her to sit at the table.

Mama, Daddy and Livvy joined her so they were all grouped on the far end where Mama usually sat.

"Livvy, I want you to tell your sister about Coy's visit to the store today."

Nothing like being put on the hot seat. But Livvy did as her mother directed, describing Coy's arrogant threat, telling her that if she agreed to be his wife, he'd help bail out her family. When she told him no, he said he'd get Ruthie to marry him.

"Well, you know what?" Ruthie replied. "I *would* marry him. He's rich and he's good looking and he likes to have fun."

"He doesn't love you, honey," Mama said.

"I know he used to have an eye for Livvy, but he has an eye for me now. There's nothing wrong with him liking me."

Livvy lost control then.

"Coy Whitaker is like a rat snake slithering into a bird nest to eat the baby birds. And you're the baby bird."

"I am not a baby bird!"

"You're only fourteen years old," Daddy said.

"You're siding with Livvy against me. You and Mama both. But if Coy asks for my hand, I'll say yes."

"You'd need our permission."

"We can go across the state line and get hitched. Coy said so."

Livvy wished she could tell Ruthie about all that Coy had done to ruin the family, but there was no way she could be trusted to keep her mouth shut. They couldn't afford to tip him off that the newspapers might be investigating the bank failure and the loan company. So she bit her tongue, letting her parents plead with their youngest daughter to come to her senses.

All it did was make Ruthie even more surly than before. Not only did she give Livvy the silent treatment, now she also spoke as little as possible to Mama and Daddy. It was clear she would bolt first chance she got.

Alone in her room that night, Livvy paced the floor. She tried reading, hoping to distract herself from the suffocating hostility. But the book lay abandoned on the nightstand. The four walls were closing in on her again. She wished she could escape to the forest but it was past midnight. At length, she couldn't stand it any longer and slipped her summer robe over her nightgown and put her shoes on.

Exiting quietly, she moved across the porch before stepping down to the ground. The house was still. The only light was the lantern streaming through her bedroom window. The sky was filled with stars, a few clouds reflecting the light from a quarter moon. Just enough light to stroll around the yard, taking slow, deep breaths, trying to calm herself.

But guilt consumed her. Every awful thing that had happened to them seemed to originate from Coy's obsession with *her*. Well, except the crop failures. But she now suspected Coy was behind her husband's death. She also suspected he may have had something to do with the refusal of the bank to give Daddy extensions on his loans. On top of that, she was certain he contributed directly to the bank failure and the creation of a loan company that wouldn't give Daddy extra time to pay the loans.

Should she sacrifice herself to save her family? If she agreed to marry him, would he keep his promise and bail her family out of the financial mess they were in? No! What was she thinking? She couldn't trust a word he said. That was not the answer. But was there an answer? Was there any way out of this horrible predicament they'd gotten themselves into?

She gazed up at the heavens, noticing a blur high in the sky. Maybe that was the Andromeda Galaxy. She wished Gordon were here now so she could ask him. She also wished he were here so she could cry on his shoulder. Except, of course, she couldn't touch his shoulder. She would hike into the woods tomorrow and make a small artwork to summon him. She needed to talk with him. Her eyes welled up and the stars blurred above her.

It was at that very instant that a horrendous boom jolted her body causing her ears to ring. She'd never heard an explosion but knew that's what it was. There was an orange light above the tree line coming from the Hopkinsville crossroads.

Her family poured out of the house, lighting lanterns as they came – Mama and Daddy, then Preston and Clara, followed by Inez, Ruthie and Preston's children. They stood in their nightclothes staring at what could only be a terrible fire lighting the night sky in the distance. Then the smell of gasoline filled the air.

"The store," Livvy whispered.

"Dear God," Inez cried.

"I'll get my car keys," Preston said, dashing back into the house.

He returned a moment later tucking a shirt into his pants. He slid in behind the steering wheel. Livvy sat beside him while Daddy and Inez piled in the back seat. They tore off down the yard and onto the road leading up the hill to the crossroads. When they rounded the curve, they were met by the sight of a terrifying inferno. The store was a ball of fire, flames leaping high into the night sky. Sparks had already drifted across the road setting fire to the school and the foundation of the new hardware store. The smell of gasoline was overpowering.

Preston pulled the car to a stop a good distance away and they silently watched the Hopkins general store burn, the flames so hot, no amount of water would've been enough to dampen the blaze, much less put it out.

Other cars appeared along the two roads that met in front of the store. Some people sat in their automobiles, others stood in the darkness, their faces lit by the blaze.

After watching for a good fifteen minutes, Preston found his voice.

"There's so much fuel, it'll burn all night long."

He cranked the car and made a U-turn, heading back to the house. Mama, Clara and the kids were waiting in the kitchen. Preston described what they'd seen before telling everyone to go back to bed and try to get some sleep.

There would be no sleep for Livvy. The fire was no accident.

But who to share her suspicions with? The Whitakers had the sheriff in their pocket. They had a banker on their team. They had an Athens lawyer to do their bidding. Were they also in cahoots with the fire chief? She should contact state fire authorities.

As soon as Preston arrived in the kitchen the next morning, Livvy asked to borrow his car so she could drive to Kinston and contact the state fire marshal's office. He said they had to get to their work site first thing if they had any hope of making the loan payment.

"But I'll send Cecil back to drive you into town. You need to contact the insurance agent too."

Sitting beside him, Inez seemed in a daze.

"I'll call the insurance company while I'm there, Inez."

Her sister didn't respond, didn't look up from her plate.

"Unless you want to go with me and call the insurance agent yourself," Livvy added.

When Inez raised her head, her eyes were red and swollen. She was taking the loss hard.

"It'll never be the same store Grandma built," Livvy said, "but the insurance money should pay to rebuild and restock."

Inez chewed her lip before responding, her voice barely audible.

"I never added the rider to the policy after we got the gas pump."

Livvy stared at her, taken aback.

Preston shook his head in disbelief.

"But you said you would take care of it," Livvy said. "I thought you called the insurance agent."

"I did, but it was expensive. So I thought once we made a little money, I'd add the rider. But..."

"You never called him back?"

"We were being so careful, just you and me pumping the gas. I was waiting till we had a little more money in the account. And then there was the bank failure and our money was gone."

"You mean we have no insurance coverage for last night's fire?"

Inez let her chin hang nearly to her chest, tears spilling over.

"And we still owe Coy for the loan," Livvy said, a hint of desperation seeping into her voice. "Whatever you do, don't tell Ruthie," she whispered, giving Inez a sharp look.

Feeling a scream rising in her throat, Livvy rushed from the kitchen and out the side door to the yard. She didn't stop there. She ran down the driveway to the road, then jogged up the hill and around the bend until she reached the crossroads. Despite having witnessed the monstrous blaze the night before, the apocalyptic sight stopped her in her tracks.

As expected, the store had burned to the ground. All that was left was a layer of embers, still glowing red, heat radiating from them, making it dangerous to get close. The gas pump lay on the ground, blackened and misshapen. Across the street, the school was a pile of charred wood. Likewise, the new hardware store.

Livvy wasn't sure why she was here. Maybe she needed confirmation that what seemed like a nightmare was only too real. There would be no insurance settlement. The store couldn't be rebuilt. And now she and Inez – and maybe even Ruthie – were responsible for the loan Coy had given them out of the *goodness* of his twisted heart.

*

When she walked into the newspaper office later that morning Mr. Phillips was helpful, giving her the Atlanta phone number for the agency she needed to call to report a suspicious fire. She had brought cash with her from her small hidden stash to pay him for the long-distance call. She gave her name and address and told them she was part owner of the store that burned and explained that she strongly suspected the fire was set intentionally. Although it might've been a waste of time, she also called the insurance agent, hoping their policy might pay for something. It wouldn't. Not with the addition of the filling station additions. As Cecil drove her back to the farm, she feared her calls wouldn't do any good, but felt better for having reported it to someone outside Burgess County.

If home had been uncomfortable before, it now seemed like hell on earth. The men worked all day and the women avoided each other. Clara spent more time with her daughters to keep them away from Ruthie, including a couple of trips to the stream with the boys' fishing poles. Inez mostly stayed in her room, doing what, Livvy had no idea. Mama took care of chores all day long, sometimes pausing in the living room to stare at the space where her piano used to sit, mourning its loss. Livvy escaped to the woods.

She had no brilliant idea for a new creation. She just wanted to throw something together and add some of her hair, hoping Gordon would come. Once she reached the woodland, she scanned her surroundings for something to use, spotting a low-hanging branch of a small dogwood that was already turning red and weighed down with clumps of berries. She used her knife to cut it from the tree, then stuck it in the ground behind the canoe. She gathered small pinecones and arranged them in circles around the base. When it was complete, she snipped a few hairs from her head and tied them to the dogwood branch and stepped back, feeling the tremble in her body. Looking to the north, she saw the dark sky, then heard the sound of a horse coming through the forest.

When Gordon dismounted, she wanted to run to him, bury her face in his shoulder. Instead, she wrung her hands in frustration, guilty that she'd thrown together a fake sculpture because she was desperate for his sympathetic ear.

"Tell me," he said, noticing her distress at a glance.

The words poured out, all the horrible things that had happened since she'd seen him. Coy threatening to marry Ruthie, the letter from the new loan company saying Daddy only had two extra weeks to pay his loans, the store burning down, then finding out they had no insurance.

"Bloody hell," he said.

"I'm afraid my life sounds like a dime novel. It feels like I've got a noose around my neck and the chair is about to be yanked out from under me."

"This Coy Whitaker fellow sounds like a villain through and through."

"As you suggested, I'm trying to get the newspapers to investigate. If they do a story, the authorities might be more likely to look into it. The only witness who heard them talking about it has now left town. She couldn't give a statement anyway. It would be dangerous for a Black woman to speak against white men here in Georgia."

"Besides collusion, do you know of any other crimes he's committed?"

"He owns a speakeasy where they sell alcohol. Of course, it's illegal to sell alcohol. And I'm sure he's not reporting any income from the nightclub to the government."

"You need proof."

"Easier said than done."

"Considering all you've told me about this scoundrel, I would urge you to be careful. He's evidently a dangerous character."

"Deranged, I think. Even so, I can't believe he would do all this to force me to marry him. He could have his pick of any pretty young woman he wanted."

"That's one thing that doesn't surprise me – that he wants *you*."

*

That evening Livvy sat with Mama on the porch, staring into space while Mama worked on some mending. Neither said a word. What was there to say at this point? A pecan dropped from the tree in the yard, prompting Mama to comment.

"At least we'll have pecans to eat."

That's what it had come to – a constant search for food to put in their stomachs during the long winter ahead. Assuming they didn't have to find another roof to put over their heads first.

There was a second small sound and Livvy thought another nut had fallen but looked up to see Arlene walking up the driveway. She was alone, no baby on her hip, no little boys trailing behind her. Her husband's wagon was nowhere in sight. This was definitely not normal.

Livvy rose and met her friend in the yard, sensing what she had to say was for her ears alone.

"Let's walk around back to the garden," Livvy suggested.

Arlene gave a small wave to Mrs. Hopkins as they strolled around the corner of the house.

When they reached the garden, Livvy grabbed a basket and started down the first row, Arlene keeping pace behind her.

"We're leaving town," Arlene said in a hushed voice.

Livvy bent down to pick a squash, placing it in the basket. "Why?"

"We were asleep last night when Coy Whitaker showed up at our house. Wade went outside to speak with him, then told me he was leaving and would be back after a while. That's all he said. Nothing like that had ever happened before and I was scared. He looked like he didn't want to go but had to because Coy is his boss. I went back to bed, tried to sleep but couldn't. I was too worried. I was pacing the floor when all of a sudden I heard a god-awful explosion coming from the crossroads area. I stepped out onto the front porch and saw a bright light above the trees like a raging fire was coming for us."

Livvy squatted by Mama's tomato plant and plucked a ripe tomato to put in the basket before they moved along the row as Arlene continued her story.

"I thought sure 'nuff that Wade was dead. But I couldn't leave the children to go find out what happened, so I just stood on the porch and cried. I don't know how long it was but I heard someone walking up the driveway. When he got close enough, I saw it was him and ran to meet him. First thing he said was 'we gotta get out of here.' He said Coy wanted him to do a job, said he'd pay him good money. They drove to your store and Coy said he wanted Wade to start the gas pump and throw a match onto it so it would burn the store down. Wade told Coy he couldn't do something like that. Coy said nobody would be hurt. He just wanted to burn your store down. When Wade refused, Coy told him he was fired from the construction job and he better look out."

Livvy grabbed the tops of a bunch of carrots, wiggled them back and forth and pulled the carrots from the ground, adding them to the basket as they reached the end of the row.

"Wade says we're not safe here anymore. He says sooner or later, Coy will have his revenge. So we packed up our clothes, put the kids in the wagon and headed over to my brother's house. Lonnie says if Coy thinks Wade might talk, he's likely to believe Lonnie might talk. So Lonnie and his wife, me, Wade and the kids all squeezed into Lonnie's car and started to drive out of town. I told them we had to stop by here so I could tell you. They're waiting in the car for me just down the road in some trees. Wade says there's no doubt in his mind that Coy struck the match that caused the explosion."

Livvy could see the fear in her friend's eyes.

"I wish Wade could..." Livvy began.

"I know what you're thinking. But if Wade said one word against Coy to the sheriff or anyone else, it would be his word against Coy's word. And you know who would win that contest."

"You're right. Where will you go?"

"Got some friends over in South Carolina."

Livvy handed Arlene the basket and led her toward the front of the house.

"Thank you, Arlene. You've been a good friend to me."

"You were always kind to me and my family."

When they reached the road, Arlene headed away from the crossroads toward where Lonnie's car was hidden. Livvy whispered "God bless" as her friend walked away.

Gordon said it best – Coy was a villain through and through.

When Livvy returned to the porch, Mama greeted her with a mild admonition.

"That was a right nice thing you did giving your poor friend some vegetables from the garden. But from now on, you need to remember that we're poor too."

21

She walked to the crossroads Thursday morning a little before eight when they would normally open the store for business. She was waiting by the blackened remains when a car pulled up. The man behind the wheel stared in amazement at the conflagration.

Livvy ran over to the passenger window and told him she was co-owner of Hopkins General Merchandise and asked if he had a stack of *Kinston Bulletins* for her. He nodded and jumped out of the car to retrieve her allotment tied with string on the back seat.

"I'll sell them here on the side of the road," she said. "People depend on getting their paper."

He took one last look around and went on his way.

She pulled a paper from the stack and read a small item about the fire in which the Burgess County Fire Chief was quoted as saying the blaze appeared to have been caused by the gasoline storage tank exploding. He said no one was injured, as though that made the loss inconsequential.

There wasn't a single story about the bank failure or the new loan company. Mr. Phillips wasn't kidding when he said he didn't have time to do his job.

That afternoon, she was waiting once again when the truck pulled up to deliver the day's copies of the Athens newspaper. The driver turned off the engine so he could get out and study the burned remains.

"Never seen a fire this hot," he said to Livvy. "Looks like the tank melted."

"Yeah, it was awful."

Then she told him the same thing she told the other guy, that she would sell copies on the roadside, taking her stack of papers from him.

Pulling the top copy from the pile, she eagerly searched for stories. There was an article on an inside page about the fire. It was pretty much the same as the *Bulletin* story except it said an investigation continued into the cause, although the fire chief suspected a malfunction in the gasoline delivery line. The paper did have a follow-up story on the bank closure. It focused on three families who lost all their money. But there was nothing about Chason Loans and nothing about the possibility that the bank failure was triggered by collusion among several wealthy account holders.

As she did with the newspapers that morning, Livvy untied the string and set the stack on the side of the road, figuring anyone who wanted a copy could have one. They needed to cancel the subscription for both papers.

On her walk home, a dirty blue car flew past her, giving her a coughing fit from the dust it raised on the rutted dirt road. When she got home she found the same car parked under the pecan tree, a man in grey trousers and a short-sleeved white shirt and tie talking with Mama on the porch.

As she approached, he wiped the sweat from his face with a handkerchief.

"Livvy, this is Mr. Dickson, a reporter with the *Athens Journal*," Mama said. "This is my daughter Livvy."

He nodded, stuffing his handkerchief in his pocket. "I came to interview your father but your mother says he won't be home for another couple of hours." He turned to Mama again. "If you give me directions I could drive to his work site and we could talk there."

Mama seemed at a loss for words so Livvy jumped in, trying to conceal her eagerness.

"He's all over the place in his job. No telling where he is this afternoon. But you could stay for supper. You could talk as soon as he gets here. I know it's a long drive from Athens."

He looked at his watch and considered. "If I could speak with him before dinner, that would be best. Then I could head home."

"I'm sure Daddy would be glad to talk with you before he eats," Livvy said. "While you wait, we can fix you a sandwich and a glass of tea."

"Much appreciated," he said.

"That's a fine idea," Mama said, bustling into the house.

Livvy offered Mr. Dickson one of the rockers and she sat down in the other one.

"I assume this is about the bank failure?" she asked.

An uncomfortable expression flitted across his face. "I think I'd better wait and talk with your father."

"Of course," she replied, realizing he would view this as men's business.

So they made small talk while they waited. Mama brought a big glass of tea. Then a few moments later, she set a plate on a small table between the two rockers with a grilled egg sandwich and two big slices of tomato on the side. He dug in, not pausing until his plate was clean, Mama served him two cookies, warm from the oven along with a glass of milk. She knew how to treat company and he knew how to show his appreciation.

"Your food is so good, Mrs. Hopkins, I believe you could open a restaurant."

She laughed and thanked him for his kind words, never giving a hint of how ridiculous they were considering the financial setbacks everyone was facing.

Thankfully, Daddy, Preston and the boys drove into the yard as the table was being set. Livvy introduced their guest and then did what women were expected to do under the circumstances – she went inside and left the men to themselves. She heard Daddy tell Mr. Dickson that he'd like to have his son remain with him while they talked. Cecil and Vernon washed their hands and came inside to eat.

Daddy led Mr. Dickson out in the yard to sit in the shade of the pecan tree, each of the men carrying a chair to sit on. Livvy stared through the window, wishing she could hear their conversation. Since it wasn't dark yet, there was no way she could sneak around the house and find a hidden spot where she could eavesdrop. She reluctantly joined the rest of the family for a meal of fried fish – courtesy of Clara and her girls.

It was torture sitting at that table. She didn't even try to carry on a conversation, her mind on what was being said outside. Ruthie was sulking, as usual. Inez was morose. Mama was skittish. Clara kept looking toward the door, watching for Preston. The boys wolfed down their food like they hadn't eaten in a week. Nettie and Faye were arguing about which one of them had to milk the cow this evening until Clara told them to hush up, that it was Nettie's turn.

Mama had served big portions of food on Daddy and Preston's plates to make sure they got a good dinner when they came inside. The food was cold by the time the men walked through the door.

Livvy was dying to bombard them with questions but kept quiet as Mr. Dickson's car pulled out of the yard. It was only after the food was gone and the dishes were done that Daddy convened a meeting of the adults, returning to the chairs they'd left under the pecan tree.

"Mr. Dickson says his paper received an anonymous tip," Daddy began, glancing at Livvy, "about the bank failure being intentional, caused by wealthy bank customers who withdrew their money knowing it would trigger a bank run. He says the tip also mentioned that a new company had been created to buy up some of the bank's loans. He says they're investigating and have reason to believe the accusations, as he calls them, might be true."

Livvy held her hand to her chest in excitement as he went on.

"He says he's already learned that Chason Loans is owned by a Mr. Lester Thompson, an Athens attorney."

"Of course," Livvy said.

Daddy held up his hand for her to hold her tongue so he could continue.

"But Mr. Dickson says that company is owned by another company called Burgess Loans, which is owned by Merle Buchanan, McCoy Whitaker and his father, Jefferson Davis Whitaker."

"So it *is* a front company." Just like Gordon said, she thought.

"Appears so. He says the curious thing about the company is that it only bought two loans from the bank before it closed. My two farm loans. He says he's writing an article that'll probably appear in the Sunday edition."

Looks were exchanged all around.

"Y'all talked quite a while, Leon," Mama said. "What all was he asking you?"

"For one thing, he wanted to know if I had any idea why those men wanted to ruin me so bad that they would do all that."

"What did you tell him?" Livvy asked.

"Well, before I could answer, Preston butted in. Which was a good thing."

Preston spoke up at that point.

"I said we weren't sure. Which was my way of not telling him we think Coy belongs in a looney bin and that he's in love with the redheaded Hopkins daughter who keeps saying 'no' every time the idiot asks her to marry him."

Everyone looked at Livvy then like the whole mess was her fault.

"Coy Whitaker doesn't know the meaning of the word love," Livvy snapped.

"You're right, sis," Preston said, the others nodding in agreement. "Anyway," he went on, "I was afraid if Daddy mentioned any of that, Coy would see it in the paper and who knows what he would do."

Livvy wasn't sure how she felt. Relieved? Hopeful? Scared? A combination of all three? Because Preston and Daddy were right, once the article was published, who knew how Coy would react.

"You were right all along," Preston said, locking eyes with Livvy. "You always had a funny feeling about that jackass. Even when everyone was pushing you to go out with him like he was the best catch in Burgess County."

There was respect in his eyes, which meant a lot coming from her big brother.

*

Livvy was a case of nerves on Friday, unsure what to do with herself. But milking the cow was soothing. She enjoyed leaning against Buttercup's warm flank, carrying on a quiet conversation with the sweet cow while she filled the buckets. Then she churned the butter, a job she used to do but which Clara and her daughters now took care of. She picked up pecans that had fallen in the yard, then shelled them and stored them in a big jar. She took it upon herself to clean windows until her arm was sore. Everyone found chores to do so that by the end of the day, the house had been swept and cleaned as if they were expecting out of town company.

The men drove up at their usual time, tension evident on their faces. Preston handed Livvy a newspaper before stopping at the well to wash up. It was an issue of one of the Atlanta newspapers she contacted, a small story on the front page.

The headline read, "Kinston bank failure under investigation." The gist of the story was that investigators were looking into a new loan company that had bought two farm loans from the bank right before it closed its doors. The company was identified as Chason Loans. The company president was listed as Athens attorney Lester Thompson. The article said the paper had received a tip that the bank failure might've been the result of collusion by several parties and that the newspaper would have more information in the coming days.

She exchanged a worried look with her brother.

"And there's more news," he said.

"What?"

"We're not telling Mama or Clara," he said, "or the rest of the family, so keep it to yourself. We had an unexpected visitor today at the still. Sheriff Teague dropped by."

"He knows where the still is?"

"Hell, he probably gave Singletary a hand setting it up for all I know. He came to tell us from now on we owe him ten dollars a week instead of five."

"Ten dollars a week? How will you make any money that way?"

"He doesn't want us to make any money."

"What're you going to do?"

"We don't have any choice. We have to pay him. You were right about this too, Livvy. You said from the get-go that the moonshine business was a harebrained idea. You accused me of turning Daddy and my boys into criminals. You said I was risking sending everyone to prison, that it would be better to lose the farm. Now we're in way over our heads. Sad to say, we could end up behind bars."

His admission gave her no satisfaction.

"There's got to be some way out of this," she said.

"Let me know when you figure it out."

He left her standing there as he headed inside. She walked toward the bone dry field, her appetite gone. The possibility that the men in her family might all go to prison left her feeling wretched. It was one thing to lose the farm, quite another to have Daddy, Preston, Cecil and Vernon incarcerated, perhaps for years.

She wished she could talk with Gordon. He had legal training. He might have a suggestion, something that could help them. It was too late, though, to head to the woods to try to *call* him. It was midnight where he was. She would see him Sunday afternoon. She would ask him then.

The cogs in her brain kept on turning even as the men left again after supper to make a delivery. They'd be racing along those dark country roads as fast as Preston's car would go. They were working long hours, probably cutting corners to speed up the process of distilling the whiskey. She hoped they wouldn't make a mistake that could hurt someone.

Crossing her arms, she continued pacing around the farm as twilight settled, ideas racing through her head. And then something Gordon said came back to her. "Proof."

*

When the car pulled into the yard late that night, Livvy was waiting in Mama's rocker. She rose and moved out of the shadows into the yard out so they'd see her as they approached the house.

"What're you doing out here so late?" Daddy said.

"Need to talk with you and Preston for a minute."

"Y'all go on," Preston said to his sons.

As the boys trudged toward the house, Daddy spoke.

"I'm dang tired, Livvy."

"Won't take but a minute," she replied, leading the men back toward the car.

"First, have you used your real names making deliveries?" she asked.

"No," Preston replied.

"I assume all of your payments are in cash?"

"Naturally."

"Livvy," Daddy said, impatient.

"If someone accused you of running moonshine, they'd need evidence," she said.

Both men stood silently, waiting for her to explain.

"What if you moved the still and all your equipment and supplies and then blew it all to smithereens?" she said.

"The men at the clubs and stores we delivered to would recognize our faces," Preston said.

"And you would recognize *their* faces. You think they'd want to report to the revenuers that the bootleggers they usually did business with hadn't delivered the latest batch of moonshine? That would be admitting they're breaking the law."

"They'd tell Sheriff Teague."

"Even if Teague wanted to arrest you," Livvy said, "he'd need some kind of proof."

"He knows where the still is."

"You could move everything tomorrow. Someplace way off the beaten track. And then toss a match, just like that swine did to our store. Then you could bury whatever's left after the explosion."

Dead silence. Preston walked a short distance away, then turned and came back.

"Might work," he said. "But no explosion. Too loud. Too dangerous. I know a good dumping ground." He looked to his father then. "Daddy, you go on inside and go to bed. I'm taking the boys and we're going to move the still tonight."

"I'll go with you," Daddy said.

"No, we'll have more room in the car without you. Go on to bed."

Preston hurried into the house to find Cecil and Vernon while Livvy waited in the yard. When the three of them emerged, she offered to help but he refused.

She eventually settled in her bedroom, lying on top of the bedspread, unable to close her eyes, filled with worry. It was one thing to suggest your brother and his sons dump their still, but now she couldn't stop agonizing about their safety. What if they were caught? But Preston had a point – doing it in broad daylight might draw attention. Unable to lie still, she paced around her bedroom, peering out the window into the darkness every few minutes, hoping they would be all right. Finally succumbing to exhaustion, she collapsed on her bed and drifted off to sleep.

When she awoke, she was greeted by sunshine streaming through her window. She jumped up, looked out the window and burst into tears of relief when she saw Preston's car.

She washed up, throwing on her clothes before hurrying to the kitchen. Daddy, Mama, Inez, Ruthie, Clara, Nettie and Faye were eating scrambled eggs and biscuits. Preston, Cecil and Vernon's chairs were empty.

"They're sleeping in this morning," Clara said casually. "They had a late night."

Livvy was so thankful they were safe in their beds. If they'd been caught or gotten hurt, she would never have forgiven herself.

22

Clara normally deferred to her mother-in-law, but Saturday morning she took charge, bound and determined to erase all traces of the men's recent business enterprise. She collected their work clothes, washing them in a tub of hot water to remove any alcohol or corn residue. She hung them on the clothesline to dry in the sun, then collected their work shoes, washing them in soapy water and scrubbing the soles with a scrub brush. She instructed all four of them to take a bath. Following orders, they took turns in the tin bathtub in the kitchen, oldest to youngest. Last, but not least, she had the boys wash the inside and outside of Preston's automobile, including the trunk and the tires. When she was finished, there was not a shred of evidence that the Hopkins men had ever been near a still. Livvy was amazed by her sister-in-law's thoroughness.

Despite the usual morning chores accompanied by the sound of chickens clucking and the cow bellowing to be milked, nothing felt natural that day. Everyone was at home, no one headed off to work. The Athens newspaper story would be published tomorrow and nerves were on edge. Late morning Livvy hiked into the woods to begin work on her new project. She wanted to complete it today so it would be ready for the finishing touch tomorrow. She was anxious to see Gordon, to hear his reassuring voice.

Taking the wheelbarrow, she headed into the forest, imagining the wishing well she would create. She stopped along the way to collect building materials – twigs, branches and vines. When she arrived, she chose a spot near where the vine hammock had been for her new creation. Thankful there was a breeze to keep her from overheating, she started by constructing the round wall, using strips of vine to bind the twigs together. The opening of the well was about three feet in diameter. The wall was four feet high and about eight inches thick. She was so experienced by now that she had the base of the well completed in a couple of hours.

She took a short break to eat a carrot and a hard-boiled egg and began work on the roof. It was cone shaped and mounted on four pillars made of sticks attached to the base. That part was a little more complicated, but she was pleased when she laced several pinecones together with vines to attach to the point at the top of the roof. She also designed a small bucket to hang from a crossbeam. Gordon would be impressed.

If only it were real. She would toss a coin into the well and wish that all of her family's problems would disappear and that she and Gordon could meet in person and share a kiss. Admittedly, that was more than one wish. But fantasizing about a kiss made her tingle.

Who was she kidding? Now that he knew all of her family's secrets, the country girl would be off limits to someone like him. It was all imaginary anyway – a wishing well was straight from the fairy tales.

She'd been so preoccupied with her work that she missed the sounds of someone approaching. A chill ran down her spine at the crunch of footsteps behind her. Turning, she met Coy's mocking eyes. He was only twenty feet away.

"So this is the love nest where you and your boyfriend meet," he said.

Her instinct was to run. But he was much faster than she was. He would catch her in no time.

"And look at all the decorations you made." He waved his arm, gesturing at the doorway, the boat, the new wishing well and her other creations. "A romantic hideout." He laughed.

"Why are you here?" she asked, racking her brain for a nearby hiding place. Unlike when Ruthie chased her, Coy wouldn't fall behind long enough for her to take cover in the underbrush.

"After reading this morning's Athens newspaper, I figured it's time you got your comeuppance. And don't tell me you're not the tipster."

Livvy was furious with herself. The reporter had said the story would come out Sunday, not today. Too late she realized she should never have hiked into the woods alone.

"I don't know what you're talking about," she lied. "I haven't seen the paper."

He rolled his eyes.

She needed to buy herself some time – time to figure a way out of this mess.

"What have you got against my family, Coy?"

"What have I got against your family? Your highfalutin family always acted like they were better than everyone else, especially the Whitakers."

"We did no such thing!"

"Yes you did. When my daddy asked your mama to go to a dance back when they were young, she wouldn't have anything to do with him. He wasn't good enough for her."

"Good grief, Coy. My mama was Bess Jenkins back then. She didn't have anything against your father. She said no to a number of boys. She only had eyes for Leon Hopkins, that's all."

"And you! You were just like her. Wouldn't give me the time of day."

"You were two years younger than me. You were a kid to me, just like all the other kids your age. I don't remember you ever speaking to me."

"You were uppity!"

"If I was ever uppity to you, I apologize. I didn't mean to be, that's for sure."

"You thought because you were part of the high and mighty Hopkins clan that you were better than me because my family was bad off. But now the tables are turned. Your family is dirt poor and the Whitakers live in a fine house with money to burn."

"We were never rich, Coy. We had a small farm and barely got by, just like our neighbors."

"Hopkinsville. That's what this place is called."

"All that means is that the Hopkins clan breeds like rabbits. That's not exactly something to brag about."

"But you wore it like a crown."

"Hogwash!"

His nostrils flared in anger.

"Then you went and married that loser, Hank Sloan."

"Hank was not a loser. He was a good man."

"You were supposed to marry me."

"I had no way of knowing you were even interested in me!"

She was right – he was deranged. How did you deal with someone who was deranged? She had no idea. But right now, she wanted to know the truth.

"You wanted Hank dead, didn't you?"

He chuckled. "Yep. And he was only too happy to oblige, agreeing to do the blocksetter's job that day. I was working there that summer. I made sure we fed him a hard tree trunk and he couldn't get the spikes in fast enough."

"What an evil thing to do."

"Of course, that was after you came home from that junior college like you were above the rest of us. By then, my family was making money so I went to college too. Wanted everyone to see I was better than you."

She couldn't think of anywhere to hide. And screaming wouldn't do any good out in the middle of the forest. Cecil and Vernon checked their traps in the evenings, not in the heat of the afternoon. She had to keep him talking. Besides, she wanted some answers.

"You and your daddy made the bank fail just so you could ruin my family, didn't you?"

"Janie's husband told us the bank didn't have much money in the vault. He said if there were some big withdrawals, the small customers would lose all their money. It was too good to pass up. I suggested forming that little loan company and buying your daddy's farm loans. Easy as pie."

"Except the newspaper found out."

"We already explained to that damn reporter we were just moving our cash because we wanted it to be in a bank that's backed by the Federal Reserve. There's already been some failures of little banks. We told him we were only trying to avoid that kind of mess."

"You're as crooked as they come, Coy. You pretend to be an upstanding citizen, but you own that Athens speakeasy, making good money selling alcohol."

"I own several speakeasies. Best investment I ever made. Sheriff Teague was only too happy to make sure we always had reliable bootleggers to supply the product. It was only fair that he got his cut of the proceeds."

"And it was you who burned down our store!"

"I offered you another chance to become Mrs. Coy Whitaker and you said no. So that was your punishment. I got the key to the gas pump from the cash register where I saw you store it. Then I unlocked the gas pump, pressed the handle, lit a match and – boom! It was a damn fine explosion if I do say so myself."

She shook her head angrily as he gloated.

"Then I found out your sister never got insurance coverage. The three stupid Hopkins sisters. Inez, the spinster who didn't buy filling station insurance; Ruthie, who believes anything I tell her because she wants me to pull her panties down in the barn and then marry her when I get her pregnant; and Livvy, the freckle-faced redhead who always thought she was better than me until she found out otherwise."

"You disgust me!"

"Now it's time you get what's coming to you." He pulled a pistol from his pocket.

Swallowing hard, Livvy took a step back as if to run but he raised his gun. "I can shoot you before you take your second step."

She was frozen with fear, unable to draw breath. Then from behind her came the familiar sound of a shotgun being cocked.

"You shoot my sister and you're a dead man, Coy Whitaker." It was Preston.

But Livvy was standing between the two of them. Neither could shoot at the other because she was in the way. In a flash, she threw herself to the ground. There was a deafening report from behind her as Preston fired his weapon. In that split second Coy sensed what was about to happen and dropped down on all fours. Livvy crawled toward where Preston was hidden in the trees, but Coy caught up with her like a hawk catching a baby mouse.

"My gun is aimed at your back," he hissed, his hand tight on her ankle.

She kicked at him, trying to get free but he tightened his grip, dragging her to him. He stuck the barrel of his pistol between her shoulder blades. Her body stiffened, her heart pounding in her chest.

"We're gonna stand up and back away," he whispered. "You fight me and I'll pull the trigger."

He wrapped his arm around her waist and hoisted her to her feet, using her body to shield himself from Preston's line of fire. Pointing the gun at the base of her skull, he pulled her slowly backward, looking left and right, alert for any movement.

"Let her go and I won't kill you," Preston called out.

Coy ignored him, tightening his hold on Livvy's waist. She struggled, trying to loosen his grip to no avail. But the distraction allowed her to slide her right hand into the pocket of her overalls. As they moved backwards, Coy had to glance behind them from time to time to make sure he didn't trip over a log or step in a hole.

Preston called out again, this time from a different direction. "Let her go, Coy!"

Coy swung around, keeping Livvy between him and Preston. He wasn't as self-assured as he'd been moments before.

She squirmed, aggravating him so that he put his mouth on her ear, commanding her to be still.

Preston's voice rang out again, this time a little further to the left from where he'd been the second time. Coy jerked around, keeping Livvy in front of him. That's when she whipped her pocketknife from her pocket, slashing in an upward motion. The sharp edge of the blade slashed his forearm, causing him to drop the pistol. When he reached down to retrieve it, Livvy wrenched free and took off toward Preston's original position so she wouldn't be in his line of fire.

Coy fired his pistol and she dropped to the ground behind the canoe to hide. There was a boom as Preston fired his shotgun. Livvy kept her head down. Seconds passed, then a whiff of smoke reached her nose. She peeked over the rim of the boat. Coy was nowhere to be seen. The spot where he'd been standing was now engulfed in flames. She remembered what the flapper girl said at the speakeasy – Coy's always got a match. And after years of drought, the forest was a tinder box. The blaze would spread quickly.

"Livvy, stay down!" Preston shouted.

A moment later she heard someone moving toward her. It was Preston.

"Let's go!" he cried, reaching down to give her a hand. "He started the fire and took off."

The breeze she'd been thankful for earlier in the afternoon was now a curse as it fanned the flames. She took one final look at her woodland creations, knowing they would be consumed by the blaze. But there was no way to save anything.

They ran through the trees, smoke filling their lungs as they raced for home. In no time, her throat was parched and her side was killing her from the mad dash. The fire chased them at an alarming pace. They ran for their lives along with the forest animals.

As they got closer to the farm and could breathe easier, they slowed to a trot. They were too winded to speak.

She was thankful to be alive. Yet it pained her that she'd goaded Coy into admitting to all the horrible things he'd done but it would be her word against his. Even if Preston had heard any of it, he was her brother, which meant his word would be suspect.

Reaching the edge of the field, they heard screams coming from the house. In the distance, they saw Coy, brandishing his pistol as he dragged Ruthie to his car parked by the road. She was crying and screaming. The family stood helplessly under the pecan tree paralyzed by fear.

Preston rushed forward, cocking his shotgun as he ran. There was too much ground to cover and Livvy knew Coy and Ruthie would be long gone in his fancy automobile before Preston got close enough. He didn't dare fire his weapon from this distance, not with Ruthie in Coy's clutches.

Then Livvy spotted Cecil and Vernon barreling around the corner of the house. Cecil was armed with a shovel, Vernon with a hoe. They raced toward the back of the car as Coy shoved Ruthie into the open driver's side door. He was about to slide in beside her when he spotted the boys charging him. He waved the pistol in their direction. They ducked as he got two shots off in quick succession. Livvy heard Mama and Clara scream as the boys hunched down behind the car. But as Coy turned to jump into the driver's seat, Cecil and Vernon darted out again, swinging their farm tools like they were battling a bear attacking their mother. The shovel hit Coy hard on the right shoulder, causing him to fall to the ground. Vernon slammed the hoe down on Coy's hand. He groaned in pain, losing his grip on the revolver. Vernon dropped the hoe and lunged for the gun where it lay in the dirt, grabbing it before Coy could recover. Vernon took off with the pistol as Cecil stood guard over Coy, threatening to strike him again with the shovel.

Closing in on the car, Preston shouted for someone to get some rope. Nettie and Faye retrieved the rope while Ruthie climbed out the passenger door, sobbing and shaking.

Panting hard, Preston arrived, handing his shotgun to Cecil. He ordered his son to keep the weapon pointed at Coy's head while he tied him up as he lay on the ground. Mr. Beasley, who'd been standing beside Inez during the ordeal, took off in his car.

It was a long time before everyone calmed down. There was a lot of hugging and a lot of tears. Mama held Ruthie in her arms, rubbing her back and telling her everything was all right, that she was safe now. Clara wept in relief, embracing Preston and then their two brave sons. Nettie and Faye hugged their brothers, their father and their mother. Everyone hugged Livvy – they'd all been so afraid Coy would carry out his threat. Livvy wrapped her arms around Preston when all the others had had their turn and thanked him for saving her life.

"It's Mr. Beasley you need to thank," he said.

"Mr. Beasley?"

"Ask Inez. I need to go to Clara and the kids."

As the yard filled with smoke, she headed to the house to find Inez. Livvy was heartbroken that Coy had confessed everything but she still had no way to prove it. If Preston backed her up, the authorities would say he was siding with his sister and couldn't be trusted. Coy had told her everything because he was planning to kill her. If it hadn't been for Preston, he would've succeeded.

Of course, the newspaper story would likely pressure state authorities to find out the truth about the bank failure and the loan company, but there was no evidence that Coy torched the store and set Hank up for a fatal accident at the sawmill, or that he owned and operated several illegal speakeasies. Who would believe Livvy?

She found her sister in the kitchen. Inez didn't ordinarily do much cooking but this evening, while everyone tried to dry their eyes and hold their loved ones close, she was busy making a big pot of mashed potatoes, a pot of field peas and biscuits.

With her apron covered in flour, she gave Livvy a second hug and teared up for a moment.

"Preston says it was your Mr. Beasley who saved my life," Livvy said.

Inez nodded and smiled proudly. "If it hadn't been for Gib, well, I don't know what would've happened. Late this morning Coy and his father stopped by Gib's store to pick up a couple of items and they saw the Athens newspaper by the register. The story about the bank failure and the loan company was on the front page. Gib says when they left the store, they stood right outside the screen door and had some angry words, raising their voices. He heard Coy tell his father 'that uppity redhead is gonna get what she deserves.' Mr. Whitaker tried to calm him down saying now was not the time do go and do something hotheaded. He said their lawyer was taking care of things. But Gib said Coy kept getting louder and louder, talking about how the Hopkins family had always had it out for the Whitakers. When they left, Gib said he read through the article again and guessed you must be the tipster referred to in the story. He said he had a bad feeling Coy might do you harm. So he left his son to run the store and drove over here to warn you. But you were already out in the woods. Preston told him that Coy wouldn't know where to look but Ruthie fessed up that she had told him where you built your artworks. Preston got his shotgun and took off to find you. A short time later we heard gunshots and feared the worst."

"Sounds like I do owe your Mr. Beasley a debt of gratitude."

"He was so relieved when we saw you and Preston safe and sound. Then he rushed off to find a telephone to call the fire department and state police."

Livvy went back outside just as an officer arrived. After deciding Coy didn't need to be rushed to the hospital, he replaced the rope on Coy's wrists with handcuffs and put him in the back seat of his car. Officer Hensley interviewed just about everyone. As he was wrapping up, a stranger wearing dark slacks with a shirt and tie stepped forward. Livvy didn't know where he'd come from but heard him say he was in the woods when Coy attacked her. So he was interviewed as well.

She moved a little closer so she could listen. His name was Andrew Weaver. He said he was an investigator for an Athens law firm hired to follow Coy. He said he'd followed him into town that morning, overheard the conversation Coy had with his father at Mr. Beasley's store, then followed him to the woods near the Hopkins' farm.

"So you heard what was said between Olivia Sloan and McCoy Whitaker?" the officer asked.

"I heard everything. He confessed to a number of crimes. I took notes."

"You took notes?"

He pulled a small notepad from his shirt pocket.

At that point, Inez called everyone to dinner. But Livvy hung back, her eyes and ears glued to Mr. Weaver as he answered questions about what he'd seen and heard. Tears welled up as she heard him describe everything Coy said, how he pulled a gun on her and fired it before setting the forest ablaze.

At length, the officer asked Mr. Weaver if he could come by the office in Athens the following day. Weaver readily agreed.

When the officer climbed into his automobile, Livvy called out to Mr. Weaver who walked back to where she was standing.

"I couldn't help but overhear," Livvy said, gesturing at the officer's car. "I was wondering who hired you."

"I'm paid by the Athens law firm I work for. I told the officer everything and I'll turn over my notes and make another statement tomorrow. The work I normally do doesn't require me to carry a weapon so I wasn't armed. It was a scary situation out there. I'm relieved you weren't hurt. I'm sorry I couldn't be of more assistance to you."

"You've been of great assistance to me. You took notes of his confession."

"You were very brave confronting him like that."

She didn't tell him she figured if she was a goner, she might as well goad Coy into telling the truth before he shot her.

"Mr. Weaver, thank you, thank you!" She hugged him impulsively.

"Just doing my job."

He smiled as he headed for his car. Livvy was beside herself with relief. Coy had admitted his crimes and Mr. Weaver heard every word.

There were so many people she was grateful to, including Mae Glover. She wished she could thank her for revealing what she overheard at the Whitaker home. Without Mae's help, Livvy wondered if the truth would've been discovered.

Then Mama's arm slid around her shoulder.

"You need to come have a bite to eat. You're as shaky as a baby chick."

"I just need to lie down for a bit."

Mama filled the wash basin in her bedroom and brought her a glass of water to quench her thirst. In no time, Livvy was cleaned up and tucked in bed. The comforting sound of her family's voices in the distance lulled her to sleep. She didn't wake up again until after the sun rose the next morning. As she opened her eyes, she caught a fading glimpse of Grandma at the foot of her bed whispering her name.

23

Nobody could talk her out of it so Preston assigned Cecil and Vernon as Livvy's bodyguards when she hiked into the woods on Sunday. The forest was charred, the ground still smoldering, burned branches and hot embers falling from the blackened trees. But she was determined. She was supposed to meet Gordon for a picnic. Although her wishing well burned to a crisp like all of her other artworks, she wanted to create some small artwork in hopes that he would still be able to come.

They wore heavy boots to protect their feet from the blistering forest floor and hats to shield their heads from hot ash that drifted down. Daddy warned them to be on the lookout for trees that might collapse.

When they reached their destination, the mystical aura that had suffused the woodland had vaporized along with all the foliage. It was silent. There were no sounds of birds twittering in the trees. The cicadas were quiet too. The air was thick and grey. But she had to try.

Wearing work gloves, Livvy gathered burned hickory nuts, arranging them in a neat pile on a large stone. Then she rounded up blackened twigs and inserted them into the pile of nuts so that it looked a little like a picture of a sea urchin she'd seen in a schoolbook. Removing her gloves, she withdrew Grandma's embroidery scissors from her overalls and snipped a few hairs from the top of her head as the boys watched. She tied the hairs to several of the twigs and stepped back, hoping against hope, waiting for a vibration. Nothing.

Cecil and Vernon were clearly filled with curiosity but respectful enough to keep quiet as she gazed toward the north. She searched for the darkened sky, listened for hoofbeats. But the fire had not only decimated the forest, it had also destroyed the magic that existed in her sliver of the woods. She could feel a sob building in her throat. Refusing to let the boys see her cry, she walked a short distance away to regain control.

"It'll grow back," Vernon said. "Come springtime, you'll see. There'll be green shoots everywhere."

"Yeah," said Cecil. "And in a few years, there'll be saplings taller than me."

They were right. The forest would grow back, assuming someone didn't turn it into farmland. But it would be many years before the trees created the tall, thick canopy that had been here for generations. Livvy would be as old as Grandma by then.

They were about to start for home when Vernon told them to hold up.

"Look what I found." He squatted to retrieve something from the scorched forest floor. He turned it over in his gloved hands before holding it up for them to see.

It was the kind of whiskey flask that Coy carried in his pocket, now blackened by fire, its cap missing.

"That's how he got the fire to start so fast," Livvy said.

"Dang," said Cecil.

As they walked back to the farm, a deep melancholy flowed through Livvy's veins. The mysterious doorway that had existed between her world and Gordon's had closed. Whether he had been real or whether he'd been her imaginary companion, the loss hit her hard.

By the time they reached the farm, Preston and Clara had returned from Kinston where they'd gone to buy newspapers. There were front-page stories in the Athens paper and the two Atlanta papers Livvy sent letters to. They all said Coy, his father and brother-in-law were under investigation for collusion in the bank failure. They also said Coy was being held in the Athens jail pending investigations into a number of other possible charges, including attacks on Livvy and Ruthie, setting the fire that destroyed the Hopkins General Store and the fire that burned the woods west of the Hopkinsville crossroads. Authorities were also considering investigating Hank's death at the sawmill six years before, which had been classified as an accident at the time.

No sooner had Livvy and the boys returned than reporters began showing up wanting to interview half the family about the bank allegations and yesterday's events. Livvy hid in her room, preferring to let Daddy and Preston do the talking.

After supper that night, Ruthie knocked on the door of what had been their shared bedroom, asking if she could come in. Livvy sat listlessly on her bed and accepted Ruthie's heartfelt apology for all the ugly things she'd said and for siding with Coy against her own family. But Livvy didn't invite her to move her things back in. She needed more time.

On Tuesday, Livvy returned to the ruined woodland, creating another small artwork and adding a few strands of hair. Once again there was no vibration and no sign of

Gordon. It occurred to her that he might've decided after hearing all the tawdry stories she told him about her family that it was best to cut off their relationship. And from his point of view, she had stood him up on Sunday. But because there was no vibration when she inserted her hair into the artwork, it had to mean this was no longer the enchanted woodland it used to be. She wasn't sure which theory hurt the most – that the magical doorway had been destroyed by the fire or that Gordon had chosen to end their friendship. Either way, she couldn't muster the same level of relief that her family felt as the week wore on and more articles appeared in the newspapers. Regret washed over her.

From the newspapers they learned that Coy, his dad and brother-in-law were being charged with fraud, which included the creation of the loan company. The report said, if proven, that meant the farm loans wouldn't have to be paid and Daddy would no longer be in debt.

They learned that the Whitakers were under investigation for tax evasion and violating the Volstead Act – the prohibition law. Coy's speakeasies were all shut down and the whiskey stored in secret compartments was confiscated. The Whitakers and Merle Buchanan were charged with collusion for causing the bank failure. The bank president, Mr. Hilliard, was under investigation as well.

Coy was charged with two counts of arson for starting the fire that destroyed the store and the one that burned the forest. He also faced charges of attempted kidnapping for his attack on Livvy and then for trying to drag Ruthie off afterwards. Discussions were ongoing about whether to file additional charges.

The Whitaker family had their lawyer contact Inez saying the personal loan Coy had made to her and Livvy was considered paid in full. Preston guessed it was an effort to give the appearance the Whitakers had a heart before any of the cases went to court.

Sheriff Teague stopped by on Wednesday to talk with Daddy and Preston. Livvy was changing into her overalls for another trek into the woods and heard their voices on the porch.

"Missed you at church on Sunday," the sheriff said.

Neither Daddy nor Preston responded.

"Believe you owe me ten dollars," Teague went on.

"Owe you ten dollars for what?" Preston replied.

"You know what."

"Sorry, we don't know what you're talking about."

"Believe you do."

"Believe we don't."

There was a long pause. Livvy could only imagine the looks being exchanged.

"We'll just see about that," the sheriff said, clomping across the porch and walking back to his car.

After he drove away, Livvy heard Daddy's voice.

"So where'd you dump the still?"

"In an abandoned cow pond on the sheriff's property."

Daddy chuckled softly.

What Sheriff Teague didn't know was that Coy had implicated him in his rant to Livvy in the woods. Teague didn't know it yet but state police now knew he'd been taking bribes from bootleggers to look the other way. And if he pointed the finger at Daddy and Preston, he wouldn't be able to lead revenuers to a still. Livvy suspected his days as sheriff were numbered.

That afternoon, Mr. Beasley came to pick up Inez to take her over to his house for supper where she would meet his family. She was a walking case of nerves, changing her dress three times, fixing and refixing her hair and putting on a dab of lipstick. She asked Livvy if she looked all right.

"You look as pretty as an azalea in full bloom," Livvy said. "I'll bet Mr. Beasley blushes like a schoolboy when he lays eyes on you."

She was proven right a short time later. Mr. Beasley's cheeks turned pink with pleasure when Inez greeted him at the door.

While the family was optimistic they were now free from overwhelming debt, they were facing an uncertain future, trying to plan how best to put food on the table and keep a roof over their heads. Daddy visited his brother Tyrone who agreed to share water rights in exchange for some of Daddy's acreage. Daddy thought Tyrone had had a change of heart after reading all the stories in the newspapers, realizing how his brother had been targeted. Livvy thought Uncle Tyrone wanted to distance himself from his conniving old friends so he wouldn't look bad in the community.

Daddy said he would transfer ownership of the farm to Preston who had lots of modern ideas about farm management, admitting Preston was right last year when he said they should quit growing cotton because it was a losing proposition. Preston also had ideas on modernizing the house, declaring it was time to add a pump from the well inside the kitchen so they wouldn't have to haul water every time they washed dishes or took a bath. He even mentioned the possibility of adding an indoor bathroom.

Mama cried tears of joy when the church that bought her piano returned it after the pastor read all the newspaper articles. She took time out every day to sit down and play hymns and other favorite tunes.

Livvy had been offered the teacher's job at the new one-room school the county was building to replace the old one that burned down. Miss Essie Hopkins, a distant cousin who had taught there for thirty years, was retiring. Nettie and Faye would be Livvy's students. It was a relief that she could earn her keep by teaching.

It appeared Inez might at long last be leaving the nest with Mr. Beasley on the verge of asking her to marry him. They got to know each other as Mr. Beasley gave Inez driving lessons when he came to visit. Livvy suspected they sometimes pulled over in a secluded spot for a little romantic togetherness.

Interestingly, Mr. Beasley brought his son Mike along with him several times. Mike was a few years younger than Livvy, but she got the distinct impression that Gib was playing Cupid, likely at her sister's behest. Mike was easy to talk to and had a friendly manner, a lot like his father. Inez was correct when she pointed out that he was also a good looking young man whose eyes lit up in Livvy's presence.

One evening, Livvy and Clara were sitting on the porch, Clara busy with her mending, as usual. Livvy was surprised when her quiet sister-in-law struck up a conversation.

"Cecil and Vernon tell me you're a talented artist."

Livvy smiled.

"They say you created the most interesting works of art out in the woods – a boat, tree people, even a big round doorway. I wish I could've seen them."

Livvy wasn't sure what to say. She'd always thought of her artworks as private.

"The boys said the doorway looked like it might lead to another world," Clara continued.

"I thought so too. I used to call it my doorway. Sometimes it seemed like it had a magic rainbow running around the inside of the circle. Must've been my imagination."

"You never know. Might've been a magic rainbow that only you could see."

Livvy thought about it – magic that only she could see. That's what had kept her sane these last few months – the magic of the woodland. Her artworks were all designed because of a desperate need to escape a dismal life: a doorway to another world; a boat to take her there; a window through which to view that other universe; a spiral galaxy made of smooth river stones like the Andromeda Galaxy Gordon talked about; a pair of tree nymphs representing her and Gordon, the man she created as a companion during her darkest days, the imaginary man she fell in love with.

Gordon might not have been a ghost, but he might as well have been, because he existed only in her mind on the other side of the doorway. He had given her hope when there was none. He had given her joy where none existed. He had given her praise and affection when the people in her real life were too busy with their own troubles to take time for Livvy. He had listened when she poured out her heart. She had created a noble man to keep herself from losing hope. Oh, how she wished he were real. But she was lucky Grandma had instilled in her the ability to cast a spell for herself, to turn the mundane into an enchanted place where she could build a dream world that included a man like no other. Because it wasn't his handsome face and his adventurous eyes that she would remember. It was the sense of belonging that she experienced when she was with him.

But it was over. The enchantment had died in the fire. The woodland was incinerated. Gordon was gone with it. She would take the hope she'd harbored deep in her heart and build a life for herself in the real world. She could still create art. She could still imbue her creations with hopes and dreams. Remembering the day they held their palms together, so close but so far apart, she knew it would take time to mourn the loss of that special place and the man she invented for herself.

Clara remained quiet for a while, seeming to understand that Livvy was grieving. After some time, she spoke again. "How did you start creating such unusual art?"

Livvy told her the story about when she and Grandma were in the woods so long ago. How she'd arranged some pretty rocks on the brilliant golden leaves. And how Grandma told her, "magic happens all the time. You just have to look for it."

"I met your grandmother once. Wish I could've gotten to know her. I like to believe that magic happens too."

They sat quietly, Clara sewing a patch on some worn dungarees.

"I'd love to see one of your creations," she said. "Could you make one here on the farm? Maybe that little patch of trees out behind the barn. I'll help if you like."

And so they spent the next several days gathering branches, twigs and vines, searching the stand of trees and the shoulders of the roads where wild bushes and vines grew.

Unlike the privacy she was accustomed to in the woods, now she and Clara worked in the open, building the doorway at the edge of the copse of trees. As before, Livvy used a couple of trees to help anchor the doorway. Clara's kids were thrilled to see their mother working with Livvy on the new nature sculpture.

The new doorway was completed the day after Ruthie, Cecil and Vernon started school. So it was just Nettie and Faye watching as the finishing touches were added. Livvy had never seen Clara smile like she did that afternoon. She couldn't wait to show Preston and the boys and thanked Livvy profusely for teaching her this new art form.

As the air cooled after supper, Clara led everyone out back for a viewing.

"Livvy called the original one the enchanted doorway," she said. "I'd like to think that this one might be enchanted too."

"My goodness," Inez said. "You're a real artist, Livvy."

There were murmurs of assent.

"I wish I'd seen all of the creations you made," Mama said, shaking her head. "I always thought I was too busy or too tired."

"They were something to see," Cecil said. "Me and Vernon got to see them all."

"I loved the canoe," Vernon said.

"And there was this rock spiral," Cecil added.

"It looked like the Andromeda Galaxy," Livvy explained.

She smiled a bittersweet smile. She'd always been a reader, borrowing books from the bookmobile on all kinds of subjects. She'd also spent time when she was growing up reading magazines at the store. She could only guess she'd read about some of the things she'd imagined Gordon telling her. She was amazed at all the conversations she'd created out of whole cloth and the long forgotten information she'd pulled from some corner of her brain. The mind was much more powerful than she'd imagined.

"Did you add some hair?" Vernon asked, gesturing at the new doorway.

She shook her head, pulling herself back to the present.

"Why would you put hair in it?" Ruthie asked.

"Grandma said Mother Nature provided me with all my supplies, so she said I should add something of myself. She cut a few strands of my hair and I tucked them into the very first artwork I made years ago. I embedded some of my hair in the artworks I built in the woodland this summer."

"Then you need to add some of your hair to this new one," Cecil said.

"Yes, Livvy," Clara agreed.

Livvy wondered, just for a second, whether the magic might return here in this little stand of trees. No. It was over. But she did it for them, using her tiny scissors to cut several strands of red hair. Entwining them through the twigs that made up the doorway, she stepped back with the others to gaze at the new sculpture. Of course, there was no vibration, no quiver. And there was no thundering of hoofbeats, which left her with an aching feeling in her chest. She blinked furiously, keeping the tears in check.

Gradually, the family drifted back to the house, Preston and Clara holding hands like young sweethearts, their kids laughing and talking. Mama and Daddy followed, Inez and

Ruthie close behind. Which left Livvy alone with the new doorway as the stars began to twinkle in the evening sky. She couldn't help but think of Gordon as her eyes swept across the firmament. He had seemed so very real.

She strolled over to the doorway, thinking back to the first time she saw him galloping toward her. Impulsively, she stepped through the center of the door, a part of her hoping she might be transported to the imaginary world where he existed in her mind. The doorway took her nowhere. She was still standing by the trees behind the farmhouse as twilight deepened. No amount of blinking could hold back the tears now. Two large teardrops streamed down her cheeks.

Her thoughts were interrupted by a loud whirring that filled the air. It was so sudden she thought a storm must be sweeping in without warning. But as she looked up, the noise went silent, then resumed. It wasn't wind. It was an enormous flock of starlings filling the sky to the west of the farm. The shape of the flock transformed, undulating one way, then the other against a backdrop of pink clouds reflecting the last of the sun's rays. The small birds seemed to cling to each other as they rose higher, then dove toward the ground. Grandma had told her it was a starling murmuration – all of the little birds banding together at twilight as the group changed shape, some of them uttering small squawks and twitters. Grandma said it was Mother Nature's magic and whenever she spied a murmuration in the fall or winter months, she would find a place to sit and watch in awe.

Livvy stood still, eyes glued to the scene above her, wondering if it was a sign from Grandma, a sign that maybe magic did still exist. As the light dimmed, the great flock dove toward the earth and disappeared from view, the fluttering of their wings silenced.

Hearing footsteps behind her, she hurried to wipe her tears away. Her family hadn't understood the depth of her loss when the forest burned.

When she turned around, there was a man walking in her direction in a coat and tie. Mr. Beasley's son Mike all dressed up? He said he'd like to come by one evening and bring his fiddle. But there was no fiddle in his hand.

"Livvy," the man called out to her, his voice filled with eagerness.

Her heart pounded as he closed the distance between them. It wasn't Mike.

"Gordon?"

Taking long strides, he advanced toward her, only stopping when they were face to face so that she had to look up into his eyes glistening in the twilight. She thought she could only see him in the enchanted woodland, only when she added strands of hair to a new artwork. But here he stood. It was more than she could bear knowing she had conjured him, that he was only a creation of her mind.

When he took her hand in his, the shock of his touch made her sway.

"You're real!" she whispered.

"So are you."

"And you're here."

"Indeed I am."

Without another word he took her in his arms and kissed her.

24

She didn't want the kiss to end, fearing it would turn out to be an illusion. She clung to him, wrapping her arms around his neck, reveling in the solid feel of his body against hers. When they paused to look into each other's eyes, she caressed his cheek, blinking away tears of joy. He kissed her again and again.

So many questions fluttered through her mind, but for the moment she just wanted to feel his arms around her, to feel his warm lips on hers. She couldn't believe he was truly here, that he was real, that he was not a figment of her imagination, that he was not some wishful fantasy. Gordon Collins was as real as she was. If he lived in England, that meant he had traveled thousands of miles across the ocean to find her.

"My darling Livvy, I love you more than words can possibly convey." His throat was husky with emotion.

"Oh, Gordon."

Putting her hand behind his neck, she pulled his face down to hers so she could kiss him. Then she pressed her cheek into his chest to hear the beating of his heart, the breath of his lungs, so very alive. It was like the two of them were molded together as one.

"I thought I'd lost you," she whispered. "After the fire, I tried to create artworks, adding my hair like I always did. I thought the fire had destroyed the woodland magic. And then I feared I must've imagined all of our meetings, all of our conversations – that I was delusional and you didn't actually exist. I was devastated."

"I got here as fast as I could."

She looked up into his eyes, relieved beyond measure that he was here.

"I didn't mean for our meeting to be like this," he said. "I was going to court you properly. And if you reciprocated my feelings, I would've asked your father for your hand. But when I turned the corner of the house and saw you, all of that melted away. I had to hold you. I had to kiss you. Now I'm desperate for you to say you'll marry me."

"Yes, yes, yes!" she whispered. "You're the love of my life."

What followed was a sweet, slow kiss, the heartfelt promise of forever. He had been the embodiment of hope during her darkest days. Now he was the symbol of a future filled with love.

The shadows had deepened and she knew that eyes were watching from the windows. She had to introduce him to her family, taking him by the hand as they walked together.

"I said hello to your family on the porch," he said. "When I told them I had come to see you, they directed me to the back yard. But only after Mr. Weaver assured them I was a right proper fellow."

"How do you know Mr. Weaver?"

"I contacted an Athens law firm and hired Mr. Weaver, their investigator, to follow Coy Whitaker. I was greatly concerned for your safety."

"So you're the one who hired him. And he's with you now?"

"I'm paying him to be my chauffeur. I don't know how to drive on the right side of the road."

She chuckled as they passed the garden.

"I'm not sure how to explain you," she said. "What did you tell your family?"

"I thought about telling them the truth but decided they wouldn't believe me. So I told them I met you when you visited Kinston – they assumed it was our Kinston – earlier in the summer and that we had been exchanging letters since you returned to your home in Georgia. I made it clear that you're the woman I'm going to marry."

"I need an explanation too. You're right – nobody would believe the truth."

"I've been thinking about that," he said. "We could tell them I've been staying with friends near Kinston and came across you while horseback riding the day you finished the doorway. And now that I must return to England, I've asked you to marry me."

When they reached the porch, they found Mama and Daddy in their rockers, Preston, Clara, Inez and Mr. Weaver sitting in kitchen chairs around them. The kids were running through the house, Faye calling out, "We saw them kissing!"

Livvy held tightly to Gordon's hand, standing in the yard as they looked up into the shadowed faces. Inez retrieved a couple of lanterns, hanging them from hooks to give them some light.

"This is Gordon Collins," Livvy said, glancing up at him, her face radiant.

"Mr. Weaver told us he's a friend of yours," Daddy replied.

"He's much more than a friend. He's the man I'm going to marry."

You could've knocked them over with a chicken feather.

"How do you do?" Gordon said, his English accent causing the girls to giggle.

"He's from England," Livvy said.

"Kinston, England, to be precise," Gordon added.

"Ah!" Inez said. "You asked Gib if there was an Englishman living in Kinston."

"And he said there wasn't," Livvy replied. "But Gordon was staying with friends not far from *our* Kinston. We met when he came across my woodland while horseback riding the day I finished the doorway."

Daddy and Preston both stood to shake Gordon's hand while the boys retrieved a couple more kitchen chairs for them to sit on.

"Amazing that you came from one Kinston to another Kinston," Clara said with a hint of suspicion. "And now you'll be married."

"I was beguiled at first by her artworks," Gordon explained. "But by the second visit I knew it was Livvy I fancied. And before long I had quite fallen in love." He gave her an adoring glance.

"Why didn't you have him over? Introduce us?" Mama asked.

"Well," Livvy replied, stalling for a moment, "I thought you might think it a little fishy, me meeting up with a man in the woods. Of course, he's always been a perfect gentleman."

Preston spoke up then. "I think Livvy's proven she's got better sense about men than the rest of the family."

Mama, Inez and Ruthie nodded sheepishly.

"We understand you're the one who hired Mr. Weaver," Inez said.

Gordon explained that when Livvy told him about Coy's threats, he was so alarmed that he contacted a law firm in Athens to pay their investigator to keep track of Coy, and hopefully, to help protect Livvy. I'm exceedingly glad I did so considering all that transpired."

"We're eternally grateful," Daddy said.

"Now I have a feeling you're taking our daughter with you back across the ocean," Mama said, a wistful tone in her voice.

*

Over the next couple of weeks Livvy gave detailed statements to the state police and the Athens law firm Gordon dealt with about the charges against Coy, his father and brother-in-law, in the event they were needed in court. Gordon took her to Atlanta to get a passport and buy clothing more suitable to the English climate. Still, she made sure to pack her overalls and dungarees after Gordon assured her there were plenty of forest areas where she could continue to create her works of art. She also packed the old pocketknife and whetstone Grandma gave her.

After discussing it with Livvy, Gordon sat down with Daddy and Preston under the pecan tree to give them enough money to pay their tax bill and help purchase necessities for the winter. Livvy watched through the window, grateful that the man she was about to marry would be so generous.

She wore a new cream-colored suit for the small marriage ceremony at the church. Her eyes misted up as they said their vows. She still couldn't believe she had magically summoned the man of her dreams from so far away while creating her art in the woods. It occurred to her that she had ended up like Inez after all – happy and in love.

After the wedding she bid a tearful farewell to her family, hugging each of them, telling them how much she loved them and promising to write.

"But will we ever see you again?" Ruthie said.

Livvy had avoided thinking about that too much. Because, as happy as she was about spending the rest of her life with Gordon, she would miss her family terribly. Before she could reply, Gordon spoke up.

"We will visit," he said, looking from Ruthie to Livvy. "About five years hence."

Livvy slipped her arm through his, more certain than ever that she was the luckiest woman in the world.

Gordon had hired Mr. Weaver to drive them to Atlanta where they would board a train for New York City. But Livvy wanted to say one last good-bye, directing Mr. Weaver to the cemetery where her grandmother was buried.

Standing beside the grave, Gordon behind her, Livvy watched as a red leaf fluttered to the ground, landing in front of the headstone as though it had come to say farewell too. It was star-shaped like the leaves of the sweet gum tree at Grandma's old house. Livvy felt certain her grandmother was sending her a message, a message of hope and love. She suspected Grandma knew long ago that the enchanted woodland would play a pivotal role in Livvy's life. She bent down to retrieve the leaf so she could press it between the pages of the book of fairy tales packed in her trunk – the book that Grandma used to read her when she was a little girl.

During the long train ride Gordon told her there was a college not far from Kinston where she could continue her art studies. He also told her they would be living in a cottage on his parents estate, not in the house she'd seen in the picture. Which was a great relief.

When they reached New York, they boarded an ocean liner for the Atlantic crossing. Leaving the Statue of Liberty far behind, Livvy was amazed at the immensity of the sea and the light sparkling on the waves. She had dreamed of leaving dust-covered rural Georgia for most of her life. But she never imagined that one day she would stand beside the man she loved, gazing out upon the Atlantic ocean. Anticipation gave her goosebumps.

Ensconced in a pretty stateroom, it was like they were on a romantic honeymoon. But making love with Gordon was ever so much more than she had imagined. It wasn't just the passion and sensuality of the marriage bed. It was the intensity in his eyes as he gazed into hers that made her tingle.

Lying in each other's arms afterwards, Gordon whispered in her ear.

"I want to show you something. Put on your coat and shoes."

She laughed as they pulled their coats on over their nightclothes. After climbing the stairs to the upper deck, he wrapped his arm around her waist as they leaned against the railing. Then he kissed her cheek and said, "lift your eyes to the heavens."

The sight took her breath away. Stars filled the night sky from horizon to horizon with an immense arc above them of purple, blue and gold spattered with dark and light.

"The Milky Way," she whispered in wonder.

They couldn't take their eyes from the awe-inspiring view, holding onto each other as a brisk ocean breeze ruffled their hair.

"See that smudge?" Gordon said, his cheek touching hers as he pointed toward the south.

"Mm-hm."

"That's the Andromeda Galaxy."

"At last I get to see the spiral galaxy."

"When we get home, you can look through my telescope. And one day we'll visit the Royal Observatory in Greenwich to see the night sky through a truly magnificent telescope."

She clapped her hands at the prospect.

He tugged her closer. "See that bright star right there?" he said, pointing north.

"Yes."

"It's actually a binary star – twin stars. Two stars that orbit each other, drawn together by gravitational forces."

"Drawn together by gravitational forces," she whispered. "Like you and me."

"Exactly so, my love. We were destined to find each other, destined to come together as one."

"It's like Grandma said. Magic happens all the time."

"You just have to look for it," he whispered before kissing her with great ardor.

The End

Review it

Thank you for reading *Livvy and the Enchanted Woodland*. If you enjoyed it, please help spread the word by posting a brief customer review. Or tell your friends, in person or on social media. Thanks very much!

Note from the author

The Great Depression lasted from 1929 to 1939. That's what we call it now, but in 1930 average folks in the US and around the world had no idea they'd entered such a long-lasting economic downturn. In the year my novel takes place Georgia farm families like the Hopkins suffered a triple whammy as they were hammered by the financial recession, a years-long drought and devastation of the cotton crop by boll weevils.

Livvy creates a type of art now called Land Art, Earth Art or Environmental Art.

Sign up for author updates and get your FREE copy of

The Engagement Ring, A short story

When Ethan pops the question, Lydia pops some questions of her own. A 21st century take on a marriage proposal with a pinch of humor and a dash of the unexpected.

Sign up here: www.connielacy.com

Also by Connie Lacy

A Suffragette in Time

Thrown back in time to the 1850s, Sarah Burns becomes a suffragette who finds danger and romance where she least expects to.

The Time Capsule
An unlikely journey through time brings Hannah Myers face to face with a man like no other. But she doesn't belong in 1918 with a killer flu epidemic raging and the KKK targeting the newspaper reporter she's fallen for. Can she rewrite history to protect the man she loves?

The Going Back Portal
She avoided the Trail of Tears. But can a young Cherokee Indian woman of 1840 survive the white man intent on owning her? Can a time traveler from the 21st century help?

The Time Telephone
What if you could save your mother's life by calling her in the past on a time telephone? An intriguing coming of age story. Teen/Young Adult Fiction

VisionSight: a Novel
Seeing the future is a curse for Jenna Stevens. A heartfelt novel of secrets and unexpected love.

A Daffodil for Angie
It's 1966. Angie's got a lot on her plate – the women's rights movement, school integration, the Viet Nam War, a cocky anti-war activist and a sexy quarterback. A coming of age story that drops you right into the social upheaval of the 1960s. Teen/Young Adult Fiction

The Shade Ring Trilogy
A compelling Climate Fiction trilogy set against a backdrop of runaway global warming. A love story in a hotter, more dangerous world.
The Shade Ring, Book 1
Albedo Effect, Book 2
Aerosol Sky, Book 3

About the author

Connie Lacy writes time travel fiction, speculative fiction and historical fiction, all with a dollop of romance. She worked for many years in radio news as a reporter and news anchor. She and her husband live in Atlanta.

Newsletter sign-up: www.connielacy.com

Contact/follow

www.connielacy.com
www.Facebook.com/ConnieLacyBooks
www.Goodreads.com/ConnieLacy
www.instagram.com/connielacy_author/
www.pinterest.com/cdlacy0736/

Email:

WildFallsPublishing@outlook.com
connielacy@connielacy.com